AUTHOR'S NOTE

THIS BOOK HAD A LOT OF INSANE RESEARCH, completely stretching me out of my comfort zone even though I've been writing mafia books for years. For readers who care about facts and small details that pertain to the reality and "realness" of this book, meaning *could this actually happen?* Are some of the medical terms and psychological traumas possible? The answer is yes. Thank you to Dr. Glena Andrews for answering all of my emails pertaining to brainwashing and hypnotherapy. Dr. Rachel Thomas was the resident doc on screen for this entire book, giving me notes on what different drugs I could use and basically how to get away with murder—all of this took place downtown Boise over a few glasses of wine! So readers, yes, a lot of this can happen, but I caution you, it would definitely need to be the perfect storm of physical and psychological trauma, aided only by an expert in their field. Curious yet? Keep an open mind and know I did use creative license for a few situations, but that should in no way take away from the reading experience. Once you finish the book, keep reading for information on the rest of my mafia series as well as the reading order.

To Rachel… thank you for not being weirded out when I sent you texts like, "If I want someone to drop dead within 24 hours…"
You rock!

PROLOGUE

Death answers before it is asked. —Russian Proverb

Nikolai

SHE WAS IN THE WAITING ROOM… I could see her. Hell, I could smell her. After all, scent was the strongest link to memories. She was nervous, tapping a blue pen against her leg. *Tap, tap, tap.* I felt each movement, heard each tap in my mind as if it were a clock ticking away, telling me our time was almost up before it had even truly begun.

When she stood, her dress hugged every curve of her lush body. I should have sent her away.

An intelligent man would.

But the masochist in me needed her to stay, or maybe it was just the irritating little muscle in the center of my chest, the one that modern medicine claims cannot truly feel emotion.

For the second time in my life, I felt emotion, felt her, right in the center of my chest, as if she'd been placed there, as

1

if it was my job to keep her safe.

I drummed my fingertips on the door, still watching, waiting. She looked irritated and reached for her phone.

With a sigh, I walked over to my intercom and picked up the phone. "Send her away."

****

A few months later…

Maya

"I DON'T CARE IF *you have to wipe her entire damn memory, just make her forget. I pay you to make people forget."*

The taste of blood filled my mouth, making me feel dirty. I had no idea why I felt dirty, just that I did, that something was very, very wrong. I blinked, but it did nothing, and my eyelashes got stuck against the blindfold. More metallic-tasting blood teased my tongue as I tried to lick across my dry lips.

I knew one of the voices belonged to my father.

Why he had me tied to a chair, bleeding—I had no idea.

Then again, he was a horrible human being, so there was that. I'd been afraid of him all my life—and now he was just proving to me how deranged he really was.

I was sixteen.

Two more years and I'd run away.

Two more years and I could go to college.

It was the one thing he promised me.

College—as long as I paid for it on my own.

I clung to the thought of escape even as I felt a heaviness descend upon the room.

"Damn it, Petrov, she's sixteen. Just bribe her with a new car."

"No." My father swore in Russian. "She is a liability. Make it go away or she dies, and her death will be on your hands."

My breath hitched in my chest.

Was my father capable of that? Of killing me?

Yes. I knew in my soul he was.

Because he had no soul.

"Fine," the smooth voice said in a low whisper, "but I work alone, leave me."

Shoes clicked against the ground in rapid succession.

A door clicked shut.

And I was alone.

I lifted my chin in defiance. I wasn't going to give into fear, even though it was a real tangible thing, licking across the back of my neck, causing hair to raise all the way down my arms.

I was a Petrov.

Maybe this was my father's way of punishing me for sneaking out last week. But I'd wanted freedom.

A freaking date.

Something. Anything to feel alive. To escape the black and white life that had been built around me, the crystal castle that dared me to throw something against the wall just so I could feel the break.

A warm hand cupped my chin. "You're beautiful. I think that's the first thing we should establish."

I refused to respond. He'd have to do better than that.

"Second," *his hand dropped. I hated that my face felt cold without it there.* "This is going to hurt, but you won't remember anything afterward, not even the sound of my voice. Because, Maya, I'm very good at what I do. You could say I'm the best."

He sounded young.

Almost as young as me but that would be impossible.

His voice was both smooth and gravelly as if when he spoke he had to fight to keep the words from sounding too pretty—maybe it was because what he did was ugly.

"I don't care," *I whispered.* "Do your worst."

"He said you'd be brave."

"I'm Russian." *My answer to everything.*

"No, actually." *He sighed.* "You're not."

"What?" The first slice of pain against my arm was like getting a really deep paper cut. I hissed out a breath and tried my best to glare through the blindfold.

"The first cut," he said smoothly, "Is always the easiest because you don't expect it. But there's always a second." A slow burn trickled down my wrist and then severe pain hit me again, this time on my other forearm. "Even the second isn't so horrible, because who only makes one cut? It's almost more expected than the first. But the third…" He made another slice this time on my open palm. "Is the worse because that's when you realize… it's only just begun."

"You can't break me," I hissed. "And I've done nothing wrong."

"You're right about one thing… you've done nothing wrong. Except, you were born, and that… according to your father… is a problem."

"And second?" I asked in a calm detached voice, already trying to climb into myself so I wouldn't feel the stinging sensation or the warm blood trickling down my arms.

"It takes experts seventy-two hours maximum to brainwash a person, to wipe their memory, to make them a whole new individual."

"So?" I croaked, jerking against the chair.

"Ah, Maya… it rarely takes me twelve hours."

My heart slammed against my chest.

Warm lips brushed against my ear. "The minute you were brought in… you were already broken."

I woke up from the dream in a cold sweat. It was always the same. Someone slicing my arm, and a smooth voice taunting me. The message was always the same.

I will break you.

I shivered and looked at my clock.

It was time to call in a favor. I was tired of the nightmares, but more tired of putting my life on hold… I needed to finish my research if it was the last thing I did. So with dread, I picked up my cell and dialed my father's number.

CHAPTER ONE

The Pier killer is at it again, claiming its first victim in two years… — The Seattle Tribune.

Maya

THE CLOCK IN THE CORNER CHIMED noon. I waited in anticipation for the doors to open. His secretary had said he'd be out in five minutes. It had been six, not that I was crazy OCD or anything, I was just a bit freaked out that I was about to meet *the Nikolai Blazik*. He was considered a god in the medical community.

And he was considered royalty if you asked anyone else.

Graduated with honors from Harvard at the ripe old age of fifteen, went on to get a degree in Human Sciences and Technologies, which basically meant he was a certified genius. His research on disease and its effects on the body gave him the freaking Nobel Prize at nineteen.

Which was naturally followed by a cover on Time

Magazine, followed by Forbes, I think you get the picture. He was ridiculously smart and extremely hard to pin down for an interview.

The only reason he was even giving me the time of day was because my father had made a call, and my master's thesis was based on Mr. Blazik's newest research on STDs.

I exhaled and looked at the clock again.

Eight minutes.

He was three minutes late.

What if he wasn't going to do the interview? I needed to finish my thesis in order to graduate—and I had to graduate in order to pay off my student loans. Regardless of how much money and power my father had, he was adamant that I make my own way.

Except in this particular situation.

I'd had to damn near sell him my own kidney in order for him to arrange the meeting. Leaving wasn't an option. He'd told me no on several occasions and then finally, picked up the phone this morning and said to be at the Blazik offices downtown at noon.

I wasn't sure why he'd finally given in after all these years of basically ignoring me. My family was dysfunctional. I stopped trying to figure them out years ago. My brother Pike had died a few weeks ago, leaving my mother heartbroken, and it was always rumored that my sister had been killed by another crime family when she was an infant, leaving just me.

I felt like the disappointment of the bunch, not that my father ever said a word about me being a disappointment. His words were always brittle, cold, and indifferent, I would have killed for some sort of emotion from the guy, but I had nothing but empty smiles and arched eyebrows.

With another sigh I tucked my dark brown hair behind my ears and drummed my fingertips along my black skirt.

I'd put on my new Nordstrom business suit, hoping it

would give me confidence, and when that failed to work—after I looked in the mirror and saw the petrified look on my face—I put on a red thong and crossed my fingers.

Underwear always did the trick. Like a secret nobody knew about... I could walk in the office confident that although I looked prim and proper on the outside—I was scandalous underneath.

The phone ringing caused me to almost fall out of my chair.

"Miss Petrov?"

I stood, my knees hitting the glass table in front of me. "Yes?"

Her smile was tight, almost as tight as the bun currently torturing her hair. "He's waiting."

He's waiting? As if *I* was the one that was late and had been sitting here wasting *his* time?

"Thank you," I managed to choke out, making my way toward the large black doors.

She opened both of them, making my entrance look a lot more grand than it really was.

Floor to ceiling windows lined every inch of wall except for the one behind me leading back into the lobby.

A large oak conference table was in the left corner and a desk that looked more like a spaceship about ready to take flight than an actual desk, had been placed in the very middle of the room.

Two black leather couches rested against the right wall with a white fur rug topping off the masculine look.

The office screamed money.

And for some reason that made it seem cold.

The door clicked shut behind me.

I did a circle, my heels clicking against the marble tile. "Um, hello?"

"Um," came a dark menacing voice from somewhere in

the room I couldn't locate. "Isn't a word. Try again."

"My name is—"

"I know who you are," the voice snapped impatiently. "Now, try again."

I tried to get my shaking under control, hoping it wouldn't show through with my next few words. "Where would you like me to sit? For your interview?"

Static filled silence followed for a few seconds before I heard a sharp irritated exhale.

"Are there not enough options, Miss Petrov?"

I licked my lips and glanced quickly around the room trying to decide what would be best, finally I settled on the couch, setting my purse on the floor and pulling out my notebook.

"Interesting." The voice contained little humor, and I would bet my right eye he found my choice in seating anything but interesting. Whatever, not my problem. I had expected him to be nicer, or at least, you know, present?

Did he get off by acting like the Great and Powerful Oz? I still didn't know where the heck he was or why he was choosing not to show his face.

First he's late.

Then it's somehow my fault.

And now he's mocking me from afar.

Screw you, Oz. I clicked my pen and waited.

"I would have taken you for a conference table type of girl," the smooth voice said, this time sounding closer. "Then again, the couches are more comfortable."

I opened my mouth, but words didn't come out. Instead, a croak or a crackle or something that sounded a lot like a strangled gasp emerged when Mr. Blazik walked through what I'd thought was a wall but was actually a door leading into another part of the office.

Shirtless.

Well not shirtless, I mean he had a shirt *on*—high-end black silk—but it wasn't buttoned. He was in the process of doing that, covering taut abs and well-defined pecs.

And I was watching him.

Shamelessly.

I quickly averted my eyes and stared at the blank notebook in front of me as my cheeks sizzled with awareness.

His approach was silent. I couldn't hear him, but I felt him, felt his body heat. Still I didn't look up. I studied his nice Italian shoes, black, shiny, they looked new, expensive.

"Are you planning on interviewing my feet?" A dark chuckle emerged from him. "Or can we get on with it?"

Get on with… yes, the interview. I blinked, then slowly inched my gaze up his body.

Black trousers that were more fitted than should be decent hugged muscular legs, leading up to a broad partially exposed, bare chest, wide shoulders, large biceps, and strong jaw.

I paused at the jaw, almost afraid to finish what my eyes had started, fearful that he really was going to be as good looking in person as he seemed.

His jaw was sharp, defined, shadowed like he'd forgotten to shave or maybe just possessed a crap load of testosterone meaning he had to shave every day.

I took a steadying breath as I finally lifted my gaze to his startling amber eyes. Brown hair curled around the nape of his neck, like a caress. He was dangerous perfection.

He smiled.

And my stomach clenched like I was going to be sick.

I hadn't planned on him being this gorgeous in real life. Because in real life men had gaps in their teeth and weird body odor, at least in my experience, there were always a few flaws, which made them human.

So my only conclusion after taking in his perfect muscled

six-foot frame was that Mr. Blazik was an alien… sent to torture the women of earth with his perfection.

I mean, what else would explain eyes so hypnotic that I wasn't just physically drawn to him, but emotionally? Or skin so smooth it looked like it had just been waxed? Even the line of his damn jaw was perfect.

He was busy buttoning up his perfectly fitted red shirt, my eyes trained on his fingers. I hated to admit that I wondered what else he did with those hands. With a gulp, I suppressed a shiver and tried to regain my focus.

"You're different than he described you." Mr. Blazik tilted his head to the side. "More… mousy." He made a disgusted face that made me want to kick him in the shin.

Ding ding ding! We have a winner! The great flaw has been discovered! He suffered from jackass syndrome. Pity, with that face… I sighed and clicked my pen again.

"I think it's on." He chuckled.

I contemplated stabbing him in the thigh, but offered a smile instead. "Do you always make a habit of dressing in front of grad students or is today my lucky day?"

He made a show of slowly licking his lips and sat, his knees touching mine. I quickly pulled away. "That depends. Do you often make a habit of disrespecting your elders before asking them for an interview?"

"You're thirty-two, hardly my elder." I said in a sweet voice. Great, now I was arguing with him. So far, the interview? Not going so hot.

"Unfair." He folded his hands together and leaned in. "You know my birthday and I don't know yours."

"Yeah well, I'm not all over the Internet." In fact, thanks to my father, my virtual thumbprint was nonexistent. I cleared my throat. "So, I just have a few questions about your research regarding the prostitution rings here in Bellevue and your findings."

His face betrayed nothing, but his eyes? His eyes seemed to darken even more. He clenched his teeth and leaned back, creating much needed space between our bodies. "Do you know why you're here?"

"To interview you." I nodded slowly. "For my master's thesis. Is that your way of making sure I know my place? Or are you really just curious?"

"You are your father's daughter." His lips curved into a delicious smile, "You resemble each other, not in looks, but definitely in attitude." His gaze was unapologetic as he tilted his head and started raking his eyes from my feet up my legs until finally settling on my face. I clenched my legs together tightly and forced a smile.

"If you don't mind, Mr. Blazik, I'd really like to get on with the interview, I know your time is precious."

As was mine, I wanted to stress, but didn't, just barely restraining myself and clenching my teeth to keep from giving him a much-needed verbal lashing.

"I blocked out my entire day."

Did he want applause? "Right, well, I assure you I can be fast."

His dark laugh had me shivering and wanting to lean forward all at once. Men that good looking shouldn't be blessed with chuckles like that—a freaking sirens call that's what it was.

"Amazing… You truly don't know why you're here, do you?"

How many times did I need to repeat myself and why was I getting the sudden impression that the guy was on some seriously hard drugs? I looked closer; didn't pinpoint pupils mean he was high or something?

"I assure you I'm not drunk, nor high, if that's what you're thinking." He chuckled again and rubbed his hands together. "Though the idea does have merit, all things considering." A muscle clenched in his jaw.

Oh good, so he was a doctor who liked drugs and had more money than God. That should go over well for addiction problems.

I scooted back against the leather and clicked my pen for, oh, I don't know, the tenth time. "If you aren't going to answer my questions, I should probably go."

"You won't be going anywhere," he said in a quiet voice. "And for that I'm truly sorry." His eyes met mine, and they seemed... apologetic.

"Pardon?" Was he threatening me? Warning bells went off in my head as adrenaline shot through my system.

"Your father..." He tilted his head. "He owes me a debt... of gratitude... I asked for something irreplaceable, something that's been owed to me for a very long time."

My stomach sank as my heart started hammering against my chest.

"What exactly did my father give you?" I choked out, hating that I probably knew the answer, because my father was ruthless, he was a business man after all, and he never backed out of a deal. It was business over family and our business was darkness itself, horrible, something I blocked out because it made me feel better when I woke up in the morning and fell asleep at night.

"Well..." Mr. Blazik stood. "I thought that would be obvious." He turned his back to me and walked over to his desk then pressed a button causing blinds to creep down all the windows. When he turned, the room was already starting to blanket in darkness, making it so that his teeth practically glowed. "He gave me you."

****

The night previous

Downtown Seattle

DRIP, DRIP, DRIP. THE *sound was a rhythmic cadence to the madness that threatened to destroy my existence. Drip, drip, drip. The blood was fuel, it was life. It was also death.*

The woman's face was void of emotion, yet I knew she felt every single slice of the knife as I worked.

Finally, I removed the diseased organ and shook my head. "You've been very, very bad, haven't you?"

A lone tear ran down her cheek.

I tossed the organ away, disgusted with the type of woman she was, with the type of human being she represented.

Sick.

Diseased.

A complete waste of humanity.

"Now." I reached for my scalpel. "I'll tell you exactly why you're going to die."

More tears.

"For your sins." I brought the blade to her throat. "For selling your very soul to the devil. I'm sending you to the pit of hell."

I sliced.

A gurgle.

And she breathed no more.

I rocked back on my heels and exhaled as the world righted itself again. One less disease walking the streets.

One less.

Because of me.

CHAPTER TWO

The local police force is asking for anyone with information about the Pier Killings to please come forward. The reward has been raised to fifty thousand dollars. —The Seattle Tribune

Nikolai

SHE WAS A PUZZLE, one I would enjoy unraveling, playing with, touching. Damn, getting my hands on her would be a sweet sin—something I couldn't do, something I had to deny myself no matter how much I wanted to touch, to feel, anything human, anything warm. Maybe that's when you know you've actually lost all of your humanity—when you crave a stranger's touch more than you crave your next meal or drink of water.

She would be water to me.

But it would be poisoned.

Touching her would end in both our deaths; he made sure of that, the bastard.

I cleared my throat and managed to keep my expression calm even though my heart was going into overdrive. She'd grown into a beautiful woman, soft where it counted. She had hips, full lips, a complexion that boasted of her rich heritage, and high cheekbones that accented her large eyes.

My admission had frightened her.

I could almost taste the fear in the air. It was a gift, being able to read people, being able to measure the emotions in the room and control them in order to benefit myself.

I toyed with the idea of letting her go for maybe a second. If I wasn't so selfish I'd give her a new ID with a passport and send her on her way.

But I'd always been a selfish bastard, and she was my prize.

The one I'd waited for, but more than that, part of the contract stated she had to be in the right mind before she was freed, and I knew that even my work wasn't always a guarantee.

I bent and pressed the remote switch beneath the table top and brought the lights up. I'd expected her to blink, momentarily disoriented. Instead, she leveled a stare on me.

"I don't understand," Maya said calmly.

She would be calm in this situation. She was always the type to fight rather than give up—I at least remembered that much about her.

"I'm not asking you to," I said simply, my eyes focused in on her smooth neck and then her lips. "And you have no choice in the matter, no say, no voice."

Her jaw clenched.

My heart raced. I loved the fight. It was like waving a flag in front of a bull. I braced myself against my desk, my fingers digging into the mahogany as I evened my breathing.

"I'm not something you can own or buy or purchase." Her nostrils flared, "I'm leaving."

"You can't," I said softly.

She stood, her knees knocked together, and then she sat and reached into her purse.

She was going for her phone.

Because a part of her believed me, which was fine because all I needed was a part of her. I didn't want her to be whole, and it wasn't my place to take more than she had to give.

I wanted a piece.

In order to give her peace.

In order for her to discover herself.

And in order for me to die without regret, without what I did hanging over my head.

Funny, I'd always believed myself to be a sociopath. Doctors couldn't figure me out. My own parents were terrified of my intelligence. It made me too damn good at what I did.

And for a while I had been okay with it.

Until her.

And then, my world, the world that had always been so very black and white, started dripping with red.

Maya Petrov had been my game changer, but I still wasn't sure if I was going to make her pay, atone for my sins, or destroy us both.

But what's the fun in playing chess when you already know all the moves?

With shaking hands she dug around her purse.

Her hair was longer than I remembered, her body fuller. Alexander Petrov had known what he was doing when he sent her. I imagined him on the other side of the chess board, grinning like a damn fool. I sighed and looked away, mumbling under my breath. "Check mate."

CHAPTER THREE

Love is evil. It will make you fall in love with a goat—Russian Proverb

Maya

MY BREATHING WAS ERRATIC, OUT OF control actually. I knew running would do nothing, plus I wasn't really that type—a runner. My father had taught me that—the same father who had just sold me to the highest bidder. I paused, had there been an auction for my life? My body? My stomach clenched as memories assaulted me—I knew what he did, what he involved himself in.

My father worked for the Russian mafia it wasn't a secret in our family or something we tried to hide. After all, he fought too hard to do things the right way, supported all the right universities, went to all the political parties. We were, from the outside, normal.

But there were always those times when I'd overheard

conversations between my parents that I wondered… was my dad as good as he wanted people to believe or was it all a lie?

I got my answer when the very first boyfriend I had in high school lost his hand in a tragic accident.

The same hand that my dad had seen said boy place on my body just as I tried to shove him away.

I didn't think much of it at the time, until every time I complained about something, an accident would happen. It was why I kept people away, because when they got close, they got hurt.

It was also why I was a certifiable nerd, pouring everything I had into studying and getting away from my family's hold on me.

With a sigh, I pulled out my cell.

"I wouldn't." Mr. Blazik had somehow made his way from the desk to the couch again and was holding my hand, keeping me from dialing. "I really wouldn't."

"He's gone too far." I jerked my hand away and dialed my father's number. It didn't ring.

Instead, a chipper voice informed me that the number I was currently dialing was no longer in service.

With shaking hands I shoved the phone back into my purse and stared at the floor. "How much?"

"How much, what?" The couch dipped under pressure as Mr. Blazik sat down.

"Am I worth?" I whispered, voice hoarse.

He was quiet for a few seconds before answering in a hoarse voice. "For a man like me? Everything."

My breath hitched in my chest. Everything hurt, from the betrayal of my father, to the fact that I probably wouldn't be able to finish my education because somewhere along the way I'd turned into a pawn instead of a daughter.

"You're not crying," Mr. Blazik observed. "I expected more… emotion."

"Would that make you feel better about owning me?" I snapped. "Or are tears the only thing that get you off?"

"You'll be taken care of." He ignored my rampage as he pulled out a new iPhone and placed it on the table. Then he opened a black folder, laid a sheet of paper next to the phone, and handed me a pen that probably cost more than some people's cars. "Sign on the dotted line please."

"Are you seriously asking me to sign my life away right now?"

"It's not yours in the first place…" His soft sigh was filled with resignation "It's mine. I own you… but I'd rather you be a willing participant."

"You're just as sick as he is," I whispered, reaching for the pen and scribbling my name across the bottom of the contract without reading it.

"I hope you'll come to regret saying that." He barely glanced at the paper now bearing my signature. "Now, let's discuss your… services."

"I'm not servicing you."

His eyebrows shot up to his forehead. "I'm sorry, did I ask you to?"

"N-no, but—"

He held up his hand. "You'll report to work every morning at eight a.m., you'll leave when I say you can leave, and everything you do for me is top secret. If any information is leaked to the public… well…"

Yeah, I knew that look. *I'd* be leaked to the public—in a very accidental way.

"So I work for you?" I stood and crossed my arms. "For how long?"

His smile was wicked, "A year." He reached out and tilted my chin toward his mouth. "Perhaps more… if I find you agreeable."

"I'm not sleeping with you."

"I don't recall asking you to."

My eyes narrowed. "So that's it? You just need a glorified secretary?"

"Something like that…" He ran his hands through his hair and reached into his pocket, pulling out a key. "Shall we have lunch?"

"Wait." I shook my head. "That's it? My evil father basically sells me to you, and now we're going to go to Wendy's?"

"I hate hamburgers."

I clenched my teeth together.

"But if that's your preference…" He placed his hand on the small of my back and directed me toward the door. I moved to pick up my discarded phone. "Leave it, that's your old life, Maya."

I hated that he not only knew my first name, but that the way he said it made me shiver.

"My old life?" I croaked. "And today is what? The first day of the rest of my life?"

His eyes darkened. "Let's just hope you live long enough to enjoy it, hmm?"

CHAPTER FOUR

Another murder has taken place, this one reportedly, near Starbucks on Pike street. Police ask that Seattle residents trust them to solve the case, the reward for the Pier killer has been raised to seventy five thousand dollars. Any information is helpful. —The Seattle Tribune

Maya

A BLACK FOLDER WAS SLAMMED ONTO the table in front of me, it may was well have been a gavel, the sound emitted carried a certain type of finality. The nail in the coffin. The fat lady singing. The pig flying. It was my end, and I was horrified that the powerful man in front of me had a say in it.

I couldn't decide if I was terrified or simply scared.

"Aren't you going to read it?" Mr. Blazik asked, his eyes alight with humor. Most likely at my expense, the ass.

I shoved the folder even harder into my purse and glared. "I'd rather not."

"Your loss." He shrugged, pressing the penthouse floor.

"I thought we were going to lunch." The elevator started to move. Panicked, I braced myself against the wall.

"We are," he answered, pulling his cell phone from his pocket and firing a text off. "Tell me, are you always this silent?" He shoved the cell back into his fitted black pants and leveled me with a curious stare.

"Yes," I snapped. Maybe if I was horrible to him he'd leave me alone, or release me from whatever contract he'd made with my father.

With a smirk, he nodded his head once and pressed the emergency stop on the elevator.

In most movies or books that's where the girl either dies or gets the crap kissed out of her.

I wasn't sure what I was hoping for, or why my body had any business arching as he neared, but arch it did, as if ready for his touch.

Which was ridiculous.

Because he owned me.

Quite literally.

And honestly, I don't care what anyone says, it may appear sexy when you see it on TV—but it's not, it's horrifying. Absolutely degrading. It makes you feel like less of a person, less of a woman, more of a possession.

And I'd been fighting my whole life to be something more than that.

Because that was exactly how my father always treated my mom.

And I despised him for it.

"Listen." Mr. Blazik braced his hands on either side of the wall.

The beeping in the elevator was starting to make my ears ring. My head swam, and I realized I'd stopped breathing. I sucked in a lungful of air that smelled like his spicy cologne.

"This doesn't have to be difficult."

"Then let me go," I hissed, pushing at his chest.

He looked down at my hand, still resting against his body, almost curiously, as if he hadn't been touched in all his thirty-two years. "Your hands… they're warm."

I jerked my hand back. "What? Only used to working with corpses?"

His eyes flashed as his body pressed mine hard against the wall. My head nearly collided with a light fixture as I gazed up into his cold eyes. "As of right now, I don't give a shit who your father is, or who you are. You work for me. I own you. Give me attitude, and it's only going to make things harder—for both of us. Now," he said, stepping back and tugging at his collar. "Let me at least feed you since I can hear your stomach growling from here. Then I'll show you where you'll be staying for the next year."

My stomach dropped. "Staying as in…" I gulped. "Living?"

"What is living… really?" He shrugged and pressed the red button, and the elevator continued to move up, finally stopping at the penthouse floor. "After you." He nodded.

I stepped into the hallway. The floors were a black marble, the walls were a matching gray, and again, it felt cold, like someone had decorated it with only one thought in mind—that it would be easy to clean the mess left by victims of gunshot—or other—wounds from the tile rather than carpet.

"It's—" I swallowed hard. "—nice."

"It's hideous." He stepped around me. "Yet absolutely necessary."

"Right." I blew air between my lips. "Because of the vampires?"

His hand froze on the lock. "So you do have a sense of humor."

"Only with friends."

He turned his head, affording me a glimpse of the slight shadow of his jaw and his full lips. "I don't have many of those."

"Shocker." I crossed my arms.

With a smirk, he twisted the lock and pushed the large black door open.

White.

Everything was white. If the hallway was the location of a vampire coven, then the apartment was something straight from heaven.

White leather sections covered half the space in front of the living area with a flat screen TV. Large gray fur rugs covered the white marble.

White drapes hung over the floor to ceiling windows.

A diamond chandelier hung above my head.

It almost burned my eyes to blink, everything was so bright. I did a small circle, my eyes resting on the full gourmet kitchen. Stainless steel double oven, gas stove, and an incredibly large fridge that looked like it could hold at least four people inside, dwarfed the rest of the kitchen.

"Do you like it?" Mr. Blazik asked, setting the key on the white granite countertop.

"It's... something." I shivered. "No color?"

"Not here," he barked, though his eyes seemed to penetrate right through me, like he was waiting for me to run or scream.

I held up my hands, seriously, one minute the guy was calm, not necessarily warm but at least somewhat kind, the next he looked ready to turn a knife on himself—I shivered—or on me.

"Mr. Blazik—"

"Nikolai," he corrected. "If you don't mind."

I ground my teeth together. "Nikolai, is there a reason we're here?"

"To eat." He flashed me a white toothy grin that matched perfectly with the décor around us. "And to make sure you get settled in."

He moved effortlessly through the kitchen and began pulling things from the dinosaur fridge—I couldn't help thinking of it as T-rex, the thing was so huge—he set some cheese, bread, and grapes on the counter, then pulled out some sliced meat. Everything looked like it had been prepared or catered for a specific event.

I really hoped I wasn't that special event, but I had a sinking suspicion I was.

I quietly set my purse down on the white couch and made my way over to the kitchen.

Nikolai retrieved a bottle of chilled champagne from T-rex, popped the cork, without injuring me or anything else in the apartment, and poured two glasses.

My hands were still shaking when he gently shoved the glass against my trembling fingers. I hated that I gave myself away so easily—but what woman, I don't care how strong, wouldn't be freaking out?

It was all like a bad dream.

Gorgeous billionaire kidnapping me from my drug lord family? Hah, right, I think I read that somewhere in a book.

But this wasn't a book.

It was as real as death, and something warned me that if I pushed him too far, he'd break—and I'd be caught in the storm, unable to save myself or anything around me.

The terror was coming back full force. I had no idea who this man was—outside of reading magazines and watching interviews on TV. He was brilliant, he was rich, and something about him was clearly… off.

"Let's make a toast." Nikolai said, his dark eyes trained on my mouth. "Shall we?" His eyes jerked away from my mouth as if I'd done something offensive like try to breathe or something.

"A toast," I repeated. "Am I supposed to pretend like this is a happy moment in my life?"

Nikolai set down his flute and pressed his palms flat against the granite, his expression hard, his mouth set in a grim line. "Life doesn't always go as planned. Think of it this way, you wanted to interview me, and now you have an internship. Make it through the next year, and who knows what doors may open for you?"

"So that's it…" I held the champagne to my lips. "You want me to pretend I'm okay with this for a year—and when I'm finished being your secretary I get my freedom?"

"Freedom…" He lifted his glass again, his dark gaze finding mine, penetrating to my very soul. "…has to be earned."

"So," I said, irritated that my voice came out in a hoarse croak, "how do I earn it?"

He took a long swig of champagne and grinned. "Maybe you should read what's in that folder… ask and you shall receive, Maya."

I finished the entire glass of champagne in one gulp.

"Eat." He tapped his manicured fingertips against the counter. "I'll be back in three hours to check on you and make sure everything is agreeable." He started walking toward the door then paused. "Oh, and Maya? I'd really read that folder if I were you."

"If I read it that means this is really happening." My voice was shaking, I couldn't control it anymore than I could control my emotions.

Nikolai hung his head. "Sweetheart, some things have been set into motion for centuries, things you can't fathom or understand. This moment right here, this is taking place because of things that you have no control over. You coming here today is proof of that. When you sin…" His eyes flashed.

"It's only a matter of time before you're asked to repent."

"Repent?" I repeated. "But I didn't do anything!"

"Maybe not." He jerked open the door. "But your father did. And the daughter carries the sins of her father..." With one final glance in my direction he shut the door behind him.

And locked it.

I ran over to the counter top searching frantically for the key.

Nothing.

Maybe it only sounded like a locking mechanism, I rushed to the door and pulled. No such luck.

I banged my fists against the wall. What if there was a fire? What if I started choking on a peanut and needed 911?

"Bastard!" I hissed, kicking the door with my high heel and stomping back into the living room.

I couldn't enjoy the beauty because it felt so wrong, so...t rapping, so final, like a high-priced cage with invisible bars. For the most part I felt like I was handling things. I mean, I didn't have a nervous breakdown, but I wasn't the type of person to do that.

I was logical, a realist. It only made sense that what he was doing was illegal, but I knew firsthand men like Nikolai, men like my father, they were above the law, they had the law in their back pockets.

With a shudder, I walked over to the kitchen and poured myself another glass of champagne to settle my nerves. My eyes fell to the couch and my purse with the black folder sticking out.

Blowing out a heavy breath, I chugged the rest of the glass and made my way over to the couch.

I could do this.

Reading. I could read. The words had no power over me and Nikolai had no power over me—regardless of what he believed.

The folder was thick and heavy. I sat on the couch and opened it to the first page.

It was the contract he'd asked me to sign, I imagined he would have made copies of it so tearing it up would do no good. It was a basic NDA saying if I spoke to the press or anyone about the happenings of Blazik Enterprises I'd be sued.

I skipped the fine print and went on to the next page.

Job Title: Intern.

Hah! So, he wasn't lying about that part. Feeling a bit more optimistic I kept reading underneath the bold print.

—**Don't ask questions. Ever.**

—**Don't give your opinion.**

—**Dress Code: Black. If an error occurs during operations and you need to get something dry cleaned, you must wait before sending it in.**

—**No outside phone calls.**

—**Eight-hour work day. Vacation available but travel must be first approved by Mr. Blazik and will be monitored**.

I scrunched up my nose, what did that mean? Monitored? At least he was going to let me vacation though I had a sinking feeling we had two very different definitions of the word.

—**No relationships.**

—**No family.**

—**No Internet.**

Seriously? So I was basically going to be locked up in a fancy apartment for an entire year, wearing black, and doing... what? His laundry? I grit my teeth and read the next line, my eyes nearly fall out of my head at the next line.

—**No sexual relationships. Must stay pure the entire year**.

My cheeks heated with embarrassment. How in the world did he know I was still a virgin, and what business was it of his in the first place? Rage overtook me as I threw the papers across the table and cursed.

It wasn't for lack of trying—the whole virginity thing. But my father had made sure no man touched me. And every time I did date it was like the men in my life panicked and backed off. The one and only time I'd gotten close to hooking up with a random guy from a bar—don't ask, low point in my life—I went home with him and he had a freaking heart attack—at twenty-eight—in my bedroom.

He lived.

But blamed me.

What? Like my mere presence caused his heart to stop?

Tears stung at the back of my eyes as I glared at the papers. I wanted a life away from my father, away from his control, away from my family. This morning I'd been so excited about my research, about meeting a man who was my idol.

It sucked.

Meeting someone you idolized for five years only to find out he's not the hero after all—but a complete monster in disguise.

Two and a half hours—and my monster would return.

I'd be ready.

I just needed to say that in the mirror about fifty more times after finishing that bottle of champagne.

CHAPTER FIVE

Police suspect the Pier Killer may be a woman based on the hate crime toward women's reproductive organs, reports reveal — The Seattle Tribune

Nikolai

THE ELEVATOR DOORS CLOSED. I GLANCED at my reflection through the smooth metallic surface and looked away.

My entire life I'd avoided mirrors, shiny surfaces — anything that would reveal to me what I already knew about myself.

That I was a monster.

The eyes are the window to the soul, and I knew better than anyone else that mine was a very dark place. In bartering for Maya's life, I hadn't once thought about what I would do when I was finished with her.

Granted, she had to survive that long.

And so many pieces had to fall into place for that to happen that I knew getting attached would damn near kill me, destroy possibly the last shred of humanity I had left.

When the doors opened, I forced a smile across my lips—it felt awkward—it always did because happiness was such a foreign emotion I wasn't sure I would even recognize it if it came and hit me upside the head.

"Mr. Blazik." Tom Mikelson, one of the board members, walked by me giving a slight wave of his hand.

"Tom." I nodded and forced the smile wider. "How's your wife? Recovering from hip surgery?"

"Oh yes." Tom rocked back on his heels then pushed his spectacles up on his large nose. He resembled a younger version of Santa Claus, with graying hair, ruddy cheeks and pronounced lips and nose, he was the closest thing to a friend I had.

Which was pathetic when I really thought about it.

"She loved the flowers." He nervously tapped his pen against his leg as he was prone to do when I engaged in conversation with him. He was fidgety, always fidgety when approached by authority. "You didn't really have to do that."

"I did," I said in a soft voice, trying to put him at ease. "And I'm happy she's doing well."

"Yes well." Tom cleared his throat.

"Was there something else?"

He sighed and shoved his hands in his pockets. "Mr. Petrov is waiting for you in your office. I noticed him waltz in when I was coming down to deliver some contracts."

"Thank you." I touched his shoulder. "I'll deal with him. Why don't you take a long lunch?" I pulled back. "In fact, take off the afternoon, visit that wife of yours."

His eyes narrowed in the protective way they often did when he suddenly felt the need to come to my defense, I might be the boss but he had a son my age, and always felt the need to step up to the battle if called. "Listen Nikolai, if Petrov is sniffing around again I can—"

"It's fine." I chuckled. "I promise. Now, go take care of your wife, and I'll see you tomorrow."

He licked his lips, his eyes darting back and forth with uncertainty before he stepped back and nodded. "Right. I'll do that."

"Good afternoon, Tom."

"Nikolai."

He rarely called me by my first name. It still made him uncomfortable to do so, and he only threw it out there when he was concerned. I thought of it as a paternal instinct, but I wouldn't know. Both my parents were dead.

I straightened my tie and made my way to my office.

Sheila, my assistant, shared a look of disdain with me before shaking her head and grabbing her purse.

"An hour should be adequate." I opened the door for her to leave and listened to her heels click against the marble floors. Typically, she took her breaks whenever Petrov was in the building. I didn't want her asking questions, and I sure as hell didn't need her to know what was going on so that she could incriminate not only herself but my entire company.

I reached for the door to my office and pulled it open.

Classical music floated through the air. The distinct smell of expensive cigars and my finest whiskey gave way to the familiar scent of Petrov. He was seated at my desk as if he owned the damn world, twirling a cigar between his fingers.

"How did it go?" he asked.

"As well as could be expected." I walked over to the sidebar and poured myself a healthy glass of whiskey and sat on the couch, showing him my ease at his visit even while I was wondering in the back of my mind if he really would keep his end of the bargain.

"Good." He stood. "I was worried."

"Bullshit." I took a swig of whiskey. "Try again."

He pulled his lips back, revealing even white teeth as he

formed a menacing smile against his pale complexion and dark hair. Petrov was a large man, he enjoyed the finer things in life and it showed in his skin and inability to wear a suit that wasn't made strictly for his large body.

"Can a father not be concerned for his daughter?"

I pressed my lips together to keep myself from insulting him and stood. What about his other daughter? The one that was currently dying from cancer? Did he care for her? Just thinking of Andi made me want to run my fist through the man's arrogant face, but now wasn't the time to act, not yet. "So, now that you know she's just fine, you'll be leaving? Wasn't that part of the deal?"

"The deal..." he repeated, puffing out smoke from his mouth. "I've come to renegotiate."

"No." I walked slowly toward the door.

"I rarely hear that word."

"I wonder if it's because you kill the individuals before they have a chance to utter it." I tilted my head in amusement. "Now, if that's all?"

"This isn't over." Petrov put out his cigar on my mahogany desk and strutted toward the door. "Eventually you will renegotiate, you'll need a favor so I keep your little secret quiet."

It wasn't fear I experienced in that moment, more like dread. I'd fought for years to keep my identity a secret, to keep my family name in the clear.

"The contract states you have no choice." I crossed my arms. "So unless one of us breaks said contract..."

"Hah." He tilted his head back and barked out a strangled laugh. "Have you seen my Maya? I'm surprised the contract isn't already void."

"I have self control." Disgusted that my suspicions were correct, I turned away from him, giving him my back was basically like pulling a gun on the man. It was disrespectful, but it was all I had. Having him in the same building, let alone the same city as Maya didn't sit well with me. She'd always been more of a pawn than a daughter, and I was beginning to realize how much.

"Till we meet again," Petrov said in a calm voice.

The door to my office shut with a quiet click.

And I was left staring at the smoking cigar on my desk. Wondering how the hell I was going to keep my end of the bargain, when ten minutes ago I was contemplating all the ways I could break it.

CHAPTER SIX

The last female victim has been identified as Mary Smith, a drug addict and prostitute. She was HIV positive. –The Seattle Tribune

Maya

THREE HOURS LATER AND I WAS still in a state of utter disbelief. I searched the entire apartment. No computer. No phone, not even a phone jack, yes I'd actually gotten desperate enough to search for one.

I was stuck in a freaking compound.

At least I had food. And alcohol.

Pacing the marble white floor, I started chewing my thumbnail. I was a smart girl, logical, able to put pieces together, but each time I tried to make the pieces fit, it was like they rejected each other, and I was just as confused as before.

Who was Nikolai Blazik? And why was I so important?

What the hell did my father do to get on this guy's bad side? Furthermore, how was Nikolai in the type of position that he could exert power over my father—one of the scariest individuals I'd ever known?

Nothing made sense.

Except one thing… if my father made a deal with Nikolai, that meant he was a scary man, a bad man, one who would think nothing of killing me and making it look like an accident.

My head still hurt.

The sound of a lock turning had my heart speeding up like I was getting ready to witness my own murder. Funny, how I'd look back on that very moment and realize how true my own words were.

But in that moment, with the lock turning, all I could think was that it was some sort of sick joke, or that surely Nikolai would re-think his decision. I had absolutely nothing to offer him—other than my brain and couldn't he find any girl to do what he needed me to do?

Air whooshed out of my lungs at seeing him again. It should be a crime to be so beautiful, it was as if every single part of his body was in perfect sync with the universe as he made his way slowly across the marble floor, his shoes hitting in perfect cadence with my heart beat.

Slowly, his lips turned up into a breathtaking smile. One that had me staggering backward and wishing he was ugly so I could hate him.

But it was hard to hate pretty. Even I had to admit that. And Nikolai? He was more than pretty, he was beautiful. All our lives we're told that ugly, deformed, is bad—but it's a lie. Sometimes the most terrifying things you will ever encounter are also the most beautiful.

"I see you've read the folder?" He pointed down at the coffee table where I'd basically made a massacre of all the different pages.

"Yeah." I croaked. My body and voice were so not in sync

at that moment and my heart was still beating so hard I was afraid he was going to see the pulse in my neck and attack vampire style—he seemed the type. In fact, the whole scenario seemed like a vampire movie gone bad.

"Any questions?" His right hand grazed my shoulder gently prodding me toward the couch. With no other option but to listen to his crazy talk, I sat.

"Questions." I huffed. "Why can't I have access to the outside world? You do realize this is kidnapping, right?"

Nikolai pressed his lips together like he was fighting not to laugh. "Kidnapping would mean you were a mere child I'd lured here under false pretenses. Need I remind you, you spent the better part of your year calling my offices begging—"

"I didn't beg."

"—begging…" Brushing off my protest like an insignificant insect, he continued. "… for one interview, for ten minutes of my time, at first I believe you asked for an hour but when that wouldn't work you were willing to meet me for twenty minutes, fifteen, finally ten, and I think the last phone call bordered on needing a restraining order when you threatened my secretary."

Heat rushed into my face. "Well, I wasn't sure she was giving you my messages."

"She was."

Awkward. I chewed my lipstick—or what was left of it— from my lower lip. "So you're saying that I'm here by choice."

"Was it your choice to come to the office this afternoon?"

"Yes but—"

"And was it your choice to ask for an interview?"

"Yes." I gritted my teeth. "But had I known it would be you owning me, not allowing me to question you, then I would have said no."

He tilted his head to the side, his dark brown eyes going completely black. "That's a lie."

"So now I'm a liar?"

"Yes." He said it so simply, so confidently, that I wanted to strangle him. "You would have been too curious to turn me down."

"Hah, curiosity killed the cat." I made a cutting motion across my throat.

His eyes narrowed in on my neck, as if watching the very pulse that was starting to speed up again. "You have beautiful skin... it's very... soft isn't it?" Lean fingers reached out and tapped the rhythm of my pulse against my neck. "Hmm..."

"Um." My lips were trembling in anticipation of more touching. "About the job."

"It's yours," he whispered, still not taking his eyes from my neck.

"Gee thanks, because that's what I came here for, a job where I'm locked away from the Internet, can't make any phone calls or watch Netflix, oh, and am apparently prevented from engaging in any sort of sexual relationship."

His hand jerked back. "So that's what this is about?"

"Yes," I said through clenched teeth. "Being locked up in solitary doesn't piss me off, but not being able to have sex does." The asshole was insufferable!

Nostrils flaring, he turned away. "It's impossible."

"What is?"

"A relationship." He swallowed, his Adam's apple bobbing up and down that gorgeous neck of his. I really needed to stop staring. He was the enemy—not a friend.

I think in those early moments I recognized things that should have given me warning. The way he stood, the way he touched me, even his eyes. My subconscious had been warning me, but I was too horrified at my circumstances to listen.

Until it was too late.

"The pay is extravagant." He licked his lips. "Half a

million."

"A year?" I croaked out. I'd been surrounded by money my whole life, but money, as my father said, had to be earned, it wasn't freely given. Blood money above all else, was always earned.

"No." Nikolai stood. "A month."

"What?" I jumped to my feet. "Half a million a month? What the heck do you have me doing? Burying bodies!"

He threw his head back and laughed. "Would you? For half a million a month?"

"No." Yes, probably, damn it!

"Another lie." He angled his head in the other direction. "Come now, aren't we close enough that you can at least be honest about what makes you tick…?" He moved until he was chest to chest with me, until there was maybe an inch of space between our lips. I fought the urge to lean. He smelled so good and something about him, maybe it was just his indifference, made me want to pick apart all his pieces.

See? I was back at the puzzle scenario.

"I barely know you," I said in a strained voice.

"Would you like to?" His eyes hooded.

"If you let me go… I'll come back to work every day. I swear, just let me have some sort of freedom and—"

"The contract is non-negotiable, I'm afraid. You either agree or…" His features inscrutable, he offered a weak half-shrug.

"Or?" I crossed my arms, taking a step back. "You kill me and bury my body?"

"You paying me half a million?" he fired back with a smile that actually managed to reach his eyes. "Everyone has a price, Maya."

"I don't."

"You do." He nodded, and his smile dwindled a bit. "Your price was an interview, and look how generous I'm being… giving you a year in my presence."

"So now I'm supposed to say thank you?"

"It would only be polite." He smirked. "But I'm a patient man. I'll wait until you say the words."

"I never will."

"Lie after lie… Will you never learn?"

"What are you, a personal lie detector?"

His eyes drank me in for a few seconds before he whispered, "I know people."

A shiver rippled through me but I managed to suppress it. "At least give me Internet."

"I'll tell you what…" He crossed his arms, mimicking me. "I'll give you Internet… after you've worked for a few days and I find your work acceptable."

"And if it's not."

"Then we're back to burying bodies, aren't we?" Another smile lifted his lips. That meant he was joking, right?

"Okay."

"Fabulous." He rubbed his hands together. "Now, go get dressed."

"I am dressed."

"Work." He said in an 'all business' manner, "Will start this evening, only because I don't have all week to train you. I need to be in Chicago Friday."

"You get to go to Chicago while I sit in solitary confinement?"

"Would it make you happy if I gave you access to the library?"

"Library?" I perked up.

"You love the classics, am I right?"

"Stop being creepy."

He threw his head back and laughed. "I don't think anyone's ever called me that."

"To your face, probably not."

"I like you."

Schooling my expression, I leveled a cool stare on him and forced calm into my voice, even though I was ready to lose my sanity. "Well the feeling's not mutual."

He smirked. "Believe me, it will be. Now, go get dressed. The closet in the master bedroom should have adequate clothing. Wear all black and please try not to take too long, we don't want to be late."

"You're the boss. It's impossible to be late."

"Maya," he snapped. "Get dressed. Now."

Was I getting to him? A little thrill shot through me at the possibility. "Say please."

"I haven't uttered that word in ten years."

"Try."

With a long sigh he looked away and murmured. "Please."

"Better."

He pointed down the hall. "Go."

"Fine." I shuffled off into the general direction of the master bedroom and quickly found an outfit that would work. Black leggings, a long black sweater, and black boots.

Several masks lined the wall of my closet, the type that might be worn at a masquerade. Did that mean he hosted parties up here? Or was he thinking I'd somehow put on a mask, too? Well, he was in for one hell of a fight because I wasn't dressing up like it was Halloween in order to do a job I didn't even want. I accidently knocked one of the masks off the wall as I walked by. With a curse I bent down and picked one up. There was something so familiar about the white, something so... red. It made absolutely no sense but it was almost like I could see blood staining it. With a shake of my head, I stood, placing it back on the wall and put on my shoes.

Ten minutes later I stomped out of the bedroom and did a little circle in front of him. "This work?"

"It will." His eyes devoured me. "I believe you'll do just fine. Remember, no talking."

"At all?"

"To the patients."

"Patients." I froze. "Like real patients."

"No, dead ones."

I laughed.

He didn't.

"Let's go." His jaw made a clicking noise as he clenched it and led me toward the door. "We don't want to be late for our first appointment."

****

Downtown Seattle
Six hours later

"DO YOU REPENT?" THE *air crackled with excitement as the knife flickered in the moonlight streaming through the windows. "Answer me!"*

But she couldn't—answer at least, her muscles were completely useless thanks to the drugs in her system.

"No?" The knife sliced through the air. "Shall I help you repent?"

A lone tear trailed down the woman's cheek, mixing with the blood from the cut in her lip.

"Fine." The knife met skin.

It pierced.

The blood was red. Pure.

And all was right in the world once more.

CHAPTER SEVEN

The body cuts were perfect, the organs removed as if the killer has the gift of a surgeon. Police are currently working hand in hand with all the local hospitals. —The Seattle Tribune

Maya

"YOU'RE NOT WEARING BLACK," I BLURTED once we were in the parking garage, my eyes scanning over the crisp white button up and the same black slacks he'd worn to our initial meeting.

"How very intuitive of you, Maya." Nikolai mused placing his hand on my lower back.

"Ass."

His lips twitched.

At least he had somewhat of a sense of humor.

"Get in." He opened the door to a black Audi A8. I slid in to the leather seat and looked around. The car seemed heavier than normal sedans or sports cars. I'd always loved Audi's but this one wasn't like others I'd seen on the road.

Curiosity got the best of me, when Nikolai got in and

turned the key I asked. "What kind of Audi is this?"

"A safe one," he said with a simple shrug, his lips pressing together in a firm line. "Throw a grenade at it and we'd walk away without a scratch."

"You uh, get grenades thrown at you often?"

"One can never be too careful."

"Hmm." I leaned back and crossed my arms as classical music floated through the car. "So, the location of our first appointment."

"A simple office building—nothing special."

"Right." I started nervously cracking my knuckles.

"Don't." His teeth clenched as he placed a solid warm hand across mine. "Just… don't, not now."

"Um, okay." His hand hadn't left mine. "Sorry."

"You should be," he snapped then jerked away from me like the feel of my skin somehow offended him.

Right. So I was back at the crazy theory.

We drove the rest of the way in complete silence—except for the violin music in the background. It seemed melodramatic. Driving through downtown Seattle with a billionaire in a car that could withstand World War Three, only to get trained for my new job.

Where I had no rights as a human being.

Yeah I was a bad romance novel waiting to happen.

He stopped the car at Pier 44 and turned off the engine. "Shall we?"

Nikolai didn't wait for me to answer, simply got out of the car. Dumbly, I followed. What other option did I have?

He was still dressed in his tight white button up and black pants. Why was it that I had to change and he didn't? The salty wet air stung my nostrils as we walked down the pier and finally stopped in front of a red door.

I looked around while he pulled out a key and shoved it in the lock. What could a man like him possibly be doing on the pier? In the dead of night? And why did he need my help?

"Do not speak." He hissed before grabbing my elbow and jerking me through the entrance. He kept his arm wrapped around me. I wasn't sure if it was because he was nervous I'd cut and run, or because it was so freaking cold in that place it could have been a freezer.

I shivered.

"You'll get used to it," he whispered across my ear.

"But don't I want to," I muttered under my breath.

His teeth flashed in what I assumed was a smile—I didn't want to think he was gnashing his teeth at me so early on in our working relationship. Maybe I was trying to stay positive.

I shivered again and crossed my arms, trying to keep my body heat from evaporating into whatever hellish nightmare I'd just walked into.

Nikolai walked toward one of the walls and flipped a switch.

The lights flickered on one by one, reminding me of those horror movies where the buzzing of the lights being on is almost as freaky as the lights being off.

Everywhere I looked was white.

White marble floors.

White couches.

And a white receptionist desk with a red J hanging down the front. If I wasn't so freaked out, I'd probably think everything looked modern and cool, not exactly inviting but not terrifying either.

Magazines littered the coffee table in the middle of the room, and a large bay window overlooked the Sound.

"Clinical," I muttered under my breath.

The sound of a phone ringing had me nearly colliding with the nearest couch and toppling over backward.

"Phone," Nikolai said in an amused voice. "It's just a phone Maya."

I managed to croak out a weak, "yeah." But was anything as it seemed with him? No, not at all, so excuse me for freaking out over the phone ringing.

"Yes." He answered on the second ring, his gaze trained on the floor. He checked his watch then motioned for me to approach the receptionist desk. "No, no that should work out just fine, I have a new… employee." His eyes found mine.

I wasn't so sure I liked the way he said employee, like I was disposable.

Or edible.

He licked his lips, eying me up and down before glancing back at the floor again. "Give me twenty minutes, then the usual."

He hung up the phone and swore.

"Problem in crazy land?" I asked sweetly.

"I don't believe the contract you signed this afternoon said anything about sarcasm. Or speaking."

"Maybe you should have put that in then before I signed on the dotted line… sir."

His eyes narrowed. "Unfortunate…."

"What is?"

"That you don't mean that term of respect the way it should be meant… I could get used to it."

"Yeah, I bet."

"Turn."

"Excuse me?"

"Around." He placed his hands on my shoulders and twisted my body toward a white door with two windows. "I have exactly eighteen and a half minutes to teach you the basics before we have our first patient."

"I'm seeing real patients?"

Nikolai didn't answer. I'd begun to notice that about him. If he didn't want to answer he simply… refused to speak, as if he didn't owe me anything.

He opened the door leading to the hallway and ushered me through, the lights flickered on all by themselves, lighting up rooms on either side of me. Each of them looked sterile enough that I could probably lick the floors and still be safer than eating while typing on my laptop.

"And behind door number one," Nikolai whispered in my ear, causing a chill to run down both my arms.

He pushed the door open it made a suction noise and then closed behind us. He stretched his arms above his head and cracked his neck then pulled out a pair of latex gloves.

I gulped and tried to stop the sudden panic that sliced through me, "Are we, examining someone?"

He paused, his hands hovering over the sink and table facing the corner. "It would be prudent for you to remember the terms of the contract, Maya."

Right. No questions, or talking.

"Do I need gloves?"

"Is that still a question? Also, if you keep talking, I may remove your tongue, you've been given fair warning."

Did he just say he was going to cut my tongue out? Holy shit, he really was crazy! Did the medical journals know this? Society? People of earth? How did he hide this side of him? I was full on panicking at that moment.

Instead of bossing me around like I figured he'd do, he clapped his hands twice, powder flying off his gloves, more violin music began to come through an unseen sound system.

To be completely honest it was creepy.

Not soothing. Kind of like the music they play in the elevator in hopes to make you forget that you could plummet to your death at any point.

I leaned against the wall and watched him pull out metal instruments. Two scalpels, which made me think surgery. It killed me not asking, and when he pulled out a respirator and grabbed an IV bag, my hands began to shake against my body.

What exactly where we doing? Performing surgery? And in what world was I even close to being adequately capable of doing anything like that? I was studying diseases, but not in the literal sense where I cut up bodies and peered inside—that was a different major, a different type of person.

Books. I liked books.

Hands on experience? No, thank you.

"You will only aid me for a few minutes at a time. When I ask you to leave, you will walk out the door. Shut it behind you and don't look back. You don't ask questions. When the phone rings again, answer it and let him know my projected finish time in order to bring in the new patient. You'll know my projected finish time because I'll text it to the phone I gave you earlier this afternoon."

Blood roared in my ears. So much information yet none of it connected or made sense.

"Maya!" he snapped. "Pay attention."

I swallowed and nodded my head. "Shut the door, don't look back, don't ask questions, answer phone, answer your text. Got it?"

His shoulders sagged a bit.

"What if I don't get your text?"

"Now that…" He smirked. "… is a good question."

"I'm full of them, just let me ask."

"I'm sure you are." His eyebrows drew up in amusement. "If I don't text, you wait for me. If after two hours you receive nothing. You find the black box located underneath the receptionist desk and follow the instructions. It's important that you do exactly what those instructions say."

"Or else?"

"Not the right question." A muscle flexed in his jaw as he looked away and clenched his fists. "Do you think you can handle all of this?"

"No."

Nikolai tilted his head and took two steps toward me. Licking his full lips he leaned in and whispered so close to my mouth I could almost taste him. "Lie."

Afraid to breathe, I answered with a stiff nod and stepped back.

"Now, answer the door."

"But there's no—"

A loud knock sounded somewhere in the building.

"End of the hall, open the door, lead our patient in. Again, no questions."

With more confidence than I felt, since my legs were like rubber as I made my way out of the office, I slowly walked to the end of the hall and opened the door.

I don't know what I was expecting.

The boogie monster?

ET?

A friggin' zombie from Walking Dead?

But a girl about my age stood on the other side of the door. She was wearing the shortest skirt I'd ever seen in my entire life. It was black and wrapped so tightly around her thighs it looked painted on. Her heels were tall and red, matching her bright red lipstick and bright red nails.

Blond hair was piled high on her head.

She assessed me just like I was assessing her.

Her eyes narrowed.

A man about six foot seven towered behind her. He had dark sunglasses on and was wearing all black just like me. The unmarked Lexus behind them was still running.

"Um…" I found my voice. "Just this way."

"How long?" The man asked with a thick Russian accent.

"I'm not sure, I'll just have—"

He held up his hand and sneered, then rubbed his bald head with that same hand. "Never mind."

I opened the door wider and let the girl through.

She smelled like bubble gum. And she looked like a stripper, walked like a stripper, if I didn't know any better I'd think Nikolai had some sort of… agreement with his patients or they weren't patients at all. A sickening feeling started churning in my gut as I led her to the room and opened the door.

"Hey, Doc." She winked and sat on the table. "This can't take long because I have like, a few clients I need to get to tonight, big money."

"Ah, big money?" Nikolai repeated then nodded to me.

I shut the door and waited, my back leaning against the furthest wall just in case he did something that meant I needed to run away—as fast as possible.

Not that there would be anywhere I could disappear to where he or my mafia boss father wouldn't find me.

Dead if I went.

Tortured if I stayed?

I shook the thought away and watched as he engaged the girl as if she was the cutest thing on the planet.

He smiled, freaking smiled at her, flirted with her, and touched her. I wasn't jealous, just… irritated, whatever, I was tired and still freaked out.

"So, Natalia," he purred. "How has business been going? Any complaints?"

"I never get complaints." She giggled behind her hand then leaned forward, her breasts practically toppling out of her low cut sparkly white shirt. "You should know that by now…"

Gross.

"Of course I do," he said in a smooth as sin voice. "Open up for me just a bit."

She opened her mouth while he looked inside and frowned. "How long have the sores been back?"

Sores?

"A few days." She shrugged. "But you know they always

go away when you give me medicine."

"Like all good doctors." He flashed another grin. "Alright... Maya."

My head jerked to attention. "Yes?"

"Across the hall is the storage closet. Can you please get me a small vial of JR 88?"

"Sure." With a gulp, I quickly went across the hall to get the vial. The storage closet was more of a drug addict's paradise. There were enough pills to get a person high for eons—on top of that he had vials of things I couldn't even pronounce. I finally located the right one and hurried back into the room.

Just in time to see Nikolai tuck the scalpel into the lapel of his jacket and pull out a needle.

I handed over the vial and waited.

With precision, he dipped the needle into the bottle then pulled a small amount, maybe the size of a pea, into the syringe. "Now, I know you hate needles."

"Ah but your poking always makes me feel better, doc." She winked.

And I again fought the urge to puke all over his perfect floors.

"All the girls do." He winked right back.

Was I the only one not winking? Not flirting?

He licked his lips, stabbing her arm with the needle and slowly injecting whatever the hell he'd told me to grab. He quickly pulled the needle out once the medicine was gone.

She slumped back, her legs and mouth falling open as if she'd just lost the desire to rein it in. Her eyes rolled up and back, and with a snort or maybe a laugh ,she lay back.

Nikolai placed the vial onto the table, pulled out an IV and inserted it into her wrist, taping it in place.

I was still trying to figure out what he was doing when his head snapped up. "What are you still doing here?"

"I—"

"Leave." He dismissed me with a wave of his hand.

With one final look at the drugged girl, I put my hand on the door knob and twisted.

He told me never to look back.

But I was too curious not to make that attempt.

And my curiosity was only made worse when I saw the reflection of the scalpel in his hand through the window of the door.

"Maya." His tone was gruff. "Do your job."

I didn't look back but the music, the same violin music that had driven me insane, got louder, as if he needed the noise to block out whatever he was doing.

Not my business, not my problem.

I quickly made my way back into the receptionist area and sat down.

The J screen saver was on the computer. I clicked it on.

Internet!

No way

Almost too easy.

"I wouldn't," a chipper female voice said. "Then again, I always liked to push his buttons too."

I glanced up from the screen and came face to face with the most gorgeous elderly lady I'd ever seen in my entire life.

"Can I, uh, help you?"

"No." Her smile was warm. "But I think I can help you— you're my new replacement."

"Oh."

"One of thirty he's had over the last two years." Her shoulders shook with amusement. "Man can't keep a woman to save his life." And then she burst out laughing as if it was the funniest thing in the world. "And you'd think with those looks, that brain, that body." She fanned herself and peeked down the hall. "Still at it, huh?"

"Um, first of the day. Who did you say you were?"

"A friend." She smiled and held out her hand. "You can call me Jaclyn, or just Jac for short."

"Jac." I repeated shaking her soft hand. The woman had more diamonds decorating her fingers than what seemed possible. Each of them sparkled as if telling their own story of love and riches. "So, I'm the thirtieth intern huh?"

"Is that what he told you?"

"Not exactly."

"Intern." She chuckled. "Has a nice ring to it. Has he texted you yet?"

"No, but—"

"He will, he always does. Only had to use the black box once." She nodded, and her eyes fell. "But that was a long, long time ago."

"Um—"

"Oh!" She clapped her hands together, making her entire outfit shake. Wait, was she wearing bells or something? I stood and looked over the counter. The woman couldn't be any taller than five-foot-one. She had red cowboy boots with bells on the tassels and skinny jeans matched with a white sweater. What should have looked stupid looked classy and stylish, like she'd just walked out of Urban Outfitters. Huh. "Why don't I show you the schedule?"

"Alright, but Nikolai didn't say—"

"Nikolai?" Her lips pressed together. "That's allowed then?"

"What is?"

"His first name."

"Apparently."

"You must be special." She smiled brighter. "I'm the only one who calls him by that... then again I'm also the only one who's ever seen the man behind the mask."

"So there's two of them?" I joked.

"Oh, yes." She nodded seriously. "Never forget how important it is to separate the two. Here he's a god."

"As opposed to?"

"Anywhere else…" She placed her hand on mine and squeezed. "He's just a man. Never forget that, sweetheart."

With that, she released my hand and waved at her eyes as if she was going to burst into tears at any moment.

"Goodness, my emotions get me these days. Now, let's look at that schedule, and I'll try to sort out any questions you may have before that elusive text comes through."

"And then what?"

"What dear?"

"After the text?"

"Oh, you bring in the next girl."

"Are they…" I swallowed. "Prostitutes?"

"Labels really do nothing for me." She shrugged again and pulled out a chair plopping right next to me. "If you're really good, tomorrow morning I'll bring you a latte, what's your favorite?"

"Anything with caffeine."

She paused, her eyes getting misty again. "I do hope you last, dear."

"And the others? They quit?"

Her eyes fell to the keyboard as she pulled a hanky from her purse and blew her nose. "Now, the schedule…"

CHAPTER EIGHT

Stay inside, Police Chief Lopez advises. He believes that the Pier killer is preying on women who are prone to leave work late or who work alone. Stay inside, until the security from your building is able to escort you out — only if you are working late. — The Seattle Tribune

Nikolai

INCREDIBLE... HOW HABITUAL MY ACTIVITIES HAD become. I felt nothing. Even when the blood dripped down her arm, I could only glance at the red pigment and wonder what type it was.

Would it be O Negative?

AB positive?

Would taking that blood bring me any closer to a cure? Or would darkness finally consume me — making it so that my habit, my life choices, ended up killing me like they killed so many that I studied?

Her face was void of emotion.

I imagined she had a few more weeks tops.

And then she would be dead like the rest of them. I had known something was wrong with me long before medical school… long before working on the cadavers or losing my first patient in the OR.

I wiped my hands on the towel and injected adrenaline back into her system. Natalia jerked awake.

"All done?"

"Yes." I offered a smile. "The sores should disappear within a few hours, do try to be careful out there tonight."

"Always am." Her lower lip trembled just enough for me to notice. "Hey um doc?"

"Yes Natalia?"

"How long?"

"Well…" I leaned forward. "That's entirely up to you. You've known that since you started coming to the clinic."

Her eyes wavered as she chewed on her lower lip. "I still haven't decided yet, what I want to do."

"When the time comes, I'll ask you again, only you can make that choice, Natalia."

With a quick nod, she hopped off the table and made her way to the door. "The new girl…" Her hand hovered above the door knob. "She's pretty."

I sighed. "All the nurses I hire are pretty."

"Right, but she isn't a nurse, she isn't one of us."

I was quiet for a minute. Leave it to Natalia to figure out that Maya was different. She was beautiful like the rest, just more… pure and innocent in ways Natalia would never understand.

"No." I didn't owe her any more of an answer or explanation.

"I hope she stays that way." Natalia's voice was hardly a whisper. "I really do."

"Me too." I hoped it more than I could possibly describe.

It was why I put certain terms in my contract. Why she was off limits. Why I was off limits to her. I was trying to decide her life for her, form an ironclad path for her to walk through so she made it through alive.

So she made it to her next birthday without becoming exactly what her father would want for her.

Because regardless of Maya not remembering.

She was still a liability, one he kept around for leverage on my behalf.

"Have a good evening, Natalia."

She left.

And the room instantly felt cold.

I wondered how long I could keep it up—before the darkness of my reality consumed me. After all, I wasn't really living for anything except trying to leave a better mark on the world. A legacy. That's what I wanted.

And after knowing what ran through my veins?

It was about damn time someone in our family tried for something different.

Blood had always stained our hands.

I'd still die with it on mine—but hopefully it wouldn't be in vain.

CHAPTER NINE

An enemy will agree, but a friend will argue—Russian Proverb

Maya

HE TEXTED EXACTLY NINETY MINUTES LATER; his instructions were clear.

N: Bring in the next one, I'll be finished in five.

I felt my eyebrows furrow in confusion. What next one? Jac had been showing me how to do the scheduling for the past hour and a half, not that any of that made sense. There were names and contact numbers, but no last names, and no private information about their conditions.

Just first names and numbers.

Though some names had little red X's next to them. Jac said that once the patient had three X's that I was to delete them from the system. I asked if every patient eventually got three X's and she changed the subject and started talking about Christmas decorations.

"Told you he'd text." Jac nodded. "Always does."

"So…" I showed her my phone. "…where do I get the next girl?"

She paused, her lips pressing together in a smile. "Well aren't you just adorable."

"Yeah," I croaked. I'd never been called adorable in my life. Not by my parents who ignored me or the boyfriends who hated me—once my father got ahold of them.

I'd been called sexy.

Cute.

Pretty—at least a handful of times.

But never adorable. Adorable meant innocence, and I wasn't innocent, I was tainted.

"The girls will always be waiting outside the door." She pointed down the hall. "When he texts you to bring in the next girl, you simply open the door, bring her down the hall and leave when he tells you."

"Okay." I licked my dry lips and rose from my seat. "I guess I'll be right back then."

"Remember," Jac called after me, "don't ask questions."

I wasn't sure why it was so important for her to remind me of that one little rule, so I shrugged her off and sighed as I made my way down the hall.

The next girl waiting had a pixie haircut and shoved a cigarette between her teeth before looking me up and down and smirking. "You're new."

"Yup," I breathed.

"He screw you yet?" Her eyebrows shot up to her hairline.

"I'm his employee."

"They all are." She rolled her eyes, and shoved past me. "I know the way."

I followed behind her because what choice did I have? When she stopped at the room and peered in, her face softened.

The door opened.

Nikolai stepped out. "Anastasia." He grinned. "How are you feeling?"

"Better now," She said in a breathy sigh.

I rolled my eyes.

"Something bothering you?" Nikolai snapped.

Crap. He saw me.

"No." I cleared my throat. "Just tired."

His eyes narrowed. "That will be all, Maya."

"Right." I clenched my fists and walked past them, this time I didn't look back, I didn't want to know. Something was very wrong with what he was doing, I just didn't know what. And it wasn't like he had some great paper trail for me to follow on his stupid computer. All I had to go by were names, and a contact number.

When I walked back into the main lobby Jac was putting her coat back on and checking her cell phone. "It will get better," she said without looking up from her phone. "It always does."

"Right." I grit my teeth, wondering if I should take the chance and tell her about the contract, ask her if the other girls had to sign them, or even just give a lame *"Help"* in her direction and see if she would take pity on me and rescue me from his evil clutches.

"I promise." Jac leaned over the counter, placing her manicured hands on the table. "It seems overwhelming for now, but this is such a great opportunity."

"Is it?" I parroted.

"Of course!" Her eyes twinkled. "Just think of the job opportunities you'll receive after you work with Nikolai for a few months."

"A year," I corrected.

She froze. "Pardon?"

Had I said something wrong? I tucked a strand of escaped hair behind my ear and shrugged. "My contract says a year."

Her mouth opened then shut. When she spoke, her voice seemed a little strained. "A year is quite a long time."

"Tell me about it." I forced a smile. "Is um, that not normal?"

"Normal." She shrugged. "What is normal?" Pulling away from the counter she dipped her head in my direction. "I'll see you tomorrow Maya."

"Okay." The door shut behind her blanketing me back into silence as I sat there wondering what in the heck I was going to do.

My text message alert went off.

N: Done.

M: Great.

What else did he want me to say? Congratulations?

N: I'll need your help cleaning up.

M: Okay…

N: Must I spell it out for you? Maya. Come.

Muttering a curse I pushed the phone away from my hand, stood, and stomped my way down the hall.

I tugged open the door and froze when I saw him tossing away bloody gloves.

"Maya," Nikolai said without turning around. "Make yourself useful and replace the bedding."

I stuck my tongue out at his back and went to the bed, pulling the sheets from their place trying not to focus on the splatters of blood I saw on them. Why would there be blood in the first place?

No questions. Right.

"Curious, aren't you?" His smooth voice penetrated my thoughts. "I can practically hear your mind working. Careful or you'll hurt yourself with all your… theories."

"Theories?" I shrugged and tossed the sheets into the nearby hamper that said laundry. "Why would I have any theories? You're a world renowned doctor, you see patients at night, patients who look like prostitutes, and you have absolutely no paper trail on your computer. Now, what do you think I'm going to do with that?"

"I'm not sure…" His hand moved to my shoulder, and he spun me around to face him. "What are you going to do with that information?"

"Go to the police," I blurted.

His amused smile made me want to stab him. "And say what? I'm being paid half a million a month to do a job I signed up for? Oh, and by the way, my father's Alexander Petrov, perhaps you have his file on hand?"

"You're a bastard," I hissed.

"And you're…" He angled a speculative look on me. "Interesting."

"Whatever you're doing, it can't be legal."

"Ah, so the daughter of a Russian mafia boss has…. morals?" His eyes were mocking as he whispered in a gruff voice, "Such a pity."

"Did you need anything else?"

"Tonight?" He licked his lips. "Yes, I believe I do."

He moved too fast for me to prepare myself. One minute he was towering over me, the next he was pushing me against the wall, his mouth inches from mine.

"I own you."

"So you've said," I could barely squeeze the words out, my throat was so dry and tight.

"I can do whatever I want with you… and nobody would hear you scream, Maya, nobody would even care. It would be prudent of you, to remember who holds your precious life in their hands. What I do here is none of your damn business. Do the job I pay you an abhorrent amount of money for, and when this is all finished, I'll write you a glowing recommendation."

"Will that be before or after you force me to sleep with you like the rest of the girls you had work for you?" The words were out of my mouth before I could stop them.

His eyes flashed, "If I wanted you, you'd know."

That was it. That one sentence crippled me. Made me feel not only small but rejected in such a vile way I wanted to cry.

"Oh, and Maya?" His head tilted. "Just in case you can't read between the lines there is nothing about you... that I want."

Tears stung my eyes as I looked down at the white floor. My throat felt thick. He was an ass! Why did I care what he thought? The loneliness of my situation was choking.

"Will that be all, Nikolai?" I met his eyes again.

"Yes." He stepped back. "Now, turn off the lights and meet me at the front."

I scurried out of the room, wiping the stray tears away, and snatched my belongings from the table.

He followed me two minutes later.

Once the door was locked, his hand was on my back, guiding me to the "safe" Audi, and before I knew it we were driving in silence back to the office building, back to my condo, back to my horrible existence where I didn't really exist, nor live for myself but for a complete psycho stranger with a god complex.

So strange, to pass by people laughing and walking home from work, to notice the little things like lights flickering in front of buildings, people holding hands, the stupid Starbucks guy handing out free samples. All of those things were symbols of freedom—something I didn't have and wouldn't have for an entire year.

What had I done wrong? In all of my years of living, I had to have done something horrible to my father to gain this type of punishment.

Maybe that was it.

I'd simply existed. And that had been enough.

I had no more tears left. Only despair as he pulled the car into the garage and turned off the engine.

I assumed he'd accompany me to my room.

He did.

The ride in the elevator was like absolute torture. I stood on one end, he stood on the other. The music was happily chirping in my ears, and I wished the damn thing would just plummet to the earth and let me die.

When we finally reached my condo, I expected him to leave. But he didn't, instead, he opened the door, led me in, and went to the fridge, pulling out a bottle of wine.

What was his angle?

And why wouldn't he just leave me in peace?

"I assume you met Jac?" He didn't make eye contact, didn't acknowledge my existence, simply pulled out two glasses and began pouring.

"She's sweet…. beautiful."

He stopped mid pour, his hand shaking a bit before he set the wine bottle down and braced himself against the counter. "She's irreplaceable."

"I'll… try." It was all I had. "To do my best."

"They all try." He sneered. "How about you succeed where they failed?"

"How about you tell me more about your high expectations so I don't fail!" I yelled back.

His face broke out into a smile. "Ah, there you are."

"What?" I threw my hands up in exasperation. "I've been here the whole time."

"You need spirit to last… Women… when they lose their spirit, they lose everything."

"You don't make sense," I grumbled and grabbed the

glass of wine he held out to me.

Being that close to him again made me want to both strangle him and pull him even closer. He smelled so good, and even though his countenance was cold, his body heat was practically leaping at me.

Nikolai shrugged. "I don't have to make sense... to you."

"Answers to no one." I lifted my glass into the air. "Got it."

"Don't lose the fight, Maya, even when the war seems daunting... simply keep fighting, let the fight mold you, don't let it break you. Too many people give up in the face of defeat. I need someone willing to push through that."

"I have..." I swallowed and looked away. "For my entire life."

"I know," he whispered. "Which is why I need you."

It was the first time I'd heard those words from his lips. I almost dropped my glass onto the floor. Had he just said he needed me? After all the arrogance, all the bullying, taunting, bossing me around?

He took a sip of wine and smiled that blinding smile that had my heart fluttering way too fast. "Don't look so shocked."

"I am," I said pointedly. "Shocked you need anything."

He shrugged.

Apparently the conversation was closed.

"Eat something," he urged, setting his wine glass down on the granite table. "My offices, tomorrow morning, eight o'clock, remember it's the thirty-second floor."

"Right."

"Wear black."

I gritted my teeth. "Not like you gave me lots of choices in that closet anyways."

His smile was back full force. "You get choices when you prove I can trust you with them."

"You don't think I'm trustworthy?"

"Your father wasn't."

"I'm not my father."

He sighed, running his hands through his hair. "Prove it."

And that was the end of the conversation.

He walked to the door and slammed it behind him, leaving me more confused than before, which was pretty damn confused, all things considered. I decided it wasn't worth the headache—*he* wasn't worth the headache. I had exactly three hundred and sixty-four more days of hell then I could go back to normal… back to a time when I didn't know Nikolai Blazik.

Back to a time when I actually knew myself.

CHAPTER TEN

The Pier Killer is believed to be looking during the day, attacking at dusk. — The Seattle Tribune

Nikolai

THE WOMAN HAD NO IDEA WHAT she was doing. It would be so easy to break her—again.

I needed her strong.

And I gave her rules in order to keep things within my control. The worst part was that she saw me as the monster when really in this scenario? I was as close to a white knight as she was going to get.

The elevator dipped with a groan then opened on the floor just below Maya's. When the doors slid apart, the scent of bleach burned my nostrils. It was a familiar smell, one that held memories, heartache, shame—so many emotions that I found myself wanting to hold my breath and close my eyes— but it hadn't worked all those times before, it certainly wouldn't work now.

The walk to my door felt lonely.

And being lonely wasn't a feeling I was accustomed to. I'd always had my work, I'd had my goals, one of which was most likely damning me to hell at this very moment, but I'd like to think she was one I'd accomplished beautifully.

I'd saved her.

She just wasn't aware that her prison—was her freedom.

I opened the door leading into my penthouse apartment and walked numbly into the kitchen.

A glass of already poured Canadian whiskey was sitting in a glass on the table with the newspaper next to it.

I had to hand it to her—Jac never missed an evening, even if she was out doing what she did best—she always took care of me.

I never wanted for anything where she was concerned.

Yet a part of me wondered if she used that as a way to keep herself firmly attached to my life—where there was no room for any other female, regardless of how harmless she might be.

"What exactly… are you doing, Nikolai?"

Jac's voice dripped with disapproval.

"Drinking," I answered in a clipped tone. "And you?"

"The same." She chuckled. "Join me."

I knew where she would be. Sitting at the piano, drink in hand, eyes blurry with emotion.

Grabbing my glass, I made my way over to her and sat quietly, my fingers grazing the ivory keys just briefly before reaching for her hand and giving it a squeeze. "Hard evening?"

The hand I wasn't holding lifted the glass to her lips—it shook violently. "When are they not hard?"

"True."

"I'm not sure about her."

And there it was.

"You don't have to be sure about her. What she does for me has nothing to do with you and the family."

"You like her." Jac licked her ruby red lips and set her drink down. "That makes her different."

"I'm protecting her. There's a difference."

"And when protecting turns into something more?" She tilted her head and gave a slight smirk, the way the moonlight reflected across her features cast a pale glow, aging her, reminding me yet again how frail she really was. "What then?"

"Then I set her free."

Jac leaned her head back and laughed, and the sound chilled me to the bone. "When have you ever been good at setting your favorite things free? Remember that bird when you were small? You named him Fred and refused to let him out of his cage, even when we told you it was safe to let him fly around the house."

I shook my head at the memory. I'd been so fearful he'd fly away that my fear eventually killed him—or so I believed. He'd never fully matured and died at a young age because of it.

"She isn't a bird," I finally whispered. "She's a person."

"Oh." Jac patted my hand. "So now you actually see people as real people, not your own person version of Operation?"

Something was off with Jac tonight. I narrowed my eyes. "That's enough."

Her smile fell, replaced by what looked like anger, before she shrugged and stood. "We're both tired, and the night still isn't finished for me I'm afraid."

"Perhaps it should be." I never told Jac what to do, it wasn't my place, but I knew her lifestyle wore on her—the secret of it wore on us both.

"I have a legacy to continue," she said in a distant voice. "Perhaps you should start thinking about how you'll continue yours… once I'm gone."

"You're not dying." I rolled my eyes and kissed her hand.

"Not yet." She pulled her hand back and reached for her jacket. "But I will be gone and soon. What will you do then, Nikolai?"

The question had my heart ramming against my chest. I didn't know. I still hadn't made my choice. I still wasn't sure how I could fulfill my family's legacy while still keeping my own sanity intact. It seemed I was the sole heir that saw a difference between right and wrong, which was really sick when I thought about it. If I was the moral compass, what hope did my family really have to begin with? I shuddered inwardly.

"The choice will happen." Jac gave a knowing nod. "And sooner than you think. Maybe a distraction is good." She pointed toward the ceiling. "But something tells me she's hands-off, am I right?"

"They always are." I hired nursing students for three months tops, paid them, swore them to secrecy, and let them go. Maya wasn't a nursing student, and I hadn't hired her for the reasons I'd hired all the others. It was simply convenient that I could kill two birds with one stone.

"But she's different, because you wish it wasn't the case."

"Goodnight, Jac." I ignored her barb even though it still managed to sneak in between my ribs, hitting its mark quite well.

Dismissed, she gave a quick nod and walked toward the door. "Careful Nikolai, I've never lost you to something as silly as emotion before—and your colors, they're showing."

"I bleed like everyone else."

Jac held open the door and called back. "More's the pity."

Once silence once again reigned in my apartment, I

moved to my couch and looked around my apartment.

It was decorated in deep purples and blacks. I had a fascination with dark colors, maybe because it was the only thing that brought me comfort, knowing that the outside was just as dark as my insides.

It was the only peace I seemed to find.

White reminded me of what I didn't have.

Purity, innocence, and a bright-eyed Russian princess who'd stop at nothing to tempt me beyond my abilities.

Her room was white for a reason.

It was a reminder.

Thou shall not touch.

Because if I did—she wouldn't live past the first caress.

I refused to tempt fate twice.

And this time.

It would be my fault.

CHAPTER ELEVEN

Police are still investigating the slew of murders taking place down in Pikes Market. Another woman's body was found, her reproductive organs stripped from her body and on her face a hollow smile. Women are strongly encouraged to stay indoors at night. — The Seattle Tribune

Maya

SLEEP DIDN'T COME — THOUGH I PRAYED and begged for it every hour I woke up and saw the alarm clock glaring back at me.

My head hurt.

My brain hurt.

And after again ransacking the apartment for any sort of way to either escape or put a giant SOS on the window… I fell into a pit of despair. Because I knew, that in the end, I'd signed a contract, my dad had sold me. I didn't really have a leg to stand on.

Plus, just like Nikolai said, who would actually believe

me? They'd probably think I'd gone insane.

With a groan I flipped over on my side and finally managed to get out of bed. Nikolai said to report to work at eight, wearing black. I wasn't sure if work meant in his offices or the one downtown, but I figured asking questions would just get him upset all over again.

He wasn't what I had expected.

Sure, he was gorgeous, entitled, controlling, but every single thing that came out of his mouth was guarded. A part of me—the stupid part—was curious, while the rest of me wanted to push him off the highest balcony I could find.

The shower did wonders for my attitude, and when I went back into the closet to find an outfit, I admitted that he'd actually picked out some pretty ridiculously cool clothes for me. I settled on a black Diane Von Fustenburg wrap dress with some black heels and grabbed a gold chain from the nearby dresser.

I grabbed a wool coat, just in case it rained and I was somehow given leave to go outside for a break, and then went into the kitchen.

And froze.

"How was your evening?" Nikolai asked, scrambling eggs over the stove like it was the most natural thing in the world, for him to make me breakfast in my kitchen, another not-so-subtle reminder that he could enter and exit my life at will. Even my private space was not truly mine. I imagined it would never be, as long as he was in my life.

"Horrible," I said honestly. "And I hate eggs."

"Don't lie."

That was it. Just a "don't lie," and he continued tossing in chopped up peppers and cheese.

With a huff I sat on the bar stool and watched his muscles flex beneath his shirt as he moved around the kitchen. He looked good there, comfortable, not as haunted as he normally looked.

I knew I was being shameless in watching him, but it was impossible not to, the man was so beautiful that it was mentally frustrating.

Why did the beautiful ones have to be sociopaths?

His rich chocolate hair curled behind his ears, dark eyes focused on the food in front of him and his muscled body stretched and strained against the tight pale blue pinstripe shirt.

"Why are you here?" I asked, "Wasn't I supposed to meet you?"

"Got hungry." He shrugged.

"And every Starbucks within the vicinity was closed?" My eyebrows arched.

He chuckled.

A laugh escaped from between his lips.

I clenched my teeth together only because it was a nice laugh, warm like honey. Damn him.

"No." He finally turned around, smile still in place. "I actually was thinking it would be good for us to have a chat before work."

"A chat, huh?" I fidgeted in my seat.

"Yes." His smile flashed again, and my knees went weak. I licked my lips and looked away.

"So chat."

"Bossy."

"Like you should talk," I muttered.

"You look nice." He pulled out a plate and served the eggs onto it then handed me a fork. "I like black on you."

"Apparently you like black on people and white on walls."

His smile froze. "Pardon?"

"Walls." I pointed around me. "Everything you live in is pristine, white, makes a girl wonder if you hate getting dirty."

His eyes darkened as he leaned forward and flicked his tongue across his lips. "Are you asking me if I like getting dirty?"

No. No I wasn't. Because I was pretty sure we were talking about two different types of dirty, and I wasn't at all prepared for his answer, not with the way he was looking at me like he could devour me in an instant.

"Um…" I shoveled a forkful of egg into my mouth and nodded. "Good eggs."

His expression changed from predatory to innocence. "Thanks."

Were we actually having a normal non-creepy conversation? I cleared my throat and continued eating so I wouldn't ruin it by talking.

"Yesterday…" He ran his fingers through his hair. He did that a lot, almost like he used his hair for his power when he had to talk about things he didn't want to talk about. "It was a hard day…"

"Can I ask why?"

"You can ask." He shrugged, "But I'll lie."

"Alright, then." I put down my fork and folded my hands. "So it was a hard day. Doesn't mean you have a right to own a girl, make her sign over her life all within an hour of meeting her, then yell at her."

"I never yelled."

Sighing, I rolled my eyes. "Well, you sure don't like using an inside voice."

His face cracked into a smile. "Like I said before, I need someone of your talents."

"I don't have sex for money."

"Why are you so concerned with having sex with me?" He smirked, "Seriously, I want to know."

"Uh, I just, you seem like the type of man who—"

"—can't get a woman without paying for her services?"

He finished, "That type?"

"Well no, but—"

"The type of man who needs to make a woman sign a contract in order to engage in an illicit affair?"

Was he seriously asking me that? My cheeks burned with embarrassment while my heart thumped with a wild curiosity. Images of bondage and blindfolds danced through my mind… and those masks.

"That's not what this is." His eyes were kind, damn him, and I felt like crying. I could handle an ass, but someone sensitive to my feelings? Not so much. Because I hadn't experienced it much in my short life… my mother ignored me as much as she could, paying all her attention to my father. And my father, well safe to say if he was ever given a father of the year award it would be because he freaking paid for it.

"So you need me," I finally said after a few moments of tense silence. "Why exactly do you need me?"

"Your research—" He drummed his fingertips along the counter. "—amongst other things, is absolutely brilliant."

My heart soared. "You really think so?"

"Absolutely." He smiled. "I see real promise, and I want you to study under me, but some of the ways I do my own personal research isn't exactly…" He shrugged. "Legal."

"Thus the contract."

"Exactly."

"But thirty girls?"

He froze, drew a deep breath, then shrugged again. "They didn't follow the rules, therefore they got fired. I decided that what I needed wasn't necessarily an assistant to replace Jac but someone who could empathize with what I was doing."

It was the most information he'd told me in two days. I clung to it like a lifeline. "And if I do well?"

"Then the world is yours." He flashed a smile. "But all

the rules from yesterday still stand... what I deal with is very sensitive and not known to the public. Do your job, with a smile on your face, and as we build trust... slowly, I'll amend the contract."

"So I prove my trust and I get Netflix?"

He chuckled softly. "Yeah, something like that, but one thing... you still can't date... or sleep around. I can't imagine that will be a problem for you all things considering but, I can't have you mixing business with pleasure."

And all the happy moments we shared just went out the window. "I'm not a saint."

"Lie." He leaned forward and winked. "I know everything about you. Now, let's get to work. We have a short day before we go... fishing."

"Fishing?"

"In a sense." He shrugged. "For patients."

"What?"

"Keep up." He knocked the counter top with his hands. "I'll show you what you'll be doing during the day and during the evening... you're mine."

"Can't wait," I said dryly.

"Most women... would be... pleased." He shoved a pair of keys in his pocket, looking sexy as hell while doing it. "I imagine you'd rather stab me."

"Good guess." I said with a sweet voice.

"Russians." He shook his head. "Always so ruthless."

"Don't I know it."

"Prove your worth, Maya. Let's go."

CHAPTER TWELVE

Fear has big eyes — Russian Proverb

Nikolai

MY PHONE HADN'T STOPPED BUZZING IN my pocket all morning. The very second I led Maya off the elevator and escorted her into my office, I knew, something was very, very wrong.

I felt it in the pit of my stomach.

I saw it in the gray cast sky.

She was dead.

With shaking hands, I basically shoved Maya into a desk, fired off instructions about some shit research I needed done then excused myself and went into one of the conference rooms.

Seven missed calls.

All from Sergio Abandonato, cousin to one of the most influential Italian mafia families in Chicago. He was married to Andi, Maya's half sister. I'd basically grown up with Andi. While Maya was kept away from what her father did, Andi was used as a shiny tool for the FBI, infiltrating their systems at such a young age that even I had been impressed.

After selling out her father and one of the dirty agents at the bureau, the Abandonatos had offered Andi protection by marriage.

I'd expected her to kill Sergio the first night.

She hadn't.

I'd expected her to drive him insane with lust.

She had.

Their marriage was supposed to be an arrangement, a way to protect her with their family name while she fought a losing battle with leukemia.

Instead, it had turned into so much more.

I'd visited during the wedding a few months ago, and even then I knew. I saw it in the way she talked to him, her body language whenever they were in a room together. And well, she was Andi; no sane man could deny her anything.

"You love him?" I asked once we were alone in her bridal room. She did a twirl for me then shrugged her shoulders and reached out her hand. I grasped her fingertips as anger washed over me anew. Ice cold. I was a doctor. I knew what was happening to her, damn it. It was almost like I could see the sick blood in her system, and even me being who I was, one of the most brilliant minds in modern medicine, I could do nothing to stop the disease—nothing.

It was like a sharp knife getting twisted into my chest, watching her smile as if she had all the time in the world. Normal girls, on their wedding day, look in the mirror and fuss over makeup or the way the dress fits, but Andi? She didn't have a complaint in the world. And out of everyone I knew, she should complain—she never did.

"Nik?" Andi gave my shoulder a little squeeze. "You're doing that weird thing where you stare into space and you get a wrinkle between your eyes." She pressed the skin between my eyebrows and scrunched up her nose. "Penny for those dark morose thoughts?"

With a sigh, I pushed her hand away then pulled her into my arms, my mouth hovered near her ear. "He will never deserve you."

"And you did?" She fired back quickly.

I sighed and pulled away. "I guess I deserved that."

"Yup." She grinned.

I licked my lips and forced my gaze away from her mouth. "I'll do what I can to keep your father away, Andi. But you know even I can't make any promises."

"He still owns you... doesn't he?"

I didn't answer her.

"Nik, I worry for you." As she should. The Cosa Nostra was organized in a way that the Russian Mafia could only dream of, there was a certain respect amongst the Italians, a loyalty, not just based on family ties but blood.

"Don't," I said in a detached voice while I anxiously rubbed the sickle tattoo imprinted in black ink across my hand. "The last thing you need to do is add more worry to your life. Just promise me, if the Italians don't hold up their end of the bargain, you'll leave a trail of blood in your wake." I had to say it, even though I knew they would. That's just who they were.

Andi barked out a laugh. "Violent Russian."

"Half Russian." I corrected.

"Still counts." She winked, then sobered. "Are you still a Boevik for my father, Nik? Tell me..."

Emotion clogged my throat mixing with the disgust and anger already present. I had to look away. "Just, be happy Andi, and if you need anything, ever..."

"There's one thing," Andi piped up.

"Why do I have a feeling I'm not going to like what you're about to say?"

"Because you won't. Always trust your gut, Nik."

I rolled my eyes in an attempt to get her to blurt out the favor rather than concentrate on my many sins or the way the Pakhan,r her father, still held me by the balls. "What is it Andi?"

"Come to my funeral."

"Andi!"

"What? It's only fair, I invite you to my wedding, and you're really the only true family I have." Guilt gnawed at the center of my chest. That wasn't true. She had a sister, she'd just never met her. *"Please? I need mother Russia present."*

"Fine." I licked my lips forcing myself to smile when all I really wanted to do was anything but promise her that I would be at the funeral. I lived for death, it had never bothered me, until her. *"I'll do it."*

"Great, and Nik?"

"Hmm?"

"She must be really pretty."

"Damn mind-reader." I muttered pulling out a short glass and pouring whiskey into it. I was at work. Drinking. Something that, while in medical school, was clearly preached against, not that I was practicing surgery right that moment. My hands shook, making the drink in my hand nearly tip over the glass. With a curse I threw back the entire contents and called Sergio back.

"Sergio?" I barked into the phone.

He was silent for a few seconds and then. "She's gone."

Hollow, his voice was so hollow, like his world had stopped functioning properly, then again, how does the world continue its turn? Without the sun to lead it, the moon to follow?

"My offer." I licked my lips, tasting the sweet whisky still caked along them. "It still stands." A few months ago I'd told him I'd make him forget in the only way I knew how—he didn't know it at the time but it was like a handshake, a gift, an offer of service, gratitude, loyalty.

Sergio sighed heavily. "Russians."

"So?"

"I'd rather feel…" he whispered. "Because that means it

happened. And she deserves to be remembered in the most raw way possible. So, today, my answer is no. Tomorrow, my answer? It will still be no."

"If you're sure."

"She wanted you at the funeral."

"I know." I cleared my throat. It did nothing to keep the sadness dripping from my voice. "I'll make arrangements."

The line went dead.

I tossed the phone onto the counter and wiped my hands over my face as the choking sensation of loss washed over me.

Andi, the only friend I'd ever known, the daughter to one of my most hated enemies, the daughter to the man who held so much of the world in his hands, was gone forever.

I glanced over at the closed door. Maya was on the other side, oblivious to the fact that the world would forever be a bit darker without her sister in it.

I didn't want to have that conversation.

I wasn't ready for it yet. Would I ever be ready?

There were still so many secrets I was keeping from her, so many loose ends that I was having trouble remembering what to keep close and what to share. She made it impossible for me to distance myself.

And that's what I needed to do.

She'd cracked her knuckles.

Stupid of me, at such a young age, to give her such a tell, but completely necessary.

"When you feel the memories return… simply crack your knuckles and they'll be nothing but a fleeting thought. Do you understand me?"

Maya blinked hard, her eyes glassy. "No."

I held the knife to her wrist and cut slowly. "It doesn't hurt anymore, does it?"

"No." She choked out. "It feels."

"Freeing." I answered for her. "As it should. Now, what

happens when you crack your knuckles?"

Her eyes darted back and forth, unable to focus on any one thing for too long. "I…" She blinked again. "It means… it means I'm remembering but, I don't know what."

"You're remembering how much you love ice cream."

She nodded. "Yes… vanilla."

"You love vanilla."

Cursing, I pushed the memory away and stood, made sure to glance in the mirror. Every dark piece of hair was in place, my crisp black suit was tailored to perfection, my blue striped shirt buttoned in all the right places, but my eyes.

They were, as always, soulless. And today, of all days, I was bothered by that. Because it was just another reminder that the world wasn't fair.

That a man like me should be allowed to live.

When people like Andi were taken too soon.

Nothing about it was fair.

I clenched my fists. This was why I was working so hard to save Maya, why I signed that damn contract with her father, why I was fighting my ass off to keep her at a distance.

So when the time came.

The darkness didn't become her prison.

But her freedom.

CHAPTER THIRTEEN

Pier Killer still at large even though no killings have been reported in a week. –The Seattle Tribune

Maya

THAT MORNING I QUICKLY LEARNED SOMETHING about Nikolai—he had multiple personalities. No really, it was the only explanation as to why, when the elevator doors opened, what was once a commanding and terrifying individual took a plant from an elderly receptionist and watered it.

Right, he watered it.

I would have laughed had it been funny but it was more confusing than anything. It was kind of like watching a politician run an *"I'm normal just like everyone else"* campaign.

I half expected him to start kissing babies and giving away free puppies.

He calmly—and, mother of all shocks—patiently described what I'd be doing during the day in the office next door to his.

Research.

And then, like he had multiple personalities, he just... snapped. With his cell phone in hand he glanced down, paled, then fired off instructions about being worth what he was paying me.

"The newest strains of STDs." He threw a file onto my desk. "Study the information collected and research about possible cures."

He had started to sweat.

Then nearly stumbled into the wall as he made his way to that weird secret door and slammed it behind him.

My heart was hammering so hard against my chest as an uncomfortable silence descended. What was he doing?

I swallowed the lump of fear in my throat, because, he wasn't just weird, he was, completely unpredictable.

I pressed my hands firmly on the large oak desk and eyed the Keurig to my left. Well, I at least knew how to make coffee. I could do that. Having no idea when he was going to be popping out of his weird super villain room, I made two cups set one on his desk and brought mine over to my chair and began pouring over the folders.

Ten minutes after his weird outburst, Nikolai emerged through the door, his stance rigid, his fists clenched tightly at his sides.

"Everything okay?" I asked.

Ignoring me, he walked briskly to his desk stared at the cup of coffee I'd made with a frown clouding his features.

Anxiety washed over me. Was the coffee a bad idea?

"What's this?" He pointed at it, his eyebrows drawn together in what looked like utter disbelief.

"Coffee," I said boldly. "Some people need it in order to function, but being who you are, I wasn't sure if you actually needed anything other than blood and the souls of virgins to make it through the day, so I took a gamble."

His lips twitched. "I can't remember the last time someone made me coffee."

"Not even at Starbucks?"

He didn't answer, just sat at his desk, still eying the coffee, like he was afraid to drink it.

"I didn't poison it, if that's what you're wondering." I turned back to my work and continued reading through the thick folder of case studies and patients when I felt him.

I glanced up into hypnotic brown eyes. "Yes?"

Nikolai held out his coffee. "It's cold."

I arched my eyebrows. "I made coffee for you to be nice not because it's my job."

"Right." He full on grinned this time. "But things always taste better when someone else makes them."

"Why do I get the feeling you just don't want to press a button?"

"I strained my finger last night."

"Highly doubt that."

Shadows lingered beneath his eyes. And for some reason, I felt guilty. It was just a cup of coffee, and it wasn't worth arguing over. I gracefully stood, grabbed his coffee and went over to the Keurig to make another.

By three in the afternoon I'd had five coffees, Nikolai had drank the one I made him then left in a hurry, speaking in hushed tones into his phone. I stood when he left, meaning to ask him what else I was supposed to do but he gave me a warning stare that chilled me to the core.

I nearly fell out of my chair trying to sit back down then stared at the computer screen until my eyes started to blur.

At lunch time his secretary brought in a Wendy's bag with a hamburger and fries with a vanilla frosty.

Groaning in pleasure, I went for the ice-cream first. Funny because I'd always hated anything cold. Ice cream had made me cry as a child but once I hit high school I couldn't get enough of it.

Every single time I had a test in school, I had to have ice cream first; otherwise I was anxious.

When I graduated, I celebrated with more ice cream.

It was an addiction I couldn't quit; one that, when I thought about cutting out sugar or dairy to lose weight, actually caused full on panic attacks, like I would somehow die without it. Which was too stupid for words, but there it was. My one vice.

"Break time," a deep male voice said from the door. I looked up to see Nikolai holding his own Wendy's bag.

"Cute." I rolled my eyes and pushed away from the desk. "I thought you hated Wendy's."

"Yeah, well," His grin was smug. "Thought it would make you smile after staring at the computer screen for hours on end." His eyes darted to the milkshake. "You're eating dessert first?"

"Yup." I licked the spoon "Think of it as a stress reliever after such a long day, you're lucky you got the flavor right."

Something dark passed over his face before he shrugged and started digging into his own bag, pulling out a fry. "You seem more vanilla than chocolate."

My entire body went numb and heavy. "Excuse me?"

"Vanilla." The way he said it had my eyes blurring like some sort of spell was being cast into the air in front of me.

"I," My arms started stinging. Slowly, I looked down at my wrists, nothing was there except for the scars from the car accident I'd been in at sixteen.

"So," He was still talking, but his voice had changed, into something hypnotic, soft, seductive, painfully commanding. "Vanilla, has it always been your favorite?"

"My favorite." I repeated, blinking up at him through lowered lashes.

"Yes." Nikolai leaned forward, tilting his head to the side. "You're favorite ice cream."

My hands twitched, and then I cracked my knuckles, a nervous habit and he was making me feel... nervous, unsettled, like I'd just been drugged.

"Yes." I finally answered.

Nikolai nodded. "Butterscotch."

My blurry vision cleared.

"I've always been a sucker for butterscotch but they only have it at select places and since you were so keen on Wendy's." His smile was easy.

And just like that, I felt like I was normal again, back in my own body. I could count on my hand how many times I'd felt that way in my life, always during simple conversations, and always with my father.

Unnerved, I stood and started packing away my food.

"Is something wrong?" Nikolai's voice was concerned but something about the rigid way he was sitting rubbed me the wrong way.

"Yes. No." I shook my head, my gaze falling to his left hand.

The black sickle tattoo mocked me.

"Tell me," I pointed to his tattoo. "Does it bother you that he marks you too?"

"Pardon?" Nikola's jaw clenched as he stood.

"My father. Does it bother you that he marks you as well?"

"He touched you?" Nikolai's brown eyes were crazed. "Maya... don't lie to me. Did he touch you? Ever?"

"Not where anyone would see," I finally said. "And sometimes, those are the worst kinds of pain, don't you think? The scars you can't prove are usually the ones that hurt the most."

"Maya—"

"I uh…" Suddenly feeling nauseated, I stumbled back. "I need to take a longer break. Is that okay?"

"Of course." Nikolai walked me to the door. "Why don't you go for a walk and grab another coffee?"

"Hah!" I nodded. "Maybe it's the caffeine that did it to me in the first place?"

"Did what?" He asked.

I popped my knuckles and lied. "Nothing."

****

I SETTLED MYSELF IN front of the office computer again. After going for a half hour walk and grabbing a coffee, I felt seriously better, finally able to pour all my nervous energy into something. Though honestly, the fact that my dad's mark was on Nikolai's skin, didn't sit well with me. Turned my stomach, in fact. I hadn't been unaware of their loose association, but seeing that mark was a bleak reminder that caution was in order.

I had to wonder, if I couldn't give Nikolai whatever he wanted from me—because I couldn't for a second believe he was offering me a job out of the goodness of his heart—would he kill me? Or hand me back to the father who sold me in the first place?

Would I turn into one of the desperate girls with soulless eyes that went to his clinics at night?

Suddenly things started clicking into place.

The men outside the door were body guards.

The girls… I'd already guessed they were prostitutes, I must have been right.

I knew my dad owned several businesses, many of them… shady. Did he operate a prostitution ring? A chill ran the length of my spine. Did Nikolai help him?

Right. No questions.

It was hard to focus on the computer when my mind was coming up with all sorts of possibilities, and my head hurt from trying to put two and two together, because nothing was adding up. Nothing.

"Maya?" Nikolai entered the office, his face void of emotion as usual. "How has your first official day on the job been?"

Strange. Odd. Freaky. "Good. Not what I expected," I lied.

"It's a trade." He sat and leaned back against the leather chair, one of two in my office. My eyes searched his perfect face, his pristine clothes, looking for anything that would even hint of him working for my father in a more… violent manner. Most of the men I'd met who worked alongside my father were large stout men, men who you wouldn't see in the ring at a UFC fight, more like the ones reffing it, and he never had bloody knuckles, black eyes in the tabloids. I shivered. He was a doctor for crying out loud. Was I seriously trying to find hints that he was a contract killer?

"You work for me during the day, I give you everything you could possibly need to not only finish your thesis but become world renowned and you help me… at night."

I snorted and changed the subject away from me. "Right, I help you help… other women at night? Is that what we're going to call it?"

"What I do at night makes it so you're able to sit your nice ass down in this office and actually conduct research," he snapped, yet again reminding me who held the power to my future.

"Fine." I held up my hands. "I don't need to know what you do with those women behind closed doors—really I don't."

"You're right." He sighed, eyes flashing with remorse. "Things wouldn't go well if you did. Think of it as me protecting you."

"Protecting me?" I parroted. "From... you and your weird nighttime job?"

"From the world." He shrugged. "From the ugly."

"Too late, I've been exposed to the ugly for far too long... I'm jaded."

"Not this jaded." His face paled. "Believe me."

His hands began to shake. Abruptly he stood and started pacing in front of me.

I leaned closer, watching his erratic movements wondering if he was going to turn back into the condescending ass he'd been before. "Have I earned Internet yet?"

"Hell, no." He barked out a laugh, and it transformed his face from indifferent to beautiful. I tried to keep my body from physically responding to the perfection. It was damn near impossible. "But nice try."

I purposely looked away.

"Dinner," he blurted. "Tonight, I'll take you to dinner after—"

"After." I repeated. "After we finish at the Pier?"

"Yes." He didn't glance back at me; instead hightailed it toward the door and shouted over his shoulder. "Remember to keep wearing black, wouldn't want anything to get on your clothes."

"Because there's always a high risk of blood stains while sitting at a desk," I fired back.

His hands braced the doorframe. "What did you say?"

"Er, blood stains? I was making a joke, you know... doctor's office?"

He hung his head, then with a curse, walked out of the room.

By the time it was five, I was ready to call it a day, too bad I didn't have that luxury. Nikolai specifically said I needed to be ready right after work.

Busy night.

That's all the text said.

If he didn't feed me I was going to cut him.

CHAPTER FOURTEEN

The man that is full cannot understand the man that is hungry. —
Russian Proverb

Nikolai

THE DRIVE TO THE PIER WAS tense. I blamed myself. My thoughts were scattered all over the place. Petrov had sent me a text earlier that morning with the words RIP over a picture of Andi.

I almost lost my shit, drove over to his house with a bomb in my car and just... ended things, not caring if there were women, children, cats, dogs, or parakeets within the vicinity, but needing to prove a point. I would not, could not, stand him disrespecting family or friends.

And to disrespect or mock her memory?

My blood ran cold.

Guilt and anger, my constant companions, choked the life from me. Andi was the only reason I had a conscience. After I brainwashed my first victim, we went out to get ice cream with her father as if nothing had happened. At sixteen I was already better than most of the men he'd used, and I was desperate, so desperate for money to go to college.

I would have done anything for him.

Anything to be able to afford the textbooks because regardless of the schools I went to, I still needed money to live, and I was an orphan.

He'd sought me out.

At twelve.

My father had been his *Kassir*, basically helping him cook the books. When, Petrov, in a fit of rage killed him and my mother, it was me who was left to fix the books, pick up the pieces, and walk away.

Only, Petrov gave me no option in the matter, and Jac had been oblivious to what was going on, had no idea that my father was so deeply involved. Maybe it had been his own sick way of trying to establish himself outside of our dark family legacy. I didn't blame him, anything was better than where I came from—anything. Even Petrov.

"Eat!" Andi had instructed, her eyes darting between me and her father. Already she was in deep with the FBI having been "adopted" by one of the directors after he and his wife couldn't have children. What a joke.

I'd picked vanilla ice cream because it was white and a reminder that things would not always be stained with blood. One day, blood would resemble salvation instead of death.

She'd picked butterscotch.

Stupid, that at the time, it made complete and total sense to use those two flavors as trigger words.

Maya sighed loudly and tried to switch the music, I lightly slapped her hand away as I pulled into my usual parking spot.

Where Andi was light, Maya was dark, the outline of her

eyes was hypnotic, captivating, making the green of her irises look so huge it almost looked animated, fake.

Her long dark hair was pulled into a low bun.

Spending time with her was like purposefully cutting myself only to watch the blood pool at my feet in wonder. I had to protect her but by doing so, I was allowing her to be with the only person more dangerous than her father.

Myself.

The click-clack of Maya's heels was a welcome distraction from my thoughts as we made our way into the office.

Jac was waiting inside, her leather bomber jacket fitting tightly around her body. Her trademark cowboy books shimmered in the light.

Her mood was greatly improved from the last I'd seen her, meaning things must have been going well. And if they were going well, it meant she wouldn't be pestering me about taking up the family business. Blood on both sides, wasn't I lucky?

"Jac!" I held out my hands to her "It's good to see you."

"And you." She kissed my cheek then patted my other with her hand as her eyes narrowed. "You haven't been sleeping, have you?

"I sleep." Clearly a lie. One of my best friends was dead, Petrov was waiting for me to fail so he could kill his only remaining daughter, whom I had to keep my hands off, not only because of the damn contract, but because anything could trigger her past, and the last thing I needed was for her to remember.

For her sake, not mine.

Jac bit out a curse. "These nights are getting to you, I know they are. Your grandpa would—"

"—be pleased," I interrupted, irritated she was bringing up my grandfather in front of Maya. "Wouldn't he?"

"Yes." She nodded and patted my cheek again, this time

tapping her finger against my jaw meaning she wanted to speak to me later. "He'd be proud to call you his grandson, rest his soul."

I glared.

While Jac simply shrugged.

"You have two new ones this evening, Nikolai." Jac said, changing the subject. "They aren't well."

"And their symptoms?" They aren't well meant that they were getting close to the time when they were no longer necessary to Petrov.

"The same as the last few weeks… it seems to be spreading." Shit.

"Hmm." I said, pretending to think out loud, buying some time while I figured out what to do with them. "Continue to train Maya with the schedule and I'll see what I can do, if it's a red line I'll let you know."

"It's day two." Jac said in a tight voice. "A red line would—"

"I'll let you know," I snapped, slamming the door behind me, a red line meant I would eliminate the threat before Petrov did. He didn't allow women of their trade to die with dignity. I did.

CHAPTER FIFTEEN

The Pier Killer is still at large. Another unidentified body was found.
Law enforcement has no comment on the victim. — The Seattle
Tribune

Maya

JAC'S FACE LOOKED PAINED BEFORE SHE made a cross over her chest then turned to face me. Forcing a smile, she clasped her hands together. "So! Let's just pick up where we left off last night, shall we?"

"Er, okay." I scooted my chair to the side so she could sit next to me.

For an hour she explained the rest of the schedule, how to answer the phone when it did ring, and of course never to ask questions. I was to be the brains of an operation I knew nothing about—and that's how it was supposed to stay.

I was about to ask her if I was ever allowed to know what actually went on when Nikolai burst through the door, his

his eyes dark with dread. "Jac! A word."

She patted my hand and stood, then followed Nikolai down the hall.

I was too curious to stay planted in my seat. Slowly, I inched my chair back and made my way toward the door.

Nikolai was shouting.

Jac was shouting.

But it wasn't in English.

It sounded—Russian—like when I overheard my father's conversations with some of his men, but the dialect sounded off.

Footsteps sounded so I ran back to my seat.

Jac burst through the door and snatched her purse off the table. She took one last look at me, shook her head, and left.

What had just happened?

I was afraid to go to Nikolai. By the sound of his voice he wasn't happy and he'd just totally lost his indifferent composure and screamed at Jac.

I wrung my hands together and stared at the clock. This was ridiculous. If he needed help he'd ask for help, right?

Wasn't it my job to assist?

I checked the schedule; the two girls Jac had mentioned were the only names listed for the evening.

My cell hadn't gone off.

No texts.

Finally, I pushed away from my desk and stood. If he fired me over asking if he needed help then... at least I'd have Netflix, right?

Jokes. I needed to make jokes about my situation as I slowly walked down the hall.

Because if I really thought about it, I was terrified—more than terrified—that one day, I'd be like the girls checking in at the office. Obsessed with the man in the doctor coat, only to one day, simply cease to exist. All because I fell for the danger.

And he was that… dangerous.

Every cell in my body was lit up like Christmas as I reached for the metal handle of the door and pushed it open, only to find the first room empty, the one he was usually in.

Backing up, I frowned, then I went to the next room.

It was empty as well.

One room left.

"Well, here goes nothing."

CHAPTER SIXTEEN

If the doctor cures, the sun sees it; but if he kills, the earth hides it. – Russian Proverb

Nikolai

THE SOUND OF FOOTSTEPS CALMED MY breathing enough for me to put the damn scalpel down and focus in on the fact that Maya would be in my office in mere seconds, and I looked like I'd just attacked a wild boar and lost.

"Nikolai?"

"Sit," I instructed, peeling the bloody gloves from my hands. Natalia had decided against my wishes to end things, which meant Jac had to clean up the mess I'd started. The last thing we wanted was for Natalia to die on the streets or God forbid spend her last few weeks getting high and telling everyone who would listen what goes on at my offices. It was just the type of thing that would set Petrov off, and he was already a loose cannon.

Maya sat and folded her hands. "Everything okay, Doc?"

"Cute." I clenched my teeth. "Don't ever call me Doc."

"Frankenstein?"

"Let's just skip nicknames."

"Okay, asshole."

I let out a pitiful groan. "The schedule, I need you to find Natalia's name and put a red mark through it. Print out the documentation, put it in the safe, then delete her files on the computer. Can you do that?"

"Wait." Maya's ponytail did a little flip as she shook her head. "You want a paper trail?"

"For the safe. For my own purposes that you don't need information on. Delete the files on the computer only after you've printed off what I need."

"Okay…"

"And for the love of God don't read her file."

"But you just said to print it—"

"Print. You hit print. You delete once the paper comes out of the feed. Must I explain everything as if you're a toddler, or can you handle this one simple task for me?" I tried to keep my voice even. "Once the paper is destroyed, make sure that the flash drive," I pointed to the drive in the computer, "is given to me at the end of the day for inspection." Nothing was ever permanently destroyed, data had a way of hanging on, just like life, and I needed to make sure I snuffed it out in the only way I knew how.

Maya's eyes filled with tears. "Right. I'll just go do that right now."

"When you're finished, close up the front. I'll meet you in the lobby, turn the lights down."

"We're done for tonight?"

"Yes," I grumbled. "For tonight."

The door clicked shut behind her. Shit. I ran my hands through my hair then kicked the metal trash can. I hadn't meant to snap at her like that, but the more questions she asked, the more irritated I became, I couldn't allow myself to attach emotionally. It was instinctual to guard myself, to protect what I did, to protect *her*. And if by being cruel I accomplished that, well.

I shrugged out of my white jacket and pulled out my phone.

Nikolai: *Natalia will be at her usual spot.*

Jac: *I'll take care of it.*

Nikolai: *I knew you would.*

I shoved my phone back into my pocket and made my way toward the lobby of my office.

Maya's back was facing me.

Her black dress hugged every delicious curve. I drank my fill—because I knew it was all I was allowed.

I could look.

But never touch.

Her father had made certain of that.

I didn't realize I was clenching my hands until I tried to place one on her shoulder. Releasing the tension in my fingertips, I lightly tapped her shoulder. "Ready to go?"

She turned slowly, her eyes narrowing. "Listen, here." A manicured finger tapped against the middle of my chest. "I get that you're brilliant, that you have money, that everything in this godforsaken world has been handed to you on a freaking silver platter, but that gives you no right to treat me like I'm a child!"

She really had no clue, I had to force myself not to smile.

And then I had to force myself not to take her into my arms and kiss the scowl from her lips.

"I'll stop treating you like a child when you stop acting like one."

If I thought she was pissed before—she was beyond enraged now. Her eyes widened as she gave me a little shove.

"You ass hole!"

I straightened my tie. "I never promised to be anything but. Now, if you're done putting me in my place, I'd like to get to dinner. We have a reservation."

"I'm not hungry."

"Lie." I checked my Rolex, "Are we going to sit and argue all night or do you want bread?"

Her eyes lit up briefly before she turned around and wrapped her arms around her body. "Like I said, I'm not really hungry."

I walked up behind her, my chest nearly touching her back, and leaned in, my mouth brushing against her ear. "You know you could just say thank you in advance and get all this huffing over with."

"Thank you?" Her body shuddered, but she didn't turn around. "For what?"

"The best bread you'll ever have in your entire life and enough wine to go with it for you to forget how much of an ass I've been."

Maya's breath hitched. She turned, her face curious.

Not going to happen. I refused to give anything away. "Or you could just force me to pay for your company, since you're so convinced that's what I do in my spare time."

She rolled her eyes. "Fine but I'm ordering whatever I want."

"I would expect nothing less from you."

She grunted and walked toward the door. I followed her out and locked up behind me. My text alert went off.

Quickly I scanned through the message from Jac.

And then a picture popped up with the word confirmed tagged to it.

"Something wrong?" Maya asked.

I offered a practiced smile. "No, no, everything's fine."

My hands shook as I unlocked the doors and shoved the

key into the ignition. Jac was out there doing what I should be doing—what my family had been doing for years, and I was taking a girl who was completely off limits to dinner.

Not because I owed her.

Or because I owned her.

But because I genuinely wanted to spend time with her—something I'd never before experienced.

I felt it then, the change in the wind as I hit the Audi's accelerator and forced myself to calm down.

She was already getting underneath my skin.

And she had no idea how dangerous that simple action would be—for both of us.

CHAPTER SEVENTEEN

Success and rest don't sleep together — Russian Proverb

Maya

HE WAS ACTING ANGRY AND CRAZY again. He was like Jekyll and Hyde. I tried to force myself to put all the different pieces of his personality together, but really, the only visual it gave me was one of a Picasso painting. I wondered if I'd ever really know the real Nikolai, or if it was even worth trying to figure out.

Something on his phone had made him uneasy.

Or maybe it was just sadness I noticed in his eyes as we drove in silence. I tried not to stare, really I did, but it was hard not to. When Nikolai was brooding or sad, there was this enigmatic pull he threw out into the atmosphere making it almost impossible not to want to lean in and whisper, "Tell me your secrets."

He'd been sad and uptight all day, ever since he'd disappeared into his hidden office.

"Why the contract?" I finally asked once the silence got to be too much. I figured he was angry enough as it was, may as well ask what I'd been dying to ask since my fate had been sealed.

"Let's not discuss work."

"It's not work," I argued. "It's my life."

"A life I'm very graciously allowing you to live out in one of my penthouse suites." His voice was stern. "And let's not forget payment."

I ground my teeth together. "See the thing is, Nikolai... most people want to have a choice in where they live and how they live, what job they hold. I know, weird, right?"

His face cracked into a smile. "You don't get a choice."

He said it like a fact, not a question. "And why is that?"

"Tell me, do you have brothers? Sisters?"

"I can't imagine you not actually knowing everything there is to know about me and my family but if you must know... I had a sister. She died when she was an infant, and last year my brother Pike was ruthlessly murdered by some Italian bastards who clearly underestimate a Russian's desire for revenge."

"Hmm, interesting."

Fine I'd take the bait. I exhaled. "What is?"

His lips rubbed together briefly. "Your version of the story."

"Is there more than one?"

"Several." He took the exit toward Everett. "Depending on whom you speak with."

"I want your version."

"I bet you do."

"Why bring it up when you aren't going to tell me anything? Seems pointless."

His frown turned into a smirk. "Are you pouting?"

"Is it working?"

He let out a low chuckle, it vibrated through the car, attaching itself to my nerve endings, causing a shiver to course through my veins. "Perhaps."

"So?" I clenched my hands together to keep myself from reaching out to him—it would be another horrible idea considering how often the man rejected and scolded me.

"Your younger sister we will discuss at a later date." His face paled. "Your brother Pike was in the wrong place at the wrong time, and your father thought it prudent to eliminate him before the Italian mafia decided to embark on a friendly war between the two families."

"Italians," I spat.

"Saved your ass," he finished. "And are more loyal than you could possibly comprehend."

"My sister?" I asked in a hopeful voice. I'd never met her, to me she was a stranger, though still family. "What about her?"

He hesitated then said in a low whisper. "It's... complicated."

"She's dead." It felt so final, saying it out loud.

"No."

My heart skipped as my blood turned cold, "What do you mean, no?"

"No," he said again. "Not dead. At least not as an infant." He hesitated as if gauging what he should say next, his voice cracking. "For now we'll just leave it at that."

"Why?"

"Because." He closed his eyes, while still driving, then opened them and said. "Her life was very different from yours... let's eat and then we'll discuss things like your sister."

"So my father lied?"

Nikolai hissed out a breath. "What do you think? He also

sold you to a bastard like me. He's a monster. Plain and simple. Then again, I own a mirror, so…" He ended the statement with a half-hearted shrug.

"You aren't a bastard," I defended, then closed my eyes in humiliation. He didn't need me to defend him any more than I needed to be feeling sorry for him.

"We're here." The car slowed to a stop. I glanced up. We were at the Everett Pier.

"More work?" I arched my eyebrows.

"Food." He opened his car door. "I did promise you bread."

"It better be good," I grumbled opening my own door and joining him in front of the car.

The restaurant appeared small. Double iron doors were decorated with large sculpted fish handles, and a sign above the door said Confetti's. It put me immediately at ease because really who takes someone to dinner at a place called Confetti's then kills them?

Wow, was I really entertaining the thought that he was a serial killer?

I glanced at him from the corner of my eye. Good looking? Check. Brilliant? Check. Rich? Check. Possible sociopath? Double check. Great. I was dining with Ted Bundy.

My body revolted against me and shivered—the thought chilled me.

"Cold?" Nikolai shrugged out of his jacket and wrapped it around my shoulders before I could say no. And all thoughts of Ted Bundy flew out the window. The jacket smelled like it had spent the day hanging up in an expensive store only to be worn by Mr. Dead Sexy for a few hours then sprayed with the most delicious spiced cologne I'd ever smelled in my entire life.

"Are you going to smell my jacket or walk through the door, Maya?"

I released the lapel of the jacket as a flush sent warmth to my cheeks. "Sorry, thought I saw a... loose thread." You know, by the lapel, where there were officially no buttons, therefore no thread. Good one.

"Ah, pesky threads." He teased, his voice indifferent, but his posture giving way that he was amused at my expense.

Ted Bundy. Ted Bundy. Ted Bundy. I needed the distance, I needed to think the worst because for some reason his every action drew me in—caused me to question the type of man he was—and my position in his life.

"Mr. Blazik." The receptionist was a short blonde with bright red lipstick, "We have your table all ready, if you'll just follow me."

"Thank you, Carly."

I suddenly felt a warm hand on the small of my back. Every single fingertip seemed to singe into my skin making me hyper aware of his presence and again of how amazing he smelled. The hand soon left my body, causing me to feel a loss I had no right to feel. Nikolai pulled out the black velvet chair. I sat while Carly placed a white napkin over my lap.

"Still or sparkling?" She held up two glass bottles of water.

"Uh..." I nervously licked my lips and looked to Nikolai.

"Still."

Did he really make me so nervous that I couldn't decide which type of water I preferred?

"That will be all, Carly."

Dismissed, she simply nodded her head and left. I glanced around the restaurant nervously. It was completely empty.

"Is it closed?" I whispered, not really sure why I was whispering, but my voice felt too loud for some reason.

"No." Nikolai reached for my wineglass and flipped it over. As if by magic, a server appeared and poured each of us a glass of wine.

"So…" I reached for the wine, needing it more than food at the moment. "Is it going out of business?"

"No."

I glared at him. "Let's try more than a one word answer."

He leaned forward, his facial features positively glowing beneath the candlelight. Damn the man was beautiful. His full lips pressed into an easy, confident smile. "I own the restaurant. I wanted it empty tonight, therefore it's empty."

"I half expected you to snap your fingers and finish that sentence with evil laughter and maybe something like… and when I take over the world all will be mine."

Nikolai choked on his wine.

"Something I said?"

His smile was back full force. "You think?"

"You don't smile enough," I blurted before I could stop myself. The words were out into the universe, and no matter how much I wanted to take them back—I couldn't. I simply watched in fascination as they slowly sank in, causing Nikolai's smile to fade and his posture to stiffen.

"Probably not something you should notice about your employer." He leaned back in his chair. "Today has been difficult."

The darkness was back. I tried to lighten the subject. "Do all employers close restaurants so they can have alone time with their favorite employees?"

"Did I say you were my favorite?"

"I nominated myself." I nodded encouragingly then took another sip of wine.

"I see that."

"Mr. Blazik." A male server who looked to be around seventeen with a soul patch and dark black hair brought another bottle of wine and two new glasses. "For the appetizers."

A new glass replaced my old one, and an elaborate shrimp cocktail was placed on my plate.

The smell of freshly baked bread assaulted my nose. An entire loaf was placed in between us.

My mouth watered as the steam danced its way toward me.

"Go ahead..." Nikolai nodded. "Before you make a fool of yourself and start clapping your hands or something."

"I do clap before I eat."

"Most women do. I think it's in a last ditch effort to burn calories before consuming an abhorrent amount of carbohydrates."

"Hah." I reached for the bread.

Nikolai grabbed the butter and cut a generous amount from the block then took my bread and lathered it on. "Don't forget the best part."

"I should have clapped."

"Life is full of regret." He smiled. "Eat your bread, Maya."

"Eat your bread, Maya. Sign the contract, Maya. Don't ask questions, Maya. You sir, are bossy." I took a huge bite of bread and nearly passed out with ecstasy.

"I imagine you forgive me now?" He cut off his own piece of bread and watched me eat, not in a creepy way but in a way that made me think he hadn't ever seen anyone enjoy food the way I did.

Which was probably true.

Food was life. And life was meant to be enjoyed, right? At least my father got that part right. Eating was meant to be enjoyed, savored.

"What?" I swallowed the last bit of bread and reached for my white wine. "What's so amusing?"

He leaned back, pieces of dark hair falling in rock star fashion across his forehead. "I think I want every evening."

"Pardon?"

"I'm adding it in the contract."

"What are we talking about?" I reached for another piece of sourdough.

He smirked. "I want all your dinners… maybe your breakfasts too… tell me do you always eat bread with such abandon?"

"Do you always treat your assistants with such extravagance?"

"No." He sobered. "I don't think I've ever been accused of that."

"No." I licked my lips suddenly feeling shy. "It's the food… I love good food."

"And good company?"

I tilted my head. "Hmm, good company being a man who never lets me ask questions."

"How about I give you a free pass? Ask me anything you want."

I almost choked on my wine. "Seriously?"

"No, I lied." He rolled his eyes. "Yes, Maya, you get one question… choose carefully."

"Damn, so I can't ask if you're a vampire or serial killer then?"

"You're trying to trick me…" he smirked. "But I'll put your mind at ease nonetheless. No, I'm not a vampire, I can't imagine sucking anyone's blood… now their skin? I could lick and suck their skin… blood?" He shrugged, while I had a mild heart attack at the vision of him sucking… anything.

"And serial killer doesn't really knock your rocks either?"

He paused, his hand hovering over his wine glass. "Life is too precious to waste."

"Fine…" I sat back in my chair, the wine doing its job by relaxing me. "Why the contract?"

"I knew you would ask that."

"Oh, did you, now?"

"Too curious for your own good, Miss Petrov."

"Thank you, Mr. Blazik."

With an exaggerated eye-roll he lifted his hand and the bread, and appetizers were immediately removed from our table only to be replaced by two Caesar salads. "The contract keeps you safe, this you already know."

"Right." I was going to stab him if he didn't answer me with real words rather than evasions.

"Think of it this way..." His voice was just barely above a whisper. "If I have something legally signed, then the only way to get out of it is how?"

"Um... death or the contract is somehow voided?"

"So you're under contract to protect you as well as myself. I need your absolute loyalty and submission. The contract makes it so that those who wish to harm you—can't."

"And I've somehow made a lot of enemies in my short life?"

"Not you," he said cryptically.

"So it's about my father."

"Isn't everything?" His voice was tinged with a bit of sadness, maybe even regret. "The sins of the father..."

"Yeah, well, apparently being born was enough to offend him, which in turn threw me into this lovely romance novel." I lifted my wine into the air. "Cheers."

"Internet." Nikolai cleared his throat. "A flat screen and a brand new computer are already waiting for you at your apartment."

My mouth dropped open in shock. "You're lying."

"I don't lie."

"I love you."

His breath hitched, and then his smile turned sour. "Wow, and all it took was a bit of technology to win that love... seems it was too easy."

"You forgot the bread."

His eyes met mine. "Maya, I do hope you one day see… everything I do. I do for you… for your safety. To keep my secrets and to protect you from them. The number one reason you have a contract isn't to protect you from your father. But to protect you from your greatest threat." His eyes grew sad, closing before opening and looking away. "Me."

CHAPTER EIGHTEEN

You needn't be afraid of a barking dog, but you should be afraid of a silent dog — Russian Proverb

Nikolai

NOW I'D GONE AND TERRIFIED HER. The flush that I had previously been enjoying spread across her skin now turned pale. She was probably entertaining thoughts that I was just like her father, ruthless, heartless, you name it.

Though I'd given up hope long ago that I possessed a heart—I was human, meaning I still wanted to believe I had one, or wanted her to believe I was capable of having one.

Every year on my Valentine's Day Andi would send me a heart card. She thought it was funny—I'd kept every single one.

"Sir." Carly approached our table, hands clasped in front of her. "Your entrees will be out momentarily, would you like to dine on the patio with the heaters and open fire pit?"

"Yes," Maya blurted before I had a chance to speak.

I forced myself to keep the laugh in when her face returned to a crimson flush while she pretended to play with her napkin.

The day had been difficult, but she was making me laugh, just like Andi had. I needed it more than oxygen.

"What the lady wants, the lady gets." I stood and held out my hand to Maya. "Shall we?"

"Oh, if we must." Her eyes danced with humor as she clenched my hand.

Memories assaulted me in that moment. Memories of a time not so long ago when I'd been callous in my dealings with her and her father—when I'd destroyed something so beautiful—because of money, because he'd had something hanging over my head—but the worst part was there was a time when I'd enjoyed it, because I was so damn good at what I did—and I had taken too much pride in it.

"Break her," he'd said.

"Watch me," I'd all but answered back.

"Hey." Maya nudged me. "We going to walk through the nice glass door or are we going back to the theory that you're not of this world... Wow! I didn't guess ghost, should I have?"

"Hilarious," I murmured then opened the door and placed my hand on her back ushering her into the outside patio area.

A roaring fire pit flickered to the left while a miniature version of the same glowed in the center of the table we'd be eating at. Heaters surrounded us and lush fur blankets lay across each lounge chair just in case Maya got cold. In all honesty, I'd meant to cut the evening short. I'd only wanted to extend to her some kindness so she'd trust me, stop asking questions, and put me out of my misery. The more time I spent with her.

The more I wanted her.

And that was more dangerous than her working for me.

It was more dangerous than her knowing my secrets.

It was more dangerous than her knowing her past.

"Alright..." She did a quick turn then poked me in the chest. "I have another guess."

My eyebrows arched, "This should be good."

She took a step toward me, then another. I wanted so desperately to back away that for a brief moment I contemplated running.

From a harmless woman.

God help me.

"You." She took another step toward me. "Are."

One more step and she'd nearly be chest to chest.

"A."

Her next step wasn't as stable, causing her to tumble into my arms. I braced her shoulders. "A what?"

Maya's eyes locked in on mine. "I—I forgot what I was going to say." Her breathing picked up speed as her eyes darted toward my lips and lingered there.

In my mind I pushed her away.

In reality... I pulled her closer.

"Pity," I whispered, my lips brushing hers, begging her to kiss me back and push me away all at once.

"It is." She slid her tongue across her lips where mine had just touched, then leaned closer to me.

I had a choice.

We both did.

A stronger man would pull away.

A stronger man would remember the damn contract and all the reasons why it was imperative that it not be voided out.

In that moment I realized two things... I'd always wanted her, even back then.

And I wasn't as strong as I'd always believed.

I gave in to my weakness.

And kissed her.

Maya's arms wrapped around my neck as I slanted my mouth against hers, trying another angle, not because I had to, but because it wasn't enough. Every angle, every collision of our mouths, the fusion of our heat—wasn't enough.

Alarm bells rang in my head like gunshots floating through the night sky.

She was off limits.

She was dangerous.

Because she could finally be the death of not only me, but my family's legacy, my life's work, and worse yet, all of my secrets.

"Nikolai." Her tongue swept against mine.

I suppressed a groan and pulled back, setting her on her feet. Maya's eyes were heavy with lust.

My fingers itched to reach for her again.

Instead, I clasped my hands behind my back and took two steps backward. "We should eat… we have an early morning."

Rejection washed across her features before she gave me a simple nod and took her seat.

The rest of the evening went to hell.

Every time she tried a bite of something new I asked her if she liked it. Her response was a meager shrug.

Russians.

When I offered more wine…

Another shrug.

When I damn near ripped the table cloth in half and threw the glassware onto the ground in frustration, she simply yawned and said it was getting late.

Repeating my same words.

The evening ended with her closing the door to her apartment in my face, and me staring at it for a good five minutes before I went down to my own apartment and stared at the ceiling.

Which would be her floor.

I heard her walking.

And if I listened hard enough…

I could also hear her crying.

It was easy to decipher amidst the noise of her TV—because many years ago it had been ingrained in my consciousness, never to leave.

I'd caused her tears before and years ago I swore I'd never cause those tears again. And yet, here I was…

We were two days into the contract. And I'd already jumped off the cliff into oblivion. Panic choked me, because I knew if for some reason that kiss triggered anything, we'd both be dead.

God help me if I continue in that way—because it wouldn't just be guilt eating away at me—but absolute horror—that her life would be given up just like that.

Her father could never know I'd touched her.

I took one last look at the ceiling and slammed all my emotions back into a box, locked it, and threw away the key.

Off limits.

Not mine.

If I truly cared for her—I'd let her believe I was a heartless bastard with no soul. I had no choice.

CHAPTER NINETEEN

A man is judged by his deeds, not his words. –Russian Proverb

Maya

THE DINNER WAS A DISASTER... ACTUALLY no that's not right. The dinner was amazing, the food incredible, the company, however, was a disaster and I only had my hormones to blame.

Stupid, stupid, stupid hormones.

My brain says watch out he could be the next Ted Bundy.

And that very same warning bell stops chiming the minute the man licks his lips and leans in.

I met him halfway.

So technically, half the fault was mine. But only half.

My last few nights had been filled with dreams, horrible dreams about ice cream, only when the man offered it to me, offered me a taste, it turned to blood, right before it touched my lips.

"Maya!" Nikolai snapped. "Do I pay you to day dream?"

Crap. How long had he been standing there? I hadn't slept much all week. It had officially been two days since our failed dinner.

Since his mouth touched mine.

Branded mine is more like it.

And try as I might—I couldn't escape the taste of Nikolai. Nor, and I'm ashamed to admit this—did I actually want to.

"Work," he said slowly, his head nodding toward the laptop on my desk. "I need you to continue researching the newest STD strains and have a report on my desk by five this evening. Make note of anything considered resistant to treatment."

"Right." I tugged at my blouse, while he checked his watch and cursed.

That wasn't typical behavior for Nikolai. He was always poised, always polite, especially at work. So something had to be wrong, but I wasn't sure if by asking a question I was actually going to get into trouble or if he would break down and tell me what I could do to help.

A few days ago it felt like we'd made progress, and now it was back to square one.

He checked his watch again then started tapping his foot against the marble floor.

I tried to concentrate on my computer screen, but the tapping continued.

Gritting my teeth I shot him a glare. "Something wrong?"

"Everything's wrong."

"Care to bitch about it?" I said in a sweet voice.

He scowled then checked his watch again. "She's late."

"Who?"

"Jac."

I frowned. "Did you two have a meeting?"

"Chicago." He sighed. "My private plane leaves in an

hour."

"But it's your plane." I explained.

"I believe I'm aware it's mine." He rolled his eyes.

"Tell the pilot to wait." I shrugged. "Not rocket science."

The tapping stopped. He turned and slowly approached my desk. Placing his hands on the top of it, he leaned in until his face was inches from mine. "Tell the pilot to wait she says."

"Y-yes."

"And say what exactly to the people I'm supposed to be meeting with?"

"Er—"

"Or how about the dinner with investors? Should I tell them to wait as well?"

"No?"

"Are you asking or telling?"

"Um..."

"Forget it," he hissed and pulled out his cell. "Jac, it's me, I know you're probably busy doing cleanup, but you're late and I need to go. Call me when you get a chance." He threw the phone against the closest chair and cursed again. "She was going to—" After a short pause he choked out, "—assist me for the weekend, just in case I needed—" He swallowed. "—assistance."

"Got that part." I nodded then raised my pencil into the air in question.

He closed his eyes and groaned. "We aren't in class. You don't need to raise your hand when you want to speak. If you have something to say, say it!"

"I'll go."

He paled. "The hell you will."

"You've got quite the temper."

At that his face softened. "Sorry. It's just that it's... Chicago."

"Wow, two apologies in what? A week? Is it Christmas?"

"Are you trying to irritate me to death?"

I rose from my chair and grabbed my purse.

"Work ends at five."

"I'm aware."

He pointed at the large mounted clock. "It's three."

"I have to pack."

"For vacation?"

I rolled my eyes and placed my hand on his arm. "You need an assistant. I'll assist you. After all you do pay me a crap load of money. The least I can do is help you pick out your ties and look pretty on your arm while you ask billionaires to continue to invest in Nikolai Enterprises."

"You're not funny."

"Wasn't trying to be."

He hesitated and looked at his watch again while I started humming the jeopardy theme song.

"When did you stop being afraid of me? I think I liked you better when you had your theories of vampirism and ghosts."

I shoved past him.

"Mature." He reared back. "What the hell, Maya?"

"Today you showed me a chink in your armor."

"Yeah?" He rubbed his arm. "What?"

"You actually do need someone." Our eyes met briefly before he glanced away, his lips formed a thin line.

"A mistake…"

"One you can't afford to make in front of people who didn't sign over their lives via a contract." I walked toward the doors and called over my shoulder. "Give me ten minutes. I'll pack fast. You can debrief me on the plane."

"I didn't say yes."

"Didn't have to! All I need is a thank you and a cell phone to show your appreciation!" I made my way into the elevator and gave him a little wave.

The angry lines of his scowl made him look so sexy I almost let out a little whimper.

What the hell was I doing?

He could be crazy.

He could be a psychopath.

He freaking owned me.

And I was yet again putting myself in the position where I could get very hurt. Then again, what was my other option? Watching Netflix with a bottle of wine?

Crap. I should have kept my mouth closed.

CHAPTER TWENTY

Draw not your bow till your arrow is fixed. — Russian Proverb

Nikolai

I WAS WORRIED ABOUT JAC. SHE always texted. She always called. I hadn't heard from her since our fight yesterday when she'd discovered that I'd been out to dinner with Maya.

"A bit of business with pleasure?" Jac's lips turned into a mocking grin. *"Do you think that's wise?"*

"It was just dinner."

"Nothing is just dinner with you."

"I'll keep my hands off her if that's what you're concerned about."

Jac snorted. "I've read that contract. If you don't then you're screwed and you know it."

I rolled my eyes. "Did you take care of the situation?"

"Depends. Are you going to keep treating her like the little pet she is or are you going to actually tell your sweet girl what it is you

do? What it is we do?"

"We never tell our secrets." I took a large sip of wine.

"I know that… just trying to see if you still know it, too."

"Is that all Jac?"

"Keep your friends close, your enemies closer." She gave one curt nod. "Don't lose your head, Nik. I'd hate to see you get hurt over a meaningless crush."

I burst out laughing. "Crushes are for children."

"My point exactly." She shrugged. "So be a man."

I pinched the bridge of my nose and looked out the window while Maya continued to comment on every single piece of equipment she saw.

"Leather chairs!" She whispered in reverence. "Champagne." Her eyebrows arched. "Is that caviar?"

"The running commentary I could really do without, Maya," I grumbled. This is where weak moments got me. Stuck on a plane with a woman I'm not allowed to touch, on the way to a funeral I didn't want to go to. At all.

I rarely lost my focus.

And I rarely lost my temper in front of others.

What the hell had possessed me to do it in front of Maya?

"So." She plopped into the seat next to me and crossed her long legs. I fought hard to pull my eyes away. "Catch me up, what exactly are we doing in Chicago."

I opened a folder and slid it across the table. "We are doing nothing. I, however, am making a speech at… a church."

I didn't miss her snort, or the way she tried to hide her amusement.

"Something funny?"

"Yeah." She nodded. "In church."

"Where did this attitude come from?"

"You kissed me." Her eyes narrowed as she leaned back into her seat, not missing a beat as she let her gaze wander across my body like a caress. I'd be lying if I said it didn't feel good, to be desired, wanted, and it was a welcome distraction from the pit in my stomach. I really, really didn't want to go to Chicago.

"You kissed me back," I retorted.

"Doesn't matter, you still *kissed* me. The line between beast and his little toy has been crossed, therefore I kind of own you like you own me, just in a more... irritating way. I have your balls in a vise."

"Let's leave my balls out of the speech if you don't mind," I said ignoring her little ploy to get under my skin again.

"Hey." Her grin spread smugly across her pretty face. "It may just inspire the crap out of them, you never know."

This was a conversation that Andi would have loved, in fact, the more Maya talked the more I saw Andi in her, which just made it that much worse. Here Maya thought I was going to Chicago to slap hands with rich doctors and make speeches, when really, I was going because I made a promise, to a dying girl.

Just one more girl, I'd failed to save.

"Let's leave all references to body parts out of my speech, hmm?"

"I'll try."

"I am the boss."

"So you are."

"I've created a monster. Had I known feeding you would gain this response I would have tied you up in the basement with a protein bar and some Gatorade."

"It's not your fault. It's Netflix. Orange is the New Black combined with the nightmares..." She yawned and it was then that I noticed how tired she looked.

I shifted uncomfortably in my seat wanting to press things further, what kind of nightmares had she been having?

"I haven't been sleeping much. Then again I blame you for keeping me from technology for so long."

"Which brings us back full circle. I should have never given you such privileges." My voice came out in a bark.

"It's a right, not a privilege," she snapped.

"So this…" What the hell was it? A eulogy? Not really, that was Sergio, but he'd asked me to say a few words. Shit. I struggled with how to ask, I didn't know the first thing about being at a funeral, I put people in the casket, I didn't visit them after they took their last breath. My eyes stung with exhaustion. "I need you to help me write it."

"Wait…" She visibly paled. "What did you say?"

"Write." I nodded encouragingly, my anger surging, breaking through all of my carefully constructed walls. Anger had no place in my business, in my life, and anger toward her, did nothing but put her in danger. "You know, words on a paper, you put them down, I say them."

"Don't be an ass."

"Maya…" I tsked. "I am what I am."

"Put that in your speech."

"Maya." I grit my teeth together to keep myself from snapping at her. "I need a speech, something… encouraging, inspirational, happy."

Maya pulled out her laptop and opened it up. "Inspirational… I can do inspirational. When was the last time I was inspired…?" Her cheeks bloomed red.

"What was that?" I breathed, my eyes lowering to the expanse of cleavage, it was a welcome distraction from my morose and jumbled thoughts. "Didn't catch what you just said."

"I, uh, didn't say anything." She nervously tucked a piece of hair behind her ear, her cheeks pinkening even further.

"Your mouth didn't… your face did."

"Let's not talk about my mouth…"

"Why?" I leaned in. "Does it inspire you too much?"

"Ass!" she hissed.

"I think you're on to something…" I chuckled, bracing my hands on the armrests. Six inches, and our mouths would touch. I wasn't just toying with breaking the contract, I was ripping it up, burning it. Just as our mouths were about to touch, I paused, lingering where our breaths mingled, hers warm on my lips, mine ragged and needy. I was right about one thing; she would be a welcome distraction, one that wouldn't allow me to feel sad, or bothered by the fact that I was flying to a friend's funeral.

And that history, if I wasn't careful could repeat itself.

She moved, dislodging her water bottle. It landed with a soft *thump* on the floor.

I reared back and stared at it.

What the hell was I doing?

And as luck would have it, the water droplets had cascaded against my left hand, my tattoo—the mark of the sickle, the mark that would tell anyone who knew anything about the darker side of life.

What I did.

Who I worked for.

What I was capable of.

What I would do—to protect not just my own identity but those closest to me.

My phone rang.

I reached down to silence it—ready to silence it, when I noted the number. Cringing, I answered it with a smooth hello.

"You know I have eyes everywhere."

"Good afternoon to you, too."

Maya pretended not to eavesdrop.

The last thing she needed to know was that I was talking to her father—correction, receiving another threat.

This one not so baseless as the rest.

"Tell me something I don't know," I said, waiting for his response.

"She's been touched."

I rolled my eyes. "You sure about that?"

The line crackled.

"She flushes when you're near."

"Most women do."

"Cocky son of a bitch." He chuckled. "Remember the terms of our agreement, Nikolai, I scratch your back, you scratch mine. She means nothing to *me*. You are the one who has everything to lose. You've developed a god complex, but I know all your secrets. It would take nothing for me to destroy you. You signed in blood. And it will be your blood that is spilled if you go back on your promise."

My nostrils flared, heat surged through my body as I watched Maya happily pull out a magazine and cross her legs. Damn it, he was right. What the hell was I doing?

My lack of self control would end up getting her killed.

I knew that just as much as he did.

I was stuck.

And he knew it. Part of me wondered if he was aware that I'd developed a conscience—then again, I'd stopped working directly with him long ago, but it didn't mean I wasn't still owned.

"We'll be in touch." The phone went dead.

Damn Russian mafia.

And damn me for being one of the best. I didn't get the nickname The Doctor because I had a good bedside manner.

And I wondered, as I tried not to stare too hard at Maya while she read through her magazine, would she still be alive if I hadn't have taken the job that changed everything?

Had I damned her, then?

Had I truly saved her?

I let out a low growl of frustration; clenching my phone in my hand, ready to break it in half. I wanted so desperately to protect her from Andi's fate, but would it be better that she died?

My body tensed.

Would I be extending her mercy, by snuffing out her life?

Maya frowned down at the magazine, her eyebrows furrowed as the plane rose to altitude.

I didn't shake, didn't so much as tremble. I was a doctor, after all, and whenever I made a decision of life and death, I was calm. Humanity didn't slip through. I didn't have a come–to-Jesus moment, where I wondered if what I was doing would sentence me to the darkest depths of hell.

It was… clarity.

The only way I could explain it.

"Something else to drink?" I asked Maya while she popped her knuckles again. Shit, twice in a few minutes? Was there something about the plane? Or my conversation?

"Wine." She said quickly. "If you have it."

I nodded, already walking to the bar. I glanced to my left to make sure she wasn't watching me, then reached into the cupboard and pulled out a syringe of sodium pentothal. It wouldn't harm her. If anything, it would relax her more, make it so that I would be able to hold a conversation with her… without her remembering a damn thing, though the dosage needed to be precise. The last thing I needed was for her to end up unconscious.

"What time is it?" I asked while I poured the wine, keeping the small syringe in my right hand.

"Oh." Maya yawned then glanced at her watch. "It's nearing four in the afternoon, why?"

"Just thinking about our dinner plans," I lied. Two and a half hours since she'd last eaten. I mentally went over her stats, weight one-forty, height five seven. She'd need a half dose at the most.

Clearing my throat, I turned, sliding the syringe into the top of my sleeve and bringing over the two glasses of wine; hers was more full.

"Wow, generous in all areas aren't you, Nikolai?" Maya eyed the wine glass and took a long sip.

"Drink it all," I instructed with a half smile. "Doctor's orders."

"All of it?" She laughed lifting the glass into the air. "This is at least two glasses."

"At least half," I said in a more gentle tone. "You seem stressed, and I know… I'm not the easiest to travel with."

Maya blinked then took another sip of wine. "No, you think?"

"It's a…" I coughed into my hand letting the syringe slip out to the tips of my fingers. "It's not you. It's me."

"Okay," she said slowly, setting her wine down on the arm rest.

"Nope." I offered a encouraging smile. "A few more sips, trust me, you'll feel so much better."

Maya rolled her eyes but drank deeply.

The alcohol would work beautifully with the sodium pentothal. Truth serums, didn't necessarily work by themselves, they were used in conjunction with other tools and drugs, allowing the human mind to be open to suggestion.

But no human mind or body was the same, meaning, the outcome was always different.

If Maya had any sort of… secret she was keeping close, something she wanted to tell me, but couldn't or refused to, it would most likely come out at some point in the next half hour.

If she were harboring memories, dark ones, ones that scared her, and I offered her a caring ear, she'd jump at it.

And I'd know.

If she was getting triggered and how.

It sounded sick.

But it was of the utmost importance that she be kept in the dark, especially since her father clearly was still keeping eyes on her.

I told myself that as she drank more wine.

But, convincing the monster what he was doing was right, was never difficult. I'd been justifying my actions since we'd originally met.

The day after her sixteenth birthday.

CHAPTER TWENTY-ONE

Although there have been no new murders, the Pier Killer is still at large. If you have any tips or hints, please contact the police hotline.
—The Seattle Tribune

Maya

THE WINE WAS HELPING, THOUGH NOT enough for me to forget what a messed up situation I was in. Private plane or not, I was still with Nikolai, and as per usual, he was being extremely vague about why he was so incredibly stressed out and clearly not sleeping. His eyes held more darkness than before, almost like he was fighting a losing battle with some sort of life ending sickness and knew the future was bleak.

I sighed and took one more healthy drink of the red wine and sat my glass on the table next to me. Warmth flooded my veins as I closed my eyes.

Nikolai leaned forward, his eyes focused in on my mouth. Butterflies erupted in my stomach as he slowly pressed a kiss to the side of my mouth.

Searing pain erupted in my neck. A stinging, and then warmth washed over me.

"What the hell?" I shoved him away from me, knocking my wine glass to the floor as I frantically pressed my fingers against the delicate skin on my neck. When I brought them back, there was no blood. For a second there I could have sworn he stabbed me. Frowning, my vision doubled as I stared at my finger tips for any trace of... my mind went completely blank as waves of heat softly rolled across my body like a caress.

"Something wrong?" Nikolai asked in a gorgeously smooth voice, like velvet, or the most exotic wine. He was positioned directly in front of me, part of his black button down shirt was opened at the neck exposing bronzed skin and an expanse of muscle I knew dipped lower.

My gaze fell down examining his pecs, wishing his shirt was tighter. I licked my lips as my eyes focused in on his belt buckle.

"Maya?"

"Hmm?" I blinked a few times then met his gaze. "Sorry." My lips felt fuzzy. "I think that wine made me... dizzy." Wait, did I have wine? I looked down at the spilled glass. Clearly I'd had wine, I'd just drank too much. "Sorry." I repeated again, though I wasn't sure what I was apologizing for.

"You're exhausted." Nikolai's voice had shifted, something in his tone was different, something that called to me, or maybe a memory inside my head. Fear, trickled down my spine as I gripped the arm rests of my seat. "Why don't you tell me what has you so stressed, Maya?"

My name on his lips was damn sexy.

He chuckled. "Why thank you."

"Did I say that out loud?" I asked, embarrassed.

"Yes."

"Great." I smiled, though my face still felt funny. "You

have to know working under you, wait, if I was under you I'd be… a prostitute, like the ones you see. They are prostitutes, right?"

"In a way," he finally answered.

"I knew it!" I tried to push against his chest but my hands wouldn't move as fast as I wanted them. "You and prostitutes. Why is it that you flirt with them and you don't flirt with me?"

His eyebrows shot up. "That's what has you stressed? You want me to flirt with you?"

I frowned. Did I? "I don't… know." I finally said. "I mean you kiss me, then you… act like I don't exist."

"Hmm." Nikolai took a seat directly next to me and pulled my hand into his lap. "Does that hurt your feelings?"

I nodded dumbly. "Or maybe it hurts yours."

"Pardon?" His smile was devilish.

I wanted to run my tongue along his lips, so bad that I couldn't focus on anything else. I just wanted to taste him.

"Maya?" His tone was low, gravelly. "Other than the flirtation is there something else bothering you, perhaps your dreams?"

"You're in them." I didn't realize it was true until the words were out of my mouth, like my brain had chosen to remember something that every other part of me had sworn to forget. I pressed a hand against my right arm as a stinging sensation built from my wrist all the way up to my elbow.

"Scars?" Nikolai pulled my arm into his lap and ran his fingers delicately over the scars from my car accident.

I nodded. "Car accident. I was sixteen, well, almost sixteen and got in a wreck. It was my fault. All of it. My father had told me I could drive after my birthday, but my car was just sitting there. So I drove it… straight into an office building."

"Lucky to be alive." Nikolai said in a tone I could only describe as angry. What? That I was living?

I popped my knuckles nervously. "Yes, I guess so."

Nikolai gripped my hands to keep me from popping. "Why do you do this?"

"Nervous habit." I shrugged and then a memory flashed. "Or..." Popping knuckles, bloody knuckles, right in front of my face.

"Maya?"

I shook my head. "Sorry, I just have a reoccurring nightmare about bloody hands."

"Maya, this is important, are there any defining marks on these bloody hands?"

"Bloody." My heart started slamming against my chest as a choking sensation washed over me. "So much blood." I let out a whimper and began frantically clawing my way out of the airplane seat. "I have to get away! It's not safe! I'm not safe!" Tears blurred my line of vision. "He'll kill me!" I was full on screaming, unable to control the panic building in my chest. "He'll kill me, you too! He'll kill us all!"

"For what?" Nikolai asked calmly, as if we weren't about to die. "Why would he kill you? What did you see?"

"Blood." My teeth chattered, "So. Much. Blood. And she was just... laying there, after he—" Shaking, such uncontrollable shaking, I made it out of my seat and into Nikolai's lap as he started wiping the tears from my cheeks, tears I didn't even know had spilled.

"Shhh," he whispered in my hair. "It's just another nightmare."

"No," I argued. "No. It's real!"

"Maya," he said my name slowly. "Open your eyes, really open them. Look around you. We're safe, in my plane, and you're in my arms. Too much wine and you fell asleep and woke up screaming."

"But—" I glanced around, throat dry, he was right but I still, I felt... like something was missing, something important.

"Something… feels wrong."

"You were terrified, I'm sure. But I'm here now…" Nikolai's deep brown eyes searched mine as he lifted a piece of candy into the air and whispered. "Butterscotch?"

CHAPTER TWENTY-TWO

An open door may tempt a saint. — *Russian Proverb*

Nikolai

I WAS A SICK BASTARD. I'D always known it, but it wasn't until she was in my arms shaking, that I realized how far I'd actually push myself, and those I cared about in order to protect everyone involved, protect my own name, protect her sanity.

She was remembering, albeit slowly. I had a decision to make. If I hypnotized her again, I risked more trauma to her limbic system, the implications of what could happen were enough to make me pause. Hell, I really was developing a damn conscience if I was suddenly toying with the idea of letting it go.

Maya was a sobbing mess. Her eyes frantic, her breathing slow. She would remember nothing once I put her to sleep, at least I could do that for her, make her sleep. Mentally, she was exhausted; physically, her body couldn't take much more, because whenever an individual revisited specific traumatic events in their subconscious, the body physically responded as if it was happening all over again, triggering the amygdala into a fight or flight response.

Maya ducked her head against my neck. "I'm so embarrassed. I fell asleep."

"It happens to all of us," I said smoothly. The reality of what we were doing finally hit me full force. How the hell was I supposed to keep her false memories intact if just being with me was causing her to relapse? It had nothing to do with sex, as I'd originally thought, because I wasn't touching her.

Kissing wouldn't be a strong enough trigger.

Sex should be the only thing that would be strong enough to trigger the memory.

And the only way for me to test that theory.

Hell.

She wouldn't remember it in the morning, my brain taunted me, reminding me that I was doing it for her own good. Protecting her, saving her. Besides, with the way she was already arching against me, the part of her subconscious that I'd just unleashed… wanted it. I wasn't sure if I should be even more disgusted with myself or thrilled.

It would be too much of a risk.

Because if she had a breakdown on the plane, I had a feeling her father would find out, I had a feeling he truly did have eyes everywhere, it wasn't a controlled environment. I wasn't comfortable with it.

Damn it.

I had a suspicious nature.

I wondered, had he seen signs at home? Was this the reason he finally allowed me to have her? Because he knew I would fail? Because I was just another loose end he would finally be able to shut up?

Too many thoughts.

Too many possibilities that made me suddenly thankful we were flying into Chicago, because the only men who would potentially help me, were the Italians, and I understood, in that moment... that I was going to have to call in that favor from the Nicolasi boss. Dread spread throughout my chest, causing my once sluggish heartbeat to pick up speed. I needed to maintain control. Too many emotions were warring with one another. The plan had never been to bring Maya into the lion's den and ask her to calmly accept the simple fate that she had more in common with them than the average person.

I felt warm wet lips against my neck. She wasn't acting like herself. In reality, without the drug, would she kiss me? Possibly. Would she be the one all over me? No. She'd rather slit my throat.

"Maya." My voice came out hoarse and raspy. "Why don't you sleep?"

I shifted her in my arms, ready to hypnotize her with one of her triggers. Years ago I'd implanted several mental viruses. That was the easiest way to explain it. A person could live their entire lives with hypnotic messages or viruses built into their subconscious, just waiting for someone of my expertise to step in and build on them or simply call them forward. I was the best at what I did, so naturally, I made safeguards, at the time, selfishly needing to protect my name, keep myself from getting killed as well as Maya.

History.

Was repeating.

And I wasn't sure I would be able to save us both again, or at all.

I opened my mouth to start the trance, when her mouth suddenly pressed against mine, hot, hungry, open. Her hands intertwined with my hair, as her fingers dug into my skull. With an aggressive tug, she nearly pulled us both out of the chair and onto the plane floor.

"I want you," she whispered against my lips, her tongue rimming my lower lip before making its way back into my mouth adding just the perfect amount of pressure to drive me insane.

"Maya…" I tried to pull away, even though I wanted nothing more than to give into every damn feeling I'd had through the years I'd spent hidden in the shadows, watching, waiting. Keeping my emotions on lockdown around her had been more than painful. At times it had felt impossible. And now it was dangerous.

Maya stopped kissing me then pressed her forehead against mine, her lips brushing mine as she spoke. "You make me feel safe."

Shit. I closed my eyes. "Maya, you've had a lot of wine, you don't know what you're saying."

"But I do." She moved in my lap, wiggling against me in ways that aroused me beyond what I already had been.

I bit down on my tongue to keep from groaning. Her laugh, sensuous and low, made my every nerve fire, every muscle jump.

"I can feel it, you want me too."

"What man wouldn't desire you?"

She gave me her back, her ass positioned directly over me as she dug her heels into the ground and moved hard against me. The seat blocked any sort of escape, and my body wanted nothing more than to allow her to rub up and down until I couldn't take it anymore and either screwed her or died wanting to.

"Please…" Maya arched back against me. "You feel so good, you make me feel good."

I let out a hiss as she stopped moving and reached for my belt buckle. My hips drove up as she pulled the leather causing an erotic explosive friction between our two bodies.

She tugged again, sliding my belt from its loop. At this point she was still sitting on me, doing her best work without actually looking at her hands.

"Nik…" She was using my nickname. Only two people called me Nik. My grandmother and Andi.

My dead friend.

Sadness washed over me again.

When had I stopped being normal? Had I ever been normal? A normal man could take the woman he cared for without regret.

Without wondering if it would be the last decision he ever made before someone else he cared about died.

Maya was getting restless in my lap. The wine mixed with the drug was most likely causing her to lose all inhibition. Under normal circumstances, I would put her in bed or lock her in her bedroom.

But we were on a jet.

Unless I put a parachute on her and went tandem, we had one option. The one and only bedroom that I was already planning on barricading myself in.

"Let's go," I stood, she slid off of me, nearly melting into a puddle on the floor before I lifted her into my arms and walked us back toward the bedroom, slamming the door behind me as I gently placed her on the bed.

Face flushed, Maya lifted her shirt and pulled it off her head, tossing it directly at my face before falling back onto her elbows and thrusting her chest forward. "Kiss me?"

She looked so beautiful.

And I was a man.

A man who had wanted her even when it was forbidden, wanted her still.

I reached for her. "How about we make a deal?"

"Like a game?" Her eyebrows lifted. "I didn't take you for the type."

"Let's just say you bring it out in me." I confessed, trying not to let my gaze linger too long on the swell of her breasts.

"I'm in." Maya laughed softly. "What's the game."

"You know how I like rules." I sobered. "There are only two."

"Two, huh?" She bit down on her bottom lip. "Okay, I'm listening."

"First rule… no talking."

"Okay."

"Second rule." I smirked. "First scream loses."

Maya pushed off the bed then stood up on her tiptoes, her lips brushing my ear as she whispered. "You're on."

CHAPTER TWENTY-THREE

Better to be slapped with the truth than kissed with a lie. —Russian Proverb

Maya

I WAS DREAMING. I HAD TO BE. He was so… aggressive, nothing gentle about the frenzied way Nik's tongue slid against my neck as he pressed another heated kiss just below my ear. "Do you give in?"

"Never." I laughed, feeling more free than I had in years. It wasn't the wine, because the wine didn't explain *his* attitude, the way he held me in his arms like I was both the most beautiful thing he'd ever encountered—and the most dangerous.

Drunk on power, I pulled away just as he dipped his head to kiss me again.

"My turn."

"Oh, Maya," Nikolai chuckled darkly. "We haven't even begun."

"But—"

Something about that sentence felt like a bolt of electricity through my limbs, chilling me in its wake, making me collapse into his arms as images of blood flashed in my line of vision.

I jerked away.

"Maya?" Nikolai frowned. "Are you alright?"

"Yes." I nodded as fear once again trickled down my spine like I was getting a shot of ice through my veins. "Sorry, I just... thought I saw something."

"Hmm, maybe it is best you go to sleep."

"No!" I yelled, desperate for the intimacy that always seemed just out of my reach. Then I felt stupid and covered my mouth to keep myself from blurting out more truths about how I felt whenever he was near. Every single word was on the tip of my tongue just waiting to be released into the universe. It was hell trying to keep everything in, and I'd always prided myself on keeping my emotions hidden, they made me vulnerable, and that was something I couldn't be when around my father, so I'd learned the art of suppressing them.

"You know..." Nikolai slowly started unbuttoning his shirt, and my mouth went dry watching, my body on edge as it anticipated what I'd see next. I wasn't sure if I wanted to stare at his mouth and imagine all the things it could do to me, or wait to see him completely shirtless—bared to me.

The shirt fell to the floor in one fluid drop.

And my brain had trouble conjuring up any sort of thought other than sweet lord how? How was a man that built?

"Hmm, no scream?" He took a step forward then tugged me into his arms, my hands pressed against his firm, warm chest. "And I thought the shirt tossing would do it."

"Close." I breathed him in, the air stirred with electricity. "Very close."

"Can't win them all." He sighed bringing his mouth to mine in a slow tantalizing kiss that tasted like red wine. His tongue was smooth, sliding against mine, tasting and caressing in a way I'd never experienced before.

We kissed for what felt like hours. Maybe it was minutes. Who knew? Time seemed to slow down then speed up only to slow down again.

My back met the soft mattress as Nikolai held his muscled body over mine. This, this is what I wanted, him, only him.

Why did it feel like I'd always wanted him?

Like I'd always craved him?

He leaned down, brushing a kiss across my earlobe as he whispered. "Give in."

Unable to control my response, I let out a slow whimper as the memory, a very realistic memory of his hands running down my body, ran through me.

"It would be a pleasure to break you." Nikolai whispered. "I wish you wouldn't be so afraid... first comes the pain."

"And next?" It was a miracle I kept my voice from shaking.

"Only pleasure." His dark gaze met mine. "I swear it."

"Why?" I jerked against the zip ties. "Why both?"

"They go hand in hand with what you've seen, the only way to fuse the memories together... is to make you think it was you... instead of her."

"So you torture me... and then—"

"—I give you the most amazing pleasure you've ever experienced."

"Is that even legal?" I tried to joke even though my insides were screaming for me to flee, I still couldn't see his face, he was wearing a white mask, like one a person would wear at a carnival or masquerade but his eyes, his evil eyes were in direct contrast to the white.

"Nothing I do here is legal. But I can promise you this—you'll

stay pure… you have to stay pure."

"Pure?"

"Pleasure is something entirely different."

"What do I call you?" I tried changing the subject.

"Whatever you wish."

"I need a name." I was all dried up on tears, the fear had already started to dissipate along with the realization that I would walk out of there alive.

"Nik." He whispered. "Call me Nik."

I let out a gasp, surging off the bed, my head nearly colliding with Nikolai's. "It was you!"

His body went rigid over me. "Excuse me?"

"You… you, you…" I choked out the words. "I saw you, or…" I felt the memory slipping again. "I mean, the man, he had dark eyes."

"What did he do?" Nik asked calmly. "Did he hurt you?"

"Yes… at first, and then…" Heat filled me to the core, so much heat that if he touched me I was certain I would shatter into a million pieces and never be whole again. "He put me back together again."

"In what way?" Nikolai braced me with his hands as he straddled his body across mine, his lips brushed light kisses across my forehead.

"He made…" Everything was blank. "He made me forget the bad…"

"And?"

I squeezed my eyes shut. "He replaced it with good."

"I can do better." Nikolai vowed in a low voice. "Let me show you?"

I nodded, wanting the memory to go away, irritated that every time Nikolai touched me, more memories came only to disappear like I was on some sort of high, but I'd watched him pour my wine.

Each time I blinked I felt more clarity.

Until Nikolai's mouth closed over mine and every shred of logic left me. I had him.... I tasted him.... I wanted him. That's why I was laying in his arms, because in a world full of terror and uncertainty there was one thing I was certain of.

Nikolai would keep me safe.

He would.

And he would give me pleasure.

How did I know that?

My body responded of its own will as Nikolai deepened the kiss then slid his hand up my simple black dress, his fingers finding my core.

He played me like I was an instrument, a melodic harp, each finger plucking a different string, each string hitting a note that took me higher and higher into oblivion... only to stop and bring me back down.

"Come on, Maya, let go for me."

Letting go meant... something big.

Something that would mean more than what I wanted it to. But what?

"Let go." He whispered, his kiss deepening as I rode his hand, and then I felt heat, so much heat wash over me as my center of gravity fell away.

My body fell back.

Slowly, like layers of secrets were just peeled back before my very eyes, Nikolai made a familiar gesture with his head, tilting it to the side, and blowing me a kiss right before whispering. "And now you sleep...." There were words after that, but my ears closed, along with my eyes, as my head touched something soft.

And my world went black.

CHAPTER TWENTY-FOUR

The most dangerous sicknesses are those that make us believe we are well. —Russian Proverb

Nikolai

MY HANDS WOULDN'T STOP SHAKING. TWO hours had passed, and my body was still conniving against me along with my brain, telling me that all I needed to do was wake her up and confess.

It sounded easy.

It should be easy.

All I needed to do was open my mouth and say the words, the words that I knew would destroy whatever friendship or relationship we'd had with one another, that the man who she dreamed of was both her hero and her villain, one in the same. Jekyll was Hyde and vice versa.

I didn't need to get into her psyche to know what would happen if I suddenly put on one of the white masks in her room. Strategically, I'd placed them there to see if they triggered anything. But as far as I knew, to her, they were simple props, costumes.

They had nothing to do with the most important twenty four hours of both our lives, and if I had it my way, they never would.

I checked my Rolex. We would be making our descent into Chicago soon. I needed to wake her up and break the news.

I sipped my wine and waited a few more minutes, not yet ready to break the spell, knowing that the minute she opened her eyes she'd remember nothing but drinking wine and then falling asleep.

It was always possible she'd remember fragments, but I could explain those away with daydreams, nightmares, take your pick.

She wouldn't remember me giving her pleasure.

And that made me borderline hostile, just thinking about the fact that she wouldn't be consciously aware that it was my kiss that made her both remember and wish she could forget, my lips that brought forth blessings, that reminded us both of the curse.

The plane took a dip. With slow movements, I rose from the chair, setting my glass on a nearby table as I made my way to the back of the plane and opened the door to the bedroom.

She was just as I left her.

Shirt off.

Arm tucked beneath her head as a cascade of dark hair fell across her face, kissing her lips and brushing across her chin.

Damn it.

I hesitated, I didn't want to break the moment of bliss where I could stare at her and imagine that she'd fallen asleep because of our lovemaking, not because I'd forced it upon her.

After I'd drugged her.

I bent down and pressed a kiss across her temple and whispered into her ear. "Wake up sleeping beauty." I snapped my fingers twice and then took a step back as she stirred.

With a moan, Maya blinked open her eyes and frowned in my direction. "Where am I?"

"Thirty five thousand feet in the air, give or take a few hundred feet." I answered in a dry tone. "Maybe take it easy on the wine next time?"

Maya jerked to a sitting position on the bed then looked down and quickly covered herself with the spare blanket. "Did I get drunk?"

"No." I offered a polite smile. "Do you remember…anything?"

"Oh, no!" Maya covered her face with her hands. "Did I… attack you?"

"Define attack." I said with a soft laugh.

"No!" Maya groaned into the blanket then pressed her face into it, her voice muffled. "Tell me I didn't kiss you or just… toss my body in your general direction and ask you to catch me."

I couldn't keep my smile from widening as I sat next to her on the bed and let out a light laugh. "Nothing as horrible as that, though next time you want sex it would probably be best to ask for it sober, and not puke after making an offer."

Maya went white as a sheet.

"I'm kidding." I chuckled, "You drank two large glasses of wine, said you felt sleepy, and I walked you to the back bedroom where you fell into a… dreamless sleep."

"No." Maya frowned. "Not dreamless." She shuddered and her skin went from pale to flushed. "I mean…" She pressed a hand to her forehead. "Is it hot in here?"

"Are you alright?" Was it vain to wish she remembered something? Anything?

"Yeah," she said quickly. "I, uh, just had a few really strange dreams."

"Alcohol tends to have that effect on people." I said in a soothing and hopefully halfway convincing voice.

"How many times have you had to say that to a patient, I wonder?" she muttered.

"More than I can count."

Maya laughed, then her eyes narrowed in on my face. "Are you… never mind."

"What?"

"Nothing…" She waved me off. "It just felt really real. My dream."

"Really real, huh?"

"Hey, I just woke up, don't correct my speech."

I held up my hands in innocence. "Why don't you get dressed, then we can talk, alright?"

"Talk?"

"About our reason for being in Chicago."

"No more secrets?"

"No." At least in this I could be somewhat honest.

"What changed?"

Everything, I wanted to say. Instead, I simply ignored the question as I typically did when I didn't want to answer something. "Get dressed, Maya. We don't have much time, and I mean to catch you up before we're held at gunpoint."

She laughed.

I didn't.

"Anything is safer than my father and his thugs," she said under her breath.

"Hah!" I laughed without humor. "Then you clearly have never met the Five Families."

"Five… families?" she repeated.

"The Five Families." I tried to keep the bitterness out of my voice. "From Sicily. If you think your father is scary…

you're in for a very rude wakeup call, and I apologize in advance… they look well dressed, attractive, orderly, safe."

"Is it a ruse?"

"Wolves in sheeps' clothing… every last one. We'll talk more in a few minutes when I'm not distracted by the fact that you aren't wearing a shirt."

She glanced down.

"Maya, that only makes me want to see more."

She dropped the blanket.

That wasn't part of the plan. I clenched my fist in my hand. "What are you doing?"

"This feels familiar." Her words were hollow, like she was trying to remember.

"Are you saying I visited you in your dreams?" I asked, keeping to a light, teasing tone.

"Yeah." She snorted. "But believe me, they weren't real, no way a man is that skilled in the bedroom using his hands."

It was a direct hit to my ego.

Because it *was* me.

It *is* me.

But saying something would ruin more than I was willing to risk—at least in that moment. Soon, soon she would know.

And I'd have to pray she wouldn't run screaming in the other direction.

Or worse… point the gun and pull the trigger.

"I'll just wait outside." I shut the door swiftly behind me, my hands still shaking, like they always did when adrenaline coursed through me, like they had before my first female patient at the clinic.

Like they did whenever Jac approached me about my family legacy.

Shit… I still hadn't heard from Jac.

I made a mental note to call her the minute we landed or at least text to make sure things were under control on her end because if they weren't—then I was in for a hell of a time when I got back to Seattle.

CHAPTER TWENTY-FIVE

Make peace with man and war with your sins.—Leo Tolstoy

Maya

I HOPED I WASN'T AS RED as I felt. I'd never had graphic sexual dreams that had to do with men—or my boss for that matter, the one who was semi kidnapping me and connected to the Russian mafia in ways I didn't want to know.

Seriously? I experience my first orgasm. In. My. Sleep. By a man who swears he's never going to kiss me again? How's that for sexual regression?

I could still feel his hands on my body. I shuddered as I relived the vivid dream of him pulling his shirt over his head. Had I really conjured up what he would look like completely shirtless? What kind of hussy had I turned into?

My lips buzzed from his kiss as if the memory was burned across them. I clenched my thighs together as another shudder wracked my body.

"Maya?" Nikolai knocked on the door. "Are you ready yet?"

No, sorry just thinking about riding my boss, be right there! I mentally smacked myself and quickly pulled on my shirt, tucking it into my skinny jeans and pulling my hair back into a low ponytail. It would have to do, I knew I probably looked a hot mess, but I didn't want to keep him waiting.

In fact, I never wanted to keep Nikolai waiting.

Not because I thought he would harm me, but something about his impatience made me feel nervous.

I pulled open the door and stumbled into his arms as the plane hit some turbulence. His mouth fell open, and I stared like I'd never seen a mouth before or perfect white teeth or smooth tan skin.

His taste had been white hot, impossible to describe, I needed to experience it at least a hundred more times before I'd be able to find the right words.

Words. Why was that triggering something in my head?

"Oh, no!" I wailed. "I'm supposed to help you with a speech!"

"Maya—"

"Why did you let me drink?"

"Maya." Nikolai led me to one of the chairs, and I had no choice but to sit, "That's what I need to talk to you about."

I mentally filed through encouraging uplifting things he could say in church while he spoke, I could at least multi task that way.

"...she's dead."

"Wait..." It was getting hard to breath. "Who's dead?"

"Andi... your sister. She died."

"My sister?"

"Not your full sister, by blood." Nikolai's eyes searched mine. "Do you understand what I'm saying?"

"The one you said didn't die when she was a baby? She

was adopted instead?" I shook my head, no wait that made no sense. "But now—now she *is* dead? How did she die?"

"Leukemia...." Nikolai reached for my hand. "And, Maya, I don't know how to tell you this, but she wasn't adopted. She was Petrov through and through."

"What exactly are you saying?" I jerked my hand back.

"Your mother bore you." Nikolai nodded. "But your father... is not your father." His eyes fell to our hands, he grabbed my fingers again and squeezed. "Your mother had an affair before she became pregnant with Andi, your father, once he discovered who you truly belonged to, gave Andi away as a punishment to your mother, used her as leverage."

"But why?" I was trying to process the information but it was as if a bomb had just exploded in my mind. I'd always known about my sister but she'd been gone at such a young age and the one time I had asked about her, I'd been told she was dead. I'd just assumed... now I don't know what I assumed. Whenever I tried to conjure up memories of my past it was a giant blur as if I had some sort of mental block.

And my father? The man who had basically sold me into slavery wasn't even mine? How was that fair? On one end, I was thrilled that I shared no blood with the man who'd sell me to a complete stranger, on the other hand, a sense of loss hit me square in the chest. Where did I even belong?

"Does it really matter?" Nikolai's dark brown eyes searched mine. "The point is this... your sister, the very sister that you are related to, through your mother, is gone, and we will be attending the funeral."

Too many thoughts jumbled in my head. I wanted to mourn her, but how did I mourn someone I didn't really remember? How did I do her justice? This life that was taken? "She was young wasn't she? I remember that much."

"Twenty-two."

My stomach clenched. "Was there a chance I could

have…?" I couldn't form the words as tears welled in my eyes. *So young. She was so young.*

"No." Nikolai pulled me into his arms and hugged me tight. "You were not a bone marrow match."

"How do you know?"

Nikolai ran his hands along the scars on my arms and whispered. "I'm a doctor… and as you know I've worked very closely with your father over the last ten years. I have ways of finding out such things."

I wasn't entirely satisfied with his answer. "I have… so many questions. What was she like? Did she have a boyfriend? Was she—?"

"Please find your seats for the final descent into Chicago," the captain said over the intercom.

I buckled my seatbelt, missing the click three times before Nikolai finally took pity on me and buckled it up then pulled it tight. I felt like a little kid who was getting fussed over.

"Don't cry." Nikolai's thumbs wiped away the tears I didn't even realize had fallen. "She had… the most beautiful ending."

"A beautiful ending?"

"A happy one… bittersweet." Nikolai nodded. "And I think you'd be relieved to know your father was never able to break her or her husband."

"Husband?" She was married?

"Sergio Abandonato." Nikolai smirked.

Why did that name sound so familiar?

"Stop frowning so much." Nikolai said in a teasing tone. He was doing that more and more this trip, it made me wonder what had shifted so much in the past few hours that he wasn't all doom and gloom like he'd previously been. Maybe he took a nap too? "He's cousin to one of the most powerful mafia families in the states."

"More powerful than—?"

"Yes," Nikolai growled. "But in a more... professional way, if that makes sense."

"No. It makes no sense." Nothing made sense anymore, nothing.

"Your father would shoot one of his own men in cold blood. Hell, he'd shoot your mother and not even blink, simply wipe the prints from his gun, hand it to his right hand man, march off and allow the birds to desecrate her body."

A strong shudder rippled through my body.

"The Italians?" Nikolai said their name almost... reverently, accompanied by a soft sigh. "They would only kill blood if they had no choice, and even then, they say a prayer over them once the blood runs cold... and give the right of burial to the family. That is true professionalism, in a world surrounded by crime and murder.

The plane landed with a loud *thunk*. I gripped Nikolai's right arm, having trouble processing his words that continued to tumble over each other in my head.

We were meeting The Italians.

My sister was involved with them.

Nikolai was involved with them.

My father wasn't my father.

And the sister I'd thought had been dead, lost to me forever—hadn't been, but now she really and truly was gone.

What was I supposed to do with all of this information? How was I supposed to keep myself from having a nervous breakdown?

I took a few deep breaths. Whatever the case, I was still Russian, and Russians didn't cower when faced with impossible circumstances, I knew that much about my heritage, about my blood.

I'd stand.

I'd walk to the airplane door, head held high.

I would not panic.

Nikolai would sense it.

And something told me showing weakness to him was the same as bleeding in shark infested waters.

We taxied for a few minutes in silence, and then the doors to the plane opened.

I grabbed my purse and slung it over my shoulder.

Nikolai grabbed a black briefcase then proceeded to reach into the pocket and pull out a shiny black gun. I wanted to believe it was fake, but I knew that would be a lie. He was packing, but why?

"What are you doing?" I hissed.

He gave me a look that said shut up, put on the safety and held it open in the palm of his hand then used his free hand to guide me to the door.

It was dark except for the few lights on the private runway.

A black Range Rover.

A black Mercedes AMG.

A black Escalade.

Four men, one woman. All of them standing with their guns literally pointed at us as if we were about to start a war on the tarmac.

Waiting for Nikolai to set off a bomb? Or what?

"Just a wild guess." I spoke above the roar of the engines as my hair whipped around my cheeks. "But... the Italians?"

"Live and in the flesh," he grumbled.

"You could have told me they hate you." I gripped his hand tighter.

"What? And ruin the warm welcome for you?" His lips curved into a smile. "Never."

Slowly, we descended the stairs, hand in hand.

A large man in his twenties approached us, his reddish brown hair blowing in the wind, two semi-automatic weapons strapped to his burly chest. If I'd thought Nikolai was large, this man was downright lethal. At least six-four and over two hundred pounds of muscled rage, he sneered the minute we stepped onto the runway, as if our presence offended him so much he was having trouble breathing.

"Campisi," Nikolai said in an irritated voice. "Good evening."

The man named Campisi grunted in Nikolai's direction then turned his cold hard stare in my direction. I shrank into Nikolai's body and clutched his chest with my free hand, chilled to the core. I wasn't sure if this man wanted me to speak or was just trying to see if I'd burst into tears.

I'd seen stares like his before.

From my father.

And his idiots.

Years of training kicked in, years of needing to defend myself against jackasses, so, instead of shrinking more into Nikolai, I took a deep breath, straightened my shoulders, pulled away and stared down the beast of a man.

And the very minute I found my confidence, he smiled. "So, she really is a Petrov after all. I was worried there for a minute."

"Tex worried," a raspy voice said from behind him. "Now, that I'd like to actually see." The man, who looked about my age, pushed himself next to this Tex Campisi guy and narrowed his eyes at me. He had a lip ring, piercing blue eyes, and dark hair.

Both men had a terrifying beauty about them.

"Nixon," The man smirked. "Abandonato," he finished. "Welcome back to Chicago, Nikolai."

"I wish it were under better circumstances," Nikolai said in a low voice. "I almost didn't come but—"

"—it's what she wanted." A girl stepped forward. She had silky black hair that fell just below her shoulders, was wearing a red leather bomber jacket, black stiletto boots hugged her dark wash jeans. She at least offered me a polite smile before tossing her gun into an oversized Prada bag then winking in my direction.

She kept her gun in her Prada?

Then again, where else would she keep it? Her pocket?

Why did she have a gun?

Actually, why did any of them have guns?

"She looks nothing like her." Nixon spoke to Nikolai. "She looks like she's more related to us than Petrov."

"I did tell you her parentage." Nikolai shrugged. "How is he?"

Nixon frowned. "He's taking it as well as can be expected."

"He?" I repeated, speaking up for the first time since meeting the Italians.

"Sergio." Nixon nodded. "Your sister's husband."

My stomach clenched.

"She just found out..." Nikolai said in an apologetic voice.

"Ten minutes ago," I grumbled.

"Heartless bastard." Campisi burst out laughing. "You'll do just fine in Chicago. It's in times like these I remember why I let you live."

"You don't let me do anything," Nikolai said through clenched teeth, taking a step toward the man who seemed to have threatened him without putting it into words.

I grabbed Nikolai's hand and tugged him back. Not that I didn't think he could hold his own, but I didn't think it wise to pick a fight with someone who looked like he prayed someone would slap him just so he could have a reason to shoot.

"Enough, Tex," Nixon hissed under his breath. "We have enough issues with our own family. How about we keep the peace between the Russians that at least like us?"

"Right." Campisi sneered then took a step backward.

"Well, I can see Frank's eye twitching from here, which means we need to get a move on." An elderly gentleman next to Nixon let out a snort and started walking back toward the Escalade.

I looked to Nikolai for help.

He gripped my hand and led me to the waiting Range Rover. A man in all black stood next to the door and opened it for me. He didn't make eye contact, didn't even blink. I slid across the plush leather seats and tried to keep myself from panicking. This was normal. They were being polite or as polite as they could be, right?

Normal.

That had seriously gone out the window the minute I accepted that job with Nikolai and agreed to his ridiculous contract.

As if sensing my distress Nikolai patted my leg then whispered against my ear. "You are safe with them, safer with them than you would ever be with me."

My heart raced. What did he mean?

I was safer with the people pointing guns at my head, than I was with Nikolai? He made no sense.

At all.

And to make matters worse, just the fact that he was touching my leg was reminding me of my dreams.

Though, as we started driving away from the airport, I couldn't shake one thought... that my entire dream had involved the airplane and a bedroom that according to Nikolai, I hadn't even seen until after I fell asleep.

I frowned the rest of the drive.

CHAPTER TWENTY-SIX

Success and rest don't sleep together. –Russian Proverb

Nikolai

JAC: WHY THE HELL ARE YOU in *Chicago? So, a life was lost. You have a job to do!*

Nikolai: She was important. How is...business?

Jac: Business is not going well. Several women have stopped by the clinic only to see its doors closed for the first time in five years. I sent them away and said you would attend to them once you returned.

I let out a relieved breath.

Nikolai: Thank you.

Jac: If your grandfather could see you now...

Nikolai: Leave him out of this.

Jac: It is because of him that you have everything that you have!

Nikolai: I need to run. Thank you, Jac.

She didn't respond. I didn't expect her to. It was the first time in years I'd closed down the offices. I tried to keep my expression void of any sort of emotion, even though my insides were wound so tightly I felt like screaming. It seemed the more I wanted to help, the deeper I dug the hole.

I glanced at Maya out of the corner of my eye. Her back was ramrod straight, her eyes locked on Nixon, the Abandonato family boss, as he drove us through the ironclad gates of his house and compound.

I breathed the first sigh of relief in what felt like years, toying with the idea of leaving Maya with the only people who truly could make her disappear.

Who could keep her safe from her father.

Who could help me fake her death.

The idea had merit.

And maybe if I was a less selfish individual, I'd follow through with it, possibly wipe her memory completely of me and her past life, but I'd always wonder if the feel of my lips across hers would be strong enough to stay amongst the memories I wouldn't be able to eradicate.

Nixon pulled the SUV to a stop and turned off the ignition. I unbuckled my seat belt and motioned for Maya to follow us into the large house. It was a brick two-story mansion that had been in his family for over fifty years, though everything had been so modernized that you probably couldn't use the restroom without having a camera trained in on your ass.

Maya clutched my hand tightly in hers as we walked in silence toward the front door. Two men stood on either side, ear pieces in their ears.

I smirked, nodding my head in their direction. "I imagine the added security is for my benefit?"

Nixon rolled his eyes. "My wife's pregnant, so it's fifty percent Russian shit and fifty percent paranoia."

"Thanks." I grinned smugly at the two men, itching to start a fight, one I knew I'd finish; not much could stop me. My specialty might be more of the emotional terrorism type but my father, while he was living, had still forced me to learn how to box.

The minute we stepped into the house, all hell broke loose.

"Son of a bitch!" a woman shrieked. "Are you ever clothed?"

Maya's eyes widened as Chase, assassin by trade, hovered over the stove and lifted a wooden spoon to his mouth. "Damn that's good sauce."

"Chase Winter!" Mil yelled. "We have guests!"

"I'm making sauce, babe, I told you, no yelling when I'm making sauce!" He was, very clearly yelling just as loud as she was, though in the brief moments I'd been with any of the families I'd come to notice that was just how they communicated. Loudly. And often.

"Chase!" Mil rolled her eyes. "Can't you see we have company?"

"Russians..." Phoenix, the Nicolasi boss nodded in my direction. "...aren't truly company, more like—"

"A necessary evil?" Maya popped up.

Chase slowly turned around, his eyes zeroing in on Maya and the way she attached herself to my side. "You." He pointed with the sauce covered spoon. "You can stay for dinner."

"Chase has spoken." Frank, boss to the Alfero family walked around us and took a seat at the head of the table and began pouring himself a generous amount of wine. "Nikolai..." He cleared his throat. "How is business?"

All talking ceased.

Smoothly, efficiently, I pulled the gun from the back of my pants, slid it across the table, released Maya, then pressed my hands against the wood. "Business is too good to mess it up by getting shot… surprised you didn't search me sooner."

"Consider it an olive branch," Nixon said from behind me, his hands patting my chest, then legs, then arms.

When he was done all eyes turned to Maya.

"What?" she whispered. "You don't think…"

"I'll do it." Mil stepped forward. "Although the guys are all happily married, I wouldn't trust them not to cop a feel, especially my husband."

"Shit, Mil, you know I'm not like that."

"You're getting sauce on the floor, Chase!" she snapped while he blew her a kiss and kept stirring the pot.

Everything was filled with life, even though everywhere you looked there was death. Maya probably had no idea that we were doing just that, courting death, by simply eating dinner with these people, but we were. And I wasn't stupid enough to think that one false move wouldn't end both our lives.

It was what they were good at, the Italians, disarming the situation, making you think that you really were walking in on a simple family dinner, when in all reality each person had a different weapon trained on you, just waiting for you to make a false move so they'd have an excuse to inflict bodily harm, and smile while doing so. It was their way. So completely foreign from the way I'd always done things, the entire situation felt eerie.

"Clean." Mil stood and then winked in my direction. "Nice work, Nikolai, she's got a great ass."

Maya blushed profusely.

I cracked a smile, it took a giant effort not to burst out laughing. I'd always loved Mil. She reminded me of Andi in so many ways.

Just thinking of Andi's name made an all familiar ache to spread from the middle of my chest out toward my limbs.

And like a dark cloud, the room once again was filled with a tense silence.

"She died well," Frank said after a few seconds, his wine glass lifted halfway in the air. "She died brave."

"Did she hurt?" Maya asked, her voice barely above a whisper.

"No." Frank's blue eyes blurred with tears. "Had she been in pain, Sergio would have taken care of it."

I wanted to be angry that Sergio offered to kill Andi... but I knew, in his mind, in the mind of the mafia, it would still be an honorable death, something she deserved.

"I wish I could have met her," Maya said in a small voice.

I didn't do comfort well, wasn't sure if I was emotionally capable of doing anything more than wrapping my arm around her—especially in front of people who, up until six months ago, had been sworn enemies.

Mil was the first to speak. "She'll always be with you, she's persistent like that... Sergio says he sees her in the way rain falls, constantly hitting your face until you have no choice but to lift your chin toward the sky." Her eyes filled with tears. "Then again he also sees her in a baseball bat, so maybe he's come unhinged."

"Do I get to meet him?" Maya asked.

Phoenix shared a pointed look with me before glancing at Maya. My stomach clenched with unease. Phoenix and I had a shared pain. It was only too easy to read emotions from his face, and he seemed not only worried but tired. "It's probably best that you meet him later, at the funeral, right before you leave."

Maya didn't push him, though I'd expected her to.

"Shall we sit?" Frank motioned to the empty chairs. "Chase has prepared a meal for us to share."

I wondered if Maya understood the importance behind breaking bread with your enemy—or the significance. That if

Frank hadn't offered food, we'd be on the opposite end of a gun instead.

Once pasta had been dished up, everyone began eating, everyone but Tex. I should have known the Cappo would have his doubts about me. He was, in essence, the godfather, though young, so young that I would have laughed at his power trip. But it wasn't an act, he was a Campisi. He'd killed his own father in cold blood then shot two bullets between his eyes just in case.

He was ruthless, cold hearted, rumored to have no conscience. At times I wondered if we were related, since the same things had been said about me.

"Campisi," I snapped. "Keep looking at her like that, and I make you squawk like a chicken every time someone snaps their fingers."

Nixon chuckled behind a mouth full of bread while Tex's eyes narrowed to tiny slits. "Do it and I'll pull your intestines out through your ass."

"Lovely," a female voice said from the direction of the kitchen as she made her way along with two other women into the room. "Intestines? Really?" Mo Abandonato, Tex's wife slid into a chair next to him followed by Phoenix's wife Bee and Nixon's wife, Trace.

They made the necessary introductions with Maya.

Tex bit down on his lip then reached for Mo's hand while she whispered something in his ear.

"Squawk like a chicken?" Maya asked under her breath. "What does that mean?"

"It means," Chase interjected from Maya's other side, "that he's a freaking hypnotist, amongst other things. Heard that last year he had one of Petrov's men willingly walk into a raging fire. He burned alive, you could smell the singed skin hours later."

I groaned, clenching my teeth together in rage, while

Maya tensed next to me. Of course she did, it wasn't exactly a glowing review of my humanity.

"So, how did you two meet?" Chase changed the subject. It would have been a welcome change, except for that story wasn't exactly table conversation. I sighed. Then again, neither was talk of intestines coming out of asses.

"I work for him," Maya said in a slow and steady voice.

Frank choked on his wine and began pounding his chest.

Shit. I knew exactly what Frank was thinking.

"Employee," I said loudly. "Not a patient."

"That is your business." Frank answered.

I let out a sigh, the pasta feeling like a brick in my stomach. "She's working on her master's thesis on the spread of sexually transmitted diseases. During the day she does research for me. At night—"

"Do tell." Chase chuckled darkly. "What do you do for the good doctor at night?"

Maya didn't miss a beat. "You mean before the naked examination or after I screw him in my nurse outfit?"

His eyes widened.

Mil cackled. "You deserved that."

"Oh." He frowned. "You're kidding?"

I smiled. "I think if she was being serious it would be a lot more exciting than a simple screw on an exam table, don't you?"

Chase's eyes narrowed.

I noticed Frank check his watch out of the corner of my eye. "It is time." He stood, and the bosses followed while the spouses stayed sitting.

"Coming?" Phoenix challenged.

"Yes." I stood then reached for Maya's hand, pressing a kiss against her knuckles. "You'll be safe. I promise."

Her panic-stricken eyes didn't make it easy on me. "Where are you going?"

"Don't worry." Bee winked at Maya. "We'll watch movies and eat junk food… the guys will be just fine."

Maya wasn't used to this side of the mafia.

She was always on the outside looking in.

Never the other way around.

"I'll return," I said with a simple shrug, collected my gun from Chase and followed the men out into the darkness.

CHAPTER TWENTY-SEVEN

There is no shame in knowing. The shame lies in not finding out. –
Russian Proverb

Maya

I WANTED ANSWERS.

But I wasn't sure that the wives weren't just as dangerous as their husbands. It didn't escape my notice that Mo was cutting up slices of apple with a dagger, or that Bee had stashed a gun under the couch cushion then winked.

Trace seemed to be the most normal one. At least until she burst into tears over the tire commercial.

"First trimester." Bee said without looking in my direction. "She's having a rough time with those hormones."

"How far along are you?" I inquired, trying not to stare at her rounded belly. "If you don't mind me asking."

"Twenty-two weeks." Bee sighed. "At least I'm over the morning sickness. At this point all I want are chips. Lots and lots of chips, with extra cheese and salt. You know those ball pits on playgrounds?" I nodded. "If I could replace those with Cheetos and then just hop in and make a little Cheeto angel, my life would be complete."

"Loves her Cheetos." Mo smirked then offered me a slice of apple, I had to pull it from the tip of the knife, I tried to keep my fingers from shaking. Who were these people? It was like I'd stepped into an alternate universe.

I understood why we were there. Clearly, Nikolai had been close to my sister. But how close?

Nerves got the better of me, and I popped my knuckles.

"Are you okay?" Mo asked quickly looking down at my hands and frowning.

"Yeah." I stopped cracking my knuckles and shook my head. "It's just been a really long and confusing day."

"Welcome to the mafia." Trace spoke from the spot on the couch where she'd curled up and was hugging a pillow.

"My dad's Petrov." I felt like I needed to clear the air, I mean they probably knew that because of Andi, but still.

"You're dad's not Petrov." Mo said in a bored tone. "He may have raised you, but he wasn't your father." It surprised me that Mo seemed to know more about my parentage than I did. Then again, I seemed to be the only one in the dark and I had no idea why complete strangers seemed to have my family biography memorized while I still didn't even know who my real father was.

I choked back a sob, "Up until two weeks ago… he was still… semi-normal."

"Most monsters wear disguises until they no longer need them." Mo gave me an apologetic look. "I'm sorry to say that, but it's true."

I nodded. "Where did the guys go?"

The girls fell silent.

"Why don't we just watch the movie?" Bee turned up the

volume.

"Please?" I was desperate to know. "Is Nikolai going to be okay?"

"Hah." Bee laughed, then sobered immediately. "Do you really know so little about the man who stares at you as if you hung the moon and stars while simultaneously dancing naked in the rain?"

Heat bloomed in my cheeks. "He doesn't... look at me like that."

"He does!" all three girls said in unison.

"He'll be more than fine..." Bee answered my question. "He's Nikolai Blazik, one of the scariest bastards to ever work for the Russian mafia, not only is he notorious for his lack of conscience, but he can make anyone believe anything by the simple snap of his fingers."

"What do you mean?"

"Mentalist." Bee offered. "Hypnotist... brainwasher extraordinaire... Though my money's on alien... He's a master manipulator. Chase wasn't kidding about the whole jumping through fire and staying there until death. I'm not saying it would be a fair fight, five against one, but I am saying, they wouldn't even dream of hurting him, when keeping him on our good side far outweighs the risk of having Petrov come after us."

"But, what does this have to do with Andi?"

"Does he tell you anything?" Trace said in an agitated voice, and then yawned behind her hand. "Nikolai checks in with the bosses at least once a month... your... boss," I didn't miss how she made quotations in the air. "Is playing both sides... He's pretending to still work for your father, but feeding us the information. He even drinks wine over vodka. Chase is convinced he's going Italian."

"Someone get him a flag," Bee joked.

"But—" A choking sensation wrapped itself around my

throat. "That's impossible... he's been... out of the mafia for years, he really does work all day then run a completely legitimate business."

Raised eyebrows met my defense of him.

"Okay semi-legitimate business at night... he isn't... I mean, he's trying to keep me safe, from my father."

"Right," Trace whispered. "But who, exactly, is keeping you safe, from him?"

I didn't have an answer.

How many times had Nikolai said the same thing?

I was beginning to think that the business proposition he'd given me had been a front, a way to lead into something more. He could hire anyone for help with research—any number of interns would be thrilled to do my day job—and would work for ten dollars an hour with a cheerful smile on their faces.

The same with the night job.

Even Jac had said as much.

So why me?

And why would he bargain with me? Why would he risk losing so much with my father? And with the Italians?

Why was I worth so damn much?

"I, uh—" I stood abruptly. "I have a headache, can I lie down somewhere?"

"Sure." Bee stretched her arms above her head. "A room was already prepared for you two."

A room. Singular.

"It's at the end of the hall to the right. Your bags should already be unpacked."

Someone had rifled through my things?

"Have a good night, Maya," Bee whispered. "And remember, at least here, for now... you're safe."

"And tomorrow?" I couldn't help but ask.

"Is a new day," she offered, not making eye contact.

CHAPTER TWENTY-EIGHT

Another body was found near Pike's Market. The autopsy will take place over the weekend to discover if the Pier Killer is suspect. — The Seattle Tribune

Nikolai

"Subtle," I finally said once I was alone with Frank in the SUV. "Could you have at least made up a small white lie?"

"And tell her we were going for ice cream?" Frank laughed. "No. Besides, I do not waste my lies easily. I imagine God only gives us a few, less to men like me. No, I save my lies until I have no choice but to use them."

Leave it to the rest of the bosses to have me ride with the eldest of the five, the philosopher who was currently driving faster than everyone else put together.

"Sergio's house was infiltrated twice while Andi was staying with him. We need to know how they received the codes, and we need to know if Petrov plans on retaliating."

I took a deep breath and cracked my neck. "I could do it

blindfolded."

"I'm well aware of your skill set," Frank said in a stern voice. "Just make it fast, I have my eye on a 1955 Cabernet."

"Italians and their wine."

"Russians and their vodka."

"Touché."

Frank pulled into the darkened parking lot. Two lights flickered on the empty street, one above a metal door, the other above a garage.

"Looks inviting," I said in a hollow voice.

"Soundproof." Frank said before turning off the vehicle. "Nobody can hear the screams."

"I tip my hat to the architect."

Nixon was already opening the door to the warehouse by the time Frank and I made our way out of the car, the rest of the bosses followed in silence, the only sound was our footsteps against the dusty cement floor.

We stopped in front of a second door, still metal, but brand new. Nixon punched in a code, the door unlocked, making a sucking noise as he pulled the five inch contraption from the wall and allowed us all to get in.

There was nothing comforting about the sterile and bare room.

A single light illuminated a man sitting in a metal chair, his hands zip tied behind him, his mouth gagged.

Blood caked down his cheeks.

The minute he set eyes on me, he started shouting profanities against the gag, rocking in his chair back and forth.

"Hmm," Tex tapped his chin. "I'd say he's pissed you've come over to the dark side."

"Funny." I mused. "And here I thought I'd left it."

"Gag on or off?" Tex asked, being more helpful than I expected.

Mil, Frank, and Chase stood near the door, each of their

hands trained on a gun, watching, waiting.

"We need information, therefore we need it off, just expect lots of spit and snarling, that is until I can sedate him."

"Suki!" Boris gnashed his teeth then spat at my feet. *"Suki!"* He kept repeating the word over and over again, boring me to tears. Russian for traitor. Then again, he was truly calling the kettle black. After he'd found out as much as he could from Petrov, he'd started selling secrets to the FBI resulting in a few unseemly arrests for Petrov at a few of his ports in San Francisco. Boris was lucky the Italians had retrieved him before Petrov lit him on fire as well and forced him to jump off a building while still breathing. He'd been a *Byki* set on a future where he wasn't simply an enforcer for Petrov but one of his most trusted individuals, leading his own band of criminals around the United States.

Selling secrets was not the way to earn trust.

"Boris" I said his name calmly. "Do you remember me?"

"You." His accent was thick. "The Doctor! Petrov will kill you for this!"

"What makes you think... he has not sent me to deal with our embarrassments?"

Boris seemed to process this information, his skin paling more, the world would end before Italians and Russians would join forces but he didn't need to know that. I just needed to plant a seed of doubt to get him calm enough so I could manipulate him.

"But—" Boris eyes fell to the bosses behind me. "He would rather be in prison."

"Perhaps." I shrugged and rolled up my shirtsleeves, then very calmly breathed in and out, over exaggerating my gestures so that Boris would mimic without thought. It was always easy to manipulate those who were weak minded, and Boris's mind was Play Doh.

It would be so easy to reach into the depths of his

consciousness and squeeze.

Then again, it was easy for any of Petrov's soldiers.

Because every *Byki* was controlled... by me. Another reason that Petrov had decided I needed to live—he had fifty remaining soldiers who he had tested and altered with brainwashing, allowing me to test my theories on them until I owned them.

And I could turn those very same men on him, by the simple snap of my fingers.

By simply willing it.

"Boris..." I tilted my head to the right, my eyes searching his. "What have you been up to?"

He squirmed in his seat. They always did when you made eye contact.

"Spokoystviye," I barely whispered it before he blinked and then, blinked harder as if he couldn't keep his eyes open. "Ah, there, that's better. Don't you feel better, Boris?"

"What the hell kind of voodoo did he just do?" I heard Chase mumble behind me.

"It's the word for calm in Russian," Frank explained, surprising me with his knowledge of my language. "It's probably one of his triggers."

"Boris." I slapped him on the side of the head. "No sleeping, Boris. I'll let you sleep when you give me answers."

"I'm tired," he replied.

"Of course you are!" I laughed loudly. "You've been up for seven days straight!"

"I have?" He shook his head. "Makes sense, so tired."

"And hungry. You've been complaining about your lack of food for days now... but the worst... is the thirst, is it not?"

Immediately he croaked as if he had no spit left in his mouth. "It feels like sandpaper."

"And it will continue feeling that way until you give me the answers I need, not the ones I want to hear, but the truth, do you understand, Boris?"

He nodded, or it appeared to be a nod as his head fell forward, chin touching his chest. "Yes, Nik."

"Sergio Abandonato. You broke into his home... twice. How?"

"Which... time? Will I get water?"

"One answer, then we shall discuss water."

"Andi." His head fell forward again.

I slapped him on the right cheek. "Stay awake, and explain. Did Andi know she was helping you?"

"No." He started crying. "Thirsty, Nik, give me water!"

"Boris." My tone was demeaning. *"Vody."* I snapped my fingers in front of his face. "Good job, Boris. You've had your water, now tell me about how you broke into Sergio's house."

"Andi had a listening device sewn into her suitcase, a camera was positioned near the handle. A gift from her adopted father, it was brought in and left in the entry by the kitchen." Boris took a deep breath. "It was dumb luck."

"And the second time?" I demanded.

"Stupidity!" Boris yelled. "He did not arm the house. Italian thought he hit the right buttons, it malfunctioned. The alarm did not go off when it should have. Our plan was to trip the alarm and grab him, we knew we had seconds, and that we could disarm at least five of the men left behind. He would send men with her, not with himself."

I sighed. "You've done well, Boris."

"Thank you for the water."

"You're welcome, Boris."

"One more question and I'll allow you sleep."

"So tired, Nik."

"I know, Boris. I know." I leaned down and whispered in his ear. "Is Petrov done with the Italians?"

"For now." Boris answered quickly. "Licking wounds... his daughter needs his help."

"Daughter?"

"Maya." Boris chuckled. "He's going to kill her."

"Thank you, Boris." I slid a knife from my pocket and cut off his zip ties then handed him the same knife. "Thank you for your help."

"Can I sleep now?"

"Of course, Boris." I took a step back. "You will never wake up again."

"Thank you!" Tears streamed down his face. "Oh, thank you."

Another step back. "Slit your throat."

Before the men behind me could say anything, Boris ran the edge of the knife across his throat then fell to his death in a pool of blood.

"We could have shot him," Tex offered.

"I could not allow Russian blood to be on Italian hands."

Boris's arteries continued to pump blood through severed veins… I watched, indifferent, the medical side of me taking over as he hiccupped, struggling for one final breath.

Death, in my experience, should always be swift.

With a sigh, I walked over to him, grabbing the knife from the floor and severed the rest of the carotid artery beneath his left ear. The blood pumped more quickly, the gurgling stopped, and he went limp as the last remnants of life left him.,

"Gotta admit," one of the guys said, I couldn't tell who without turning around. "Something extremely calculating about knowing exactly what artery to cut. Know any other tricks?"

I turned to find Chase staring at me, a smirk across his face. The man loved new ways of torture, I was surprised he wasn't kneeling next to me pointing at the bloody mess and asking questions like an eager student.

"Plenty." I stood, wiping the knife on my slacks, and

making a mental note to burn the pants later, no loose ends. "But it would take a lifetime to teach you, and with the way you run your mouth I don't count on you living very long."

"He's got you there." Nixon snorted out a laugh then pushed away from the wall. "Thanks Nikolai, we owe you."

"No." I swallowed the lump of emotion in my throat, not because blood was fresh on my hands, blood was always fresh on my hands, but because I would never be able to repay them for what they did for Andi. "I believe I still owe you."

"In that case." Frank pulled out his keys. "You may buy us a case of wine."

"Always with the wine." I shook my head.

"Wine to Frank is both a peace offering and a necessity of life. I'd take it." Chase slapped me on the back.

We shuffled out of the room just as a few men walked in, I imagined they were the Cappo's cleanup crew. They spoke in hushed tones with Tex and Nixon, then gave a wide berth to Phoenix as they made their way past us in the hall.

Clearly, there was still unrest between the families if they weren't acknowledging Phoenix much. He'd taken over as the Nicolasi boss even though he wasn't Nicolasi by blood, and blood, to the Italians was everything.

Frank was silent on the way back to Nixon's. The car turned off, I reached for the handle, but Frank put a hand on my arm. "You'll speak. At the funeral."

"I was planning on it." I was also dreading it.

"This is good." Frank released my arm. "Thank you."

"How is he...?" I asked. "Really."

Frank chuckled. "Offer it all you want... your power of brainwashing, promising to help him forget her. He'll always say no. Why would he want to forget the lightest part of his existence?"

"Why, indeed." I pressed my lips together. "But the offer will always stand for him, it is the least I can do... if the pain is too much."

"The pain will always be too much," Frank whispered. "Life is full of pain, just like life is full of regret. It is how we react to pain in that very moment, that defines the type of person we will be. When you stop feeling pain… when you stop wanting to? That is when you have lost your humanity. The question then, should not be, should I make myself forget the pain? But, should I go on living, when it no longer makes me want to act?"

His words haunted me long into the evening while we shared a few bottles of wine. It had been ages since I'd allowed myself to lose control and drink more than I knew my body could handle.

But Italians and their loudness had a way of making me feel like family, something I'd never truly had.

I had Jac.

But did she really count anymore?

Blood stained us both.

Blood ruined my entire line.

I half walked, half stumbled to the bedroom Nixon had set aside for me, kicked off my boots, and tugged down my pants, then pulled my shirt over my head. Completely naked, I pulled the sheets back and gulped at Maya's sleeping form.

I drank her in.

From her toes all the way to her mouth.

And nearly had a heart attack when she opened her eyes and said my name.

"Yes?" I answered.

"You're naked."

"You're in my bed."

"Was I supposed to be naked too?"

I gritted my teeth. Hell yes. Naked. I could do a lot with her naked, writhing body, I could do so many things, things she would actually remember.

With a soft sigh, she turned on her side, her eyes boldly gazing at my body, I felt her stare, felt the heat of desire building as she licked her lips.

"Maya," I ground out. "We can't."

"Okay." She reached for me.

I tried to push her away, gently, but I wasn't controlled in my movements, and she was able to grip my hand and tug me onto the bed.

I straddled her.

I wanted to do so much more than straddle her.

"This feels…"

"Right?" I guessed.

"No." She frowned. "Familiar."

CHAPTER TWENTY-NINE

Listen more, talk less. –Russian Proverb

Maya

"BEEN DREAMING ABOUT ME, *zvezda moya*?"

Warmth filled my chest. "My mother used to call me her little star." It was one of my favorite memories of being a child, one of the rare things I actually did remember before my sixteenth birthday. Memories from before then had been… locked away, or so it seemed. I remembered fragments, my father said it was because of the car accident, apparently the trauma had been too much, and my concussion had caused long term effects.

"Maya," Nikolai whispered my name between our mouths, linking me to him, making me want nothing more than to kiss him, it wasn't just familiar, it was right, like he said, it was… as if we fit, we were meant to be.

The fear was still there.

But it wasn't from him.

It was for us.

And I had no idea why.

"Why are you frowning?" He asked, one hand caressing my face while the other cupped the back of my head, pulling me closer to him.

"You said never to ask questions," I teased.

His lips twitched. "I deserved that."

"I don't know why…" I worried my lower lip as tears pooled in my eyes. "I have no idea why my dad sent me to your offices, or why he would sign my life away… why you would take it. I'm confused more than ever about what we're really doing with the Italians and why they would swear to protect a hated enemy. There are so many questions that my head is spinning, but I know the answer to one. And if I know the answer to one, then I'm doing okay, right?"

"Absolutely." He tensed slightly, as if holding his breath. "And what is your answer?"

"You," I said simply. "It all leads to you. Everything. And I think, for now…" I leaned up, brushing my lips across his. "That's all that matters."

"And if I'm the key to both your survival and your destruction, what then?"

"You mean what if your water is poison?" I asked.

He didn't answer.

"Then I want to drink."

There were two seconds.

Two brief moments in time.

When I felt my heart race and wondered if it matched his as Nikolai took a steadying breath… then swallowed hard.

One beat against my chest, and his lips were touching mine.

Two beats as my heart picked up speed, and I could feel the heat of his mouth as he slid his tongue across my lower lip.

I moaned in response, reaching around his neck, grasping fistfuls of his hair and tugging as his body moved against mine. Without breaking the kiss, Nikolai found the hem of my cotton T-shirt, lifted it and pulled it over my head, our mouths parting for seconds before, with a sizzle of heat, they met again, and again. Each time our lips grazed it felt new, and yet familiar, like we'd shared hundreds of kisses, thousands of embraces.

He leaned back and helped me to a sitting position, his muscles flexing from holding his own weight. Moonlight shone across the planes of his firm chest. Something about Nikolai's masculine beauty was lethal, so dangerous that my heart raced even harder. He frowned, pressing his palm to my chest as if trying to calm me down.

I wasn't safe.

Not in his arms.

But I was where I belonged.

I was complete.

The sensation washed over me with such a rightness that I wanted to cry, like I'd been waiting my entire life for that very moment. Images of us kissing flashed in my mind.

I touched the sides of his face, my hands soaking in the warmth of his cheeks.

"I'll never be free of you," Nikolai turned his head, whispering against my open palm, then his head descended as he kissed slowly down my neck, each breath tickled against my skin as his tongue left wet possessive trails down to my collarbone, his lips sucked as his hands moved down to my hips and pulled my shorts free.

He was right about one thing, as his smooth hands trailed down the sensitive skin of my thighs, neither of us would be free of this moment, it was going to bind us together forever.

Nikolai's breathing increased as his hands cupped my ass, and he pulled my body farther down the bed then braced a hand on either side of me. Holding his weight off me, he continued kissing down my arm, stopping at my fingertips, then sucking each finger, like he wanted to taste every single part of me and wouldn't be satisfied with just my mouth.

I nearly bucked off the bed when he moved to my hips.

"Sensitive," he mused, I could feel his smile against my skin as he kept kissing. "I could drink you like this..." His mouth moved to my core. "And like this." I let out a pitiful moan as tingling sensations spiraled outward from where his mouth caressed me. "Every damn day."

"Nik—"

With a growl he splayed his hands across my hips forcing my body down when it wanted to go up, to move against him. It was the sweetest torture, and an ache built within me. I squeezed my eyes shut as a warm explosion washed over me.

It felt the same way it had in my dreams.

Only better.

I wanted more of those feelings, more of Nikolai. No, not more. All. I needed all of him.

CHAPTER THIRTY

Police have confirmed that the Pier Killer is not a suspect in the most recent homicide at Pikes Market. –The Seattle Tribune

Nikolai

"*MOY,*" I WHISPERED AGAINST HER SKIN. "*Moy.*" My body screamed as I branded her with kisses. Mine, mine, mine, she had always been mine.

I'd never wanted her on paper.

Never needed a contract to know who she belonged to.

Her body had always belonged to me, since that very first kiss, that very first touch, when I replaced the pain with the pleasure, when I broke her.

I inwardly cursed as I expunged the memories of a time long ago, she had been the apple in the Garden, dangled in front of me, her core so tempting and sweet. A voice whispered in the distance. Just. One. Bite.

I bit.

I tasted.

I fell.

Maybe that was where I went wrong. The minute I'd seen her, I had desired her, wanted her, and in all my existence, I'd never coveted something as much as I'd coveted her.

It was a sin.

To want someone so desperately that you would sacrifice anything, actual human lives, possibly your own soul, to have it.

I pushed the memories back into the furthest recess of my mind, focusing on nothing but her pleasure, her release, while silently hoping this would not be the catalyst to her unlocking that precious Pandora's box, I'd helped lock up so long ago.

Her body responded to my every kiss, my every touch... it was addicting to a man like me, a man who rarely showed emotion, someone who starved others of their humanity— discovering he very much wanted his own, one normal moment.

Boy meets girl.

Boy falls in love.

Girl never leaves.

Maya screamed out in pleasure, I kissed the inside of her thigh then climbed my way, slowly up her body, taking pleasure in the way she writhed beneath me, wanting more than anything to bring her to the greatest heights.

"That felt... too good." She whispered, mouth swollen.

My hardness against her softness was almost too painful to bear. She reached for me, wrapping her hands tightly around me. I hissed out a curse.

"Show me what to do."

"Your body..." I whispered, moving against her hand. "Will always know what to do."

"But—"

"Feel." I instructed as I moved against her then very

gently pulled her hands away even though they felt so good. I hesitated, enjoying the look of hate on her face as I teased her, rubbing myself against her, sucking and nipping her lower lip, moving to her breasts.

"Nik…"

I hesitated, she typically reverted to that name only when she was remembering. My entire body tensed.

"I need… more." She wiggled against me, then hooked her feet behind me.

I slid against her, chuckling into her neck, before I pressed an open mouthed kiss against her shoulder and inched slowly inside heaven.

Her head fell back against the pillow as I moved.

It wasn't enough.

It would never be enough.

What the hell was I thinking? One time with her? One moment? Had it been enough all those years ago?

No, it had fed the addiction, the obsession.

And I was adding lighter fluid to dry leaves and tossing a match into the air, praying somehow it wouldn't start a fire.

Each second that went by, I slid farther inside her, stopping when a look of pure awe slid over her face.

Our mouths met in a frenzy of hot kisses as I moved inside her, setting a fast rhythm, only to slow down as she tightened her grip on my body with her hands.

We were made for one another.

I'd always known it.

And now she did too.

I tried to stop, wanting the feeling of completeness within her to last an eternity, but it was impossible.

With one final thrust, I spent the last of my energy, perhaps the last of my soul… in that moment.

The darkness of our reality descended upon me with a choking reminder that what we'd just shared held the power to destroy everything.

But instead of screaming in horror that she'd just made love with a monster… Maya opened her eyes, as tears streamed down her face she whispered. "Just like my dreams."

If only she knew…

They were never dreams…

But actual memories.

"I love you," she whispered. "I've always loved you."

Her eyes closed.

"And now…" I said in a shaky voice. "You may sleep."

I could allow her that much.

CHAPTER THIRTY-ONE

Little thieves are hanged, but great ones escape. — Russian Proverb

Maya

MY DREAMS WERE FILLED WITH NIK... I wasn't sure why he felt so familiar in them, like I could laugh with him, cry with him, and he would embrace me, wipe my tears away and tell me everything would be okay.

His heat surrounded me, and my gaze sought the clock. It read two a.m., which meant I still had a few more hours in his arms. My heavy lids closed.

"It hurts!" I screamed. "So bad."

"Did you know..." He sounded apologetic. "That some philosophers believe pain is only another state of consciousness? That we can transcend it, if only we allowed our minds to see past the pain?"

"How?" I clenched my teeth together. "How do I see past the pain?"

"Focus on my voice," he urged, making another slice across my arm. "I will stop when you stop reacting."

"But—"

"Please." He sounded like he was in pain. "Please, just try."

"Why? You're the one who can stop everything! You're the one hurting me!"

"What if I promise you pleasure after the pain... what if I promise you something more?"

My vision blurred as the man in the white mask tilted his head, examining me, studying me.

"I said I'd try."

"I've drawn little blood, Maya."

"I'll have scars."

"Scars help us remember... they also, serve as a way to make us forget... I give you scars on your arms in order to imprint something new... it is impossible for your brain to recall events that never occurred. Therefore, I must cause the occurrence, understand?" Another slice. I screamed. "It will not stick if I do not cause either pleasure or pain."

"I choose pleasure."

He chuckled darkly. "They all choose pleasure. And I always choose pain."

"But..."

"For you..." I could almost imagine his smile behind the mask. "I'll gift you with both. The pain must happen. Otherwise, we will both be killed. But I can give you pleasure so that when you dream... it's not of darkness..." He reached for my hand and sucked each finger before kissing my open palm. "But of light."

I jerked awake with a gasp.

Nikolai was immediately gripping my shoulders, tipping my chin toward him, staring into my eyes like he expected me to turn into a monster or something.

"Sorry." I gulped as my heart slammed against my chest. "Weird dream..."

"Tell me…" His voice was hoarse, his hands digging into my arms as he pulled me back into his lap. I sat with his body wrapped around mine, his chin resting on my head while he rubbed up and down my arms. "What haunts your dreams at night?"

I shivered. "Pleasure…" I sighed. "And pain… always together."

"Some would say they are one in the same."

"You're a doctor," I stated dumbly. "What do you think?"

He was quiet. I swore I could almost hear the wheels in his head turning. "I'd have to say that one cannot exist without the other."

"Hmm."

My body felt heavy, but I wasn't sure why, almost like I'd had a drug-induced sleep, maybe that's what sex did to a person.

Just remembering the way being in his arms had felt, had goose bumps popping up all over my skin.

"Are you cold?" His mouth found my temple.

"No." I grinned. "Just thought of a really great way to forget about the weird dreams… if you're up for it."

"Maya," he growled against my ear, his hands already roaming freely all over my naked body. "Can't you tell? When it comes to you… I'm completely powerless to say no."

"Does that mean I can finally ask questions?"

"If you can speak then I'm clearly not as good in bed as I thought."

His hands flicked my breasts before he chuckled against my neck, flipping me onto my stomach as he whispered against the back of my neck. "But sure, ask away."

The delicious pressure of having him on top of me was almost unbearable, I couldn't see him, but I could feel every hard length of him as he entered me.

"I—"

"Yes?"

I had questions so many questions, and narrowing it down just seemed, pointless, but if he said he'd answer one...

"How long have you worked for my father?"

He increased his movements. I cried out as he answered. "Since you were sixteen."

"You..." I clenched my thighs together, fighting him, holding him off. "You were only twenty-three."

"I was around your age now when I began working full time for your father, yes..."

"What does he have over you?"

Another thrust. "I'd think you would know that by now."

"What?" My vision blurred as pleasure exploded all over my body.

"You." He slowed his movements pressing a kiss to my bare back and whispering, "It's always been you."

CHAPTER THIRTY-TWO

I need not fear my enemies because the most they can do is attack me.
I need not fear my friends, because the most they can do is betray me.
But I have much to fear from people who are indifferent. —Russian
Proverb

Nikolai

PETROV: *I HAVE TWO NEW GIRLS to send when you are ready, they are complaining of stomach cramps. I trust you'll take care of the matter.*

    Nikolai: *The clinic is closed until I return.*

    Petrov: *Say hi to the Italian bastards for me.*

    Nikolai: *I wouldn't provoke the very beast that stalks you, but to each his own.*

    Petrov: *I have no interest in the Italians anymore… business is too good without them sniffing around. Shall I send the girls?*

    Nikolai: *I'll text Jac, she can inject the first treatments.*

    Petrov: *Kiss my daughter.*

Nikolai: I thought that was against the rules of our agreement.

Petrov: A little bird told me it didn't matter anymore. Tick-tock, Nikolai, will you confess your sins? I await your return to Seattle.

I didn't text him back. That was what he wanted. I knew he couldn't prove shit, but I hated that I felt nothing but guilt and dread the next morning, instead of excitement.

I should feel content.

Instead I felt sick.

I was at Andi's funeral, gripping Maya's hand as tightly as physically possible, and all I could think about were those brief moments of pleasure in her arms and how I wanted more.

How, if I was given the choice eight years ago, I would have still been in the same damn position. It had always been about her. It always would be.

And I could never tell her how important she really was to me without exposing my secrets, putting her in danger, and making her hate me forever.

I released her hand then rubbed my fingers along the inside of her arms where the scars remained. Six cuts on each arm.

Twelve cuts total.

All but two were lateral.

Made with glass from the car she supposedly crashed.

The fragments of glass were pushed into her arms to make sure that they looked like they had landed there and then the cuts were made.

The perfect plan.

For seeing something she should have never seen.

The perfect plan, for forcing an eager twenty-three year old into a tyrant's service.

"A trade." Petrov shrugged. "Your father said you agreed."

My father lied, which meant, he must have owed Petrov a lot before his death. But Petrov never collected in money, he collected in blood. Regardless of how rich I was, I would never be able to pay the debt.

"Of course," I lied smoothly. I was so damn good at lying, at making anyone believe anything, that it was almost boring. "What would you like me to do Petrov? You know besides run a multibillion dollar company and make sure to help you keep your practices... private."

"Did I say I needed an accountant?"

The hairs on the back of my arms stood at attention. It wasn't good, or it wouldn't be good.

"I've been told you want to conduct illegal research on the spread of STDs, but can't manage to get your hands on enough infected women in order to test your illegal drugs."

"Those drugs," I spat, "will one day cure AIDS, you bastard!" I lunged for him, but was held back by two men then kicked in the stomach.

I doubled over, trying to catch my breath.

"Exactly." Petrov grinned. "I have girls to give you... but first, you must do something for me. It's easy, really. I've been told you can manipulate people's minds... that you've studied the power of suggestion, hypnotherapy." He shrugged. "Brain-washing."

The only souls I'd ever told had been my father and grandmother.

One or both of them had said something.

To the most dangerous individual I'd ever known.

"And?" I smirked. "Do you need me to make you forget your sins, Petrov?"

"Mine?" He laughed loudly. "No, but a few of my men... they need to be controlled... you do some work for me here and there, make sure that I have adequate control over my business, and girls will magically show up at your clinic on a nightly basis."

"A trade," I whispered.

"I scratch your back, you scratch mine. What's the harm? I

need people I can trust... and you need to save the world... why not allow me to help you do it?"

I shook hands with Satan that day, and never looked back for fear of facing my own pride and turning to stone.

"And now, a few words from Andi's good friend Nikolai Blazik." A collective gasp rang out, apparently the rest of the made men had not been made aware of my presence.

I let go of Maya's hand and slowly made my way to the front of the large Catholic church. I was still surprised I hadn't been struck mute for the things I'd done in this life.

Things I'd pay for in the next.

I hadn't written a speech.

I hoped my words would do her life justice.

"Andi," I began, my voice never wavering in its strength as I looked out over a crowd of one hundred fifty members of the oldest Italian mafia families in the United States. I wouldn't blink if someone pulled out a gun and pulled the trigger. I almost expected it, but nobody made any sudden movements.

Perhaps they were that afraid of the Cappo, or that stunned to see me, a Russian, in their precious Catholic church.

"Andi," I said again. "Was the light in the darkness, the loudness in the silence, the laughter in the wind." I cleared my throat. "Being with her was experiencing life for the first time, and I know the world is now a darker place without her in it. As a doctor, I blame myself for not having saved her. It's too easy to get deeply lost in the pride of your abilities until you are faced with something like cancer, something so devastating to the human body that you have no choice but to sit back and watch while it eats away at those you love the most. She died, but her soul lives on in the lives she touched with the five families. She may have had Russian roots, but her blood..." I smiled. "It was Italian, and God, he sees the truth, does he not?" A few chuckles. *"Bog vidit pravdu."* He sees the truth, I repeated. "And the truth is that an angel has joined the courts of heavens. *Blagosloveniya,* Andi. We will miss you." Blessings, Andi, blessings my dear friend. I kissed my fingers holding the third finger pressed to my thumb, then took my fist and pounded it against my chest. The first was an ancient gesture of blessing, the second, loyalty. She deserved both.

When I took my seat, Maya grabbed my hand and squeezed. How had I thought I could ever continue living without her?

I couldn't.

Not anymore.

Even if that meant she'd hate me forever.

I loved her enough to want her mind free.

Free to choose me.

Free to curse me.

Just…free.

"You did wonderful," she whispered in my ear.

"Moy," I whispered back. "You will always be mine. Thank you for being here."

"Ah." She smiled. "I'm getting to ask questions, and now you're thanking me?"

My lips pressed together to keep from smiling. "Yes well, don't get used to it."

"Hard assed Russian," she joked.

Never letting her go again. My heart beat for her.

Once the funeral procession ended, I made my way over to Sergio to say my goodbyes, and Maya joined me, offering her condolences.

I was suddenly thankful she hadn't met Phoenix until recently, she would notice a familiarity about him that I wasn't sure I was yet ready to reveal.

His features would remind her of her own.

Connecting the dots would be unwise.

For many reasons, the main one being that memory too, was locked inside her brain and I knew if that one came undone, everything else would follow.

Clearly sex hadn't been a huge trigger for her, but the day was emotional and trying. It wasn't over, and I knew that the more tired she became, the more she would be tempted to let her guard down.

And when the guards of your brain were down.

There was no telling what could enter... or exit.

"A walk." Phoenix nodded to me. "I'll have Bee take Maya back to the car."

I kissed Maya's hand, and we both waited until she was out of earshot.

"You asked about the whorehouses." Phoenix slid a piece of paper into my hand. "The ones my father was involved in are long gone, but there are two addresses that haven't been fully researched... Both are new constructions just outside of Seattle. Sergio hacked the cameras and was able to get a live feed. Seventeen cars in a little over two hours. All businessmen, entering the small temporary building, and then leaving."

I nodded, and my stomach turned sour. "The girls have been carrying more bruises lately, the sickness starts in sooner than it ever has before. The conditions must be dire."

"It's your only lead, but be careful." Phoenix sighed and looked back toward Maya and Bee. "Petrov won't like the fact that you're trying to save Maya and expose him to the feds at the exact same time."

"Petrov can go to hell."

Phoenix laughed, "Can't say that I disagree, but be careful. It's rarely the first hit that takes down the giant..."

"I don't mean to destroy him with one hit... I mean to injure him so I can inflict so much pain on his person that he forgets his own name." I said in a calm voice.

Phoenix's brows rose. "Alright then, on that note... I'll leave you to it, if you need a cleanup crew, let us know. It's the least we can do."

"Thank you." I held out my hand.

He shook it. "Doesn't mean we're friends."

"Russians and Italians? Don't make me laugh." I smirked.

Phoenix bit down on his lip, let out another chuckle then gave me a middle finger salute before walking off.

When I reached the car Maya was yawning into her hand and nervously popping her knuckles.

"So it begins," I said under my breath.

"Huh?" She popped her right hand then left and as if noticing for the first time she was doing it, she winced. "I'm so sorry, I know you hate that. It's bad for your joints right?"

"Yeah." I nodded. "And that's not the reason I hate it."

"Is it the sound?"

"More of what the sound reminds me of."

"Cracking joints?"

I stared straight ahead and answered. "The sound of a clock ticking."

CHAPTER THIRTY-THREE

Do not make me kiss and you will not make me sin — Russian Proverb

Maya

THE FLIGHT HOME WAS UNEVENTFUL. I kept thinking Nikolai would kiss me but every time I leaned in, he brushed a kiss across my cheek and told me I needed to go to sleep.

"What is with you and sleep?" My eyes watered as I let out a huge yawn and tried to cover it up with the back of my hand.

Nikolai's eyebrows shot up. "Tired?"

I glared.

With a light laugh he lifted me into his arms and walked me back toward the bedroom. "I'll sleep right next to you. It's been a long day. Rest."

"But I want to kiss."

"And have you yawn while I give you an orgasm?" he

joked, his mouth curved into a gorgeous smile. "Doesn't really do much for a man's ego, Maya."

"Your ego's just fine, Harvard."

"I had that coming."

"You did."

"Sleep." He kissed my forehead. "By the time you wake up, we'll be back in Seattle and you'll feel rested."

"Fine," I grumbled. "But don't leave. I feel safer with you next to me."

"You shouldn't," he said in a tired voice.

"Why?" I flipped over on my side and faced him, tracing the outline of his face with my fingertip. "You would never hurt me."

"What if I already did? Would you forgive me?"

"But you haven't." My head was starting to throb. "You've never hurt me, and I don't believe you're capable of it."

"What if I've hidden that side from you... stupidly believing that if I had you fall for the man you see in front of you, you'd accept even the darkest of secrets?"

"You told me to sleep, and now you're talking about secrets." I shook my head. "Whatever secrets you have, you can trust me."

"And if my secrets hurt us both?"

"Then we figure them out together."

"If only..." He sighed, flipping onto his back and putting his arms behind his head. "...it were that simple."

"But—"

"Rest," he instructed tapping two fingers to my temples. He was right... I was sleepy. I couldn't keep my heavy lids open any longer.

****

"I'LL BE RIGHT THERE," Nikolai said into the phone. "We just landed."

I stretched out on the bed. We'd landed? And I wasn't in a seatbelt? Was that legal?

"Told you that you were tired." Nikolai's smile was tight. "I'm going to have someone drive you back to the apartment. Something has come up at the clinic."

"I'll go." I shot to my feet feeling, then got dizzy as they made an impact on the floor.

"You're drunk on sleep. You'll be absolutely no help."

"Please?" I felt like he was pushing me away, like he had no choice, and I wasn't going to let him, not if I could help it. I was pulled to him. I felt like maybe he needed me just as much as I needed him, possibly more.

He hung his head. "Fine, but..."

"I know I'm not wearing black."

"How'd you know?"

"You have a thing with blood getting on white."

"I do." He seemed surprised I'd put two and two together.

"Actually, you just have a thing with blood being spilled, but I think it goes back to you being a doctor. Maybe it seems wasteful."

"Maybe." He was lost in his thoughts, or appeared to be so as he took my hand in his and led me down the stairs of the airplane.

Within thirty minutes we were downtown at the Pier clinic. Jac was waiting for us inside. The minute she set her eyes on me, she frowned. "What's Maya doing here?"

Nikolai opened his mouth to speak but I interrupted him. "I begged him to let me work. I didn't want to get sent home by myself."

"Home?" She repeated. "You're living together now?"

"No." I felt my face flush. "Not exactly. You know what?

I'm still really tired I think I'll go sit by the computer while you two talk."

Jac seemed, angry. Her frown was permanent, her hands shook. I turned away and headed for the computer. She walked briskly behind me, the heels of her boots slamming into the floor.

"The two new patients have been entered into the computer. Why don't you go greet them by the door like a good assistant while I talk to Nik?" Venom laced her every word.

I stood on wobbly legs and made my way down the pristine white hall as lights flickered on above me.

Two knocks on the door.

A large body guard with a shaved head was leaning against the brick wall, a cigar hanging out of his mouth. "Bout time." His words were cultured with a thick Russian accent. It reminded me too much of my father. I stepped back in a learned fear.

"*Vyydite iz avtomobilya suka!*" He spat, loosely translated get out of the car, bitch. Great. Maybe I should have gone home like Nikolai suggested.

The car door jerked open, two long tan pale legs that went for miles stepped out, the legs were attached to a tall gorgeous blonde in a skin tight black leather dress, her blue eyes flashed in recognition. She looked from the man to me, then back to the man. "Is this a joke?"

"Um, if you'll just follow me." I tucked my hair behind my ear and held the door to the clinic open.

"Bitch." She spat at me, pushing past and stalking down the hall to the right exam room. I didn't go in with her, she paused in the doorway and turned back to me. "You don't remember me do you?"

"I'm sorry…" I winced. "I don't know you."

"Oh, that's rich." She rolled her eyes. "Don't tell me your

dad brainwashed you like he did your mother."

I stared at her blankly. "I'm sorry miss, I think you have me mistaken with someone else."

"Maya." She cackled out my name. "You know I always wondered if he ended up using you like he did the rest of us, but apparently not since you work for the doctor. Then again, he works for him too so you're still a whore, just a different type of one." I lunged for her, but Nikolai grabbed me by the waist and set me on the other side of the girl.

"Maya, why don't you go check in with Jac, hmm?"

"Fine." I swallowed down the anger and marched down the hallway in a fury. When I reached the receptionist desk, Jac was already sitting there in the chair, her eyebrows rose when I sat with a thud and pulled up the spreadsheet.

"Got your panties in a twist?" she asked, her face appeared lighthearted but her words sliced through the air, almost like she was being passive aggressive.

"Not now, Jac."

She shrugged and leaned back in her chair while I scrolled through the appointments, found the correct time and went to mark the girl's first visit.

It was her third.

Hadn't Jac said they rarely made it past the third?

"She's..." I whispered then narrowed my eyes on the name. "Galina Ivanov." A vision of a little girl speeding by me on a red bike pushed forward to my consciousness.

"Galina wait up!" I yelled laughing after her. "Friends aren't supposed to cheat in races!"

"Beat you!" She giggled, her blond pigtails flying into the air. I finally caught up to her and crossed my arms.

"That was mean!" I scolded her, half tempted to push over her bike.

"Sorry, Maya. Best friends still?" She held out her pinky finger.

I shook it with my pinky and giggled. "Best friends forever, Galina, you know it!"

"Girls!" Mother called. "Come on in for a snack... Maya, you must change your clothes before your father gets home, you know how he feels about getting your clothes dirty."

I grumbled out a response and linked arms with Galina as we made our way into the house.

Impossible. I pushed back from the desk. I was having some sort of... meltdown or something. Why was my brain suddenly remembering that? And why was Galina in the clinic?

Panicked, I didn't even think about the rules. I had to know. I ran down the hall with Jac calling after me.

When I found the correct exam room, I pushed the door open and gasped as Nikolai inserted a syringe into Galina's arm.

Her eyes were open.

Like she was awake.

But she wasn't moving.

"Maya," Nikolai said in a detached voice. "Is there a reason you're in here?"

"I know her."

He froze, his movements pausing midair as he slowly met my gaze. "I'm sorry, what did you say?"

"Galina." I pointed at the motionless girl. "She was... I think... I think we were friends, when I was little. I had a red bike and she had a red bike, they both had baskets..." I tried to pull from the memory but it was slipping away.

Nikolai set down the syringe. "Don't focus on the whole picture, focus on the details, like what the air smelled like, tasted like, did she hold your hand? Did you laugh?"

"You believe me?"

"I do." His eyes were sad.

"I'm sorry." I shook my head. "I don't... I can't remember

anything else."

His shoulders tensed. "Alright, since you were friends you may as well stay in here during the procedure."

"Procedure?" I repeated.

"She's in an altered state of consciousness," he explained. "I oftentimes hypnotize the patients so that they don't remember anything that takes place afterward, they feel pain in the moment but don't remember they've felt it after. Hers will be brief, I need to draw some blood, and blood always makes her faint."

"You hypnotized her?" Fear trickled down my spine.

Nikolai licked his lips. "Yes... because at least in her altered state if I ask her a question she can answer in the affirmative, and when one is relaxed..."

"Ask her about me," I blurted, knowing full well that I was losing my mind or having some sort of breakdown. What alternate universe had I walked into? One where I had fragmented memories of a girl in pig tails? And why wouldn't my body want me to remember? I had no idea the car accident had done so much to me.

Nikolai shook his head. "No, that could be dangerous."

"Please?"

With a heavy sigh, Nikolai snapped his fingers, watching me out of the corner of his eye. Something was so familiar about his movements, like a dance, like a dance he'd taught me and I'd memorized. "Galina, it's Nik... how do you know Maya?"

"Petrov." Galina said in a pained voice. "He thought I was pretty."

The room seemed to tilt around me, leaving me breathless, blood pounding in my ears.

"Said I could make money once my parents died."

Nikolai drew another vial of blood and pulled the band off her arm then pressed a cotton ball to the inside of her elbow. "What happened, Galina? You can trust me."

Galina shook her head vigorously then started bucking off the table.

Cursing, Nikolai snapped his fingers again and said. "Sleep."

She stopped moving.

I was horrified, not by what he did, but how easily he did it... had he ever done that to me? Would he?

I couldn't look at him.

Fear and guilt gnawed at me while I stared at her expressionless face.

"My father... he wouldn't... do you think?"

"He owns several lucrative businesses that have to do with girls just like Galina... I don't just think, I know. I help as many as I can, Maya, and that is all I can safely tell you."

"Okay." I took two steps toward the door. "I'm... I need to go home."

"Tell Jac I said it was okay to close early and take you."

"Thank you." I nodded and walked away, because I didn't know what else to do, and screaming seemed to be out of the question since finding my voice was near impossible.

What was he involved in?

What type of lie had I lived?

And the bigger question... would I have ended up like Galina... had I stayed with my father?

CHAPTER THIRTY-FOUR

One does not sharpen the axes after the right time, after the time they are needed. –Russian Proverb

Nikolai

GALINA WAS SICK, VERY SICK. THE strain of syphilis had lain dormant in her body for far too long. The new strain had been rampant throughout the whorehouses, infecting at least four girls, killing two of them, though their demise wasn't because of the disease, at least not fully.

It wasn't something I could help her with. I could give her antibiotics, give her some treatments with my serum, but the infection had already weakened her heart. This new strain had become less and less responsive to any sort of drug. My worry was twofold, keeping the disease contained, but also making sure that I stayed off Petrov's radar so that I had more time to study it.

If she was still working with the rest of the girls, then

another dose of heroine, or whatever drug they gave the girls in order to keep them loyal, could stop her heart.

I didn't see any track marks, which worried me. It was the cheapest way to inject a person with the drug.

Had he moved on to something else?

Or was he simply connecting an IV to their veins and feeding the drug that way? Sick bastard.

I wiped the last remnants of blood and tried not to think about what Maya had seen. There was no stopping it now, no stopping the rest of her memories from pushing forward. Odd that one of her first strong memories would be of childhood, and not of the most traumatic experience of her life.

Galina let out a soft moan as she came to. "Nik?"

"Galina." I forced a pained smile. "I need you to move very slowly. Your body is sick. It's weak."

"Tell me something I don't know."

Sighing, I peeled off my gloves and washed my hands in the sink, my body tensing with disgust as I fought with my conscience to make her the offer I made every patient.

"How long?" she asked.

"I can't tell, but your heart could stop if they force more drugs into you… It could be tonight when you're working, it could be months from now. All I know is it will happen, eventually."

She was quiet. "I trusted him."

My stomach clenched.

"He was nice to me once my parents died, you know? Always bringing over food to my grandma's house. He even bought me a red bike to match his daughter's. He treated me like his daughter. I grew up adoring him, and then… when my *bahba* died, I had nothing. I was only fifteen."

Shit.

"He told me he had a business, but it wasn't legal to hire someone as young as me, so I'd have to sign a contract and keep quiet. But the money..." Her smile was hollow. "...was incredible. I was making more than my parents could dream of... I fell for the money, and when I started hating myself, they kept me there with drugs."

She hung her head as exhaustion washed over her features.

"Galina, you know what I'm going to ask you."

"Yes," she whispered.

"You have a choice. You can choose how you die." Why was I having trouble saying the words... offering her honor in her death? Maybe, for once in my life I was questioning if that choice was within my power to give? But going against my family's wishes, against Jac, just seemed like asking for more trouble than it was worth. Besides, at least she wouldn't live in fear, not anymore.

"Will you do it?" Galina said, surprising me.

After a quick nod, I gave her a prescription bottle of pills that by all appearances looked like morphine pills but were a placebo, sugar and powder. Then I walked her to the door.

"Done?" the guard, a new one, barked at her.

"She's clear, but I had to prescribe something for the pain. Let Petrov know that it should be the same thing he's been giving her but not to double dose her, or he's going to kill a pretty face."

The man grabbed the prescription and nodded.

"The other patient?" I asked, as I looked around the dark alley.

He rolled his eyes. "She went into the clinic hours ago, hasn't come out since, and I can't wait, put her in a taxi or let her sleep it off."

"I've only seen Galina."

"The older woman came and grabbed her, said you cleared it."

"Right." A tingling sensation washed over me. Jac had

never done that before, she knew it was against the rules, knew what would happen if Petrov discovered her involvement and how we ran our side of the business.

"Same time tomorrow night, doc." The car door slammed.

Slowly, I entered back into the building and searched every exam room for the missing girl.

Nothing.

The lobby lights were turned off, but the computer was still on. I went over to it to check the names, but only one was on the list, Galina. Who the hell had the other girl been? And where was she?

My eyes started to blur. It was time to go home, but first I needed to talk to Jac and tell her never again to involve herself in my business dealings. If I needed to put the fear of God into her, so be it. The last thing I needed was to lose more family.

CHAPTER THIRTY-FIVE

In order to prevent crime downtown, law enforcement has doubled its cops on duty during the late evening hours. –The Seattle Tribune

Maya

JAC HAD TAKEN ONE LOOK AT my pale face and motioned for me to follow her to the door.

"Nikolai said you could take me..." My voice wouldn't stop shaking. Damn it! What was wrong with me.

"Sure thing, honey." Jac said in a sweet voice, like a switch had been flipped from earlier. I immediately felt comfortable once we were in her black Buick Encore.

I shivered even though I wasn't cold.

Once we'd been on the road for a few minutes Jac started to hum, it was... eerie, the fact that she wasn't talking.

I opened my mouth to say something when she reached over and gripped my arm, her fingernails digging into my skin. "So now you know."

"Know?" I repeated. "What do you mean?" I tried to pry my arm free but she was freakishly strong for being in her late sixties.

"What he does, sweetheart." Her words were nice; her voice, however, sounded… bitter, angry, and hurt. "He works with the girls who spread their legs, it is why his research is so good. Have you never wondered? He is the only doctor in existence that can study diseases the way he does, who can use his own brands of medicine not approved by the FDA. What he does is important, what you do with that information will either save your life or end it."

Finally she released my arm.

I rubbed it and slid further away from her so the door and seatbelt were poking into my lower back. "I would never betray him."

"Good." Jac nodded. "Sometimes though, a promise is not enough. Who's to say you wouldn't rat him out if your father threatened your life?"

"My father…" I kept my voice indifferent. "…couldn't care less about me. Trust me, I'm the last person in the world he cares about."

"Smoke and mirrors." Jac cackled.

Holy crap, she was crazy! Did Nikolai know?

I looked down at my arm and frowned, there was a bloodied handprint where Jac had been gripping my arm.

And two more handprints on the steering wheel of the car.

We pulled up to the building.

I calmly, opened the door, offered my thanks, and moved as fast as my legs would take me to the elevator pushing the button harder than necessary.

"Come on, come on." I stomped my foot a few times, then nearly had a heart attack when the doors actually opened and a person shuffled past me.

I was being ridiculous. I wasn't some lost virgin in a horror movie, running up the stairs instead of down, or hiding in the basement. It was Jac, she'd been working with Nikolai for years.

Just as I was straightening my shoulders and getting ready to walk in the elevator a hand grabbed my shoulder from behind.

I turned around and screamed.

Jac took a step back, a smirk across her lips as she dangled my purse in front of me. "I figured you'd want your things."

"Sorry." I placed my hand against my chest while my other grabbed the purse. "Jumpy tonight."

"I'll say." Her frozen smile didn't crack. With a tilt of her head she gave me a nod then walked back to the running car.

Her hands were clean of blood.

And when I looked back down at my arm, it only had a faint remnant of red.

Had I imagined it all?

Or was she really bat shit crazy?

My nerves were shot by the time I made it onto my floor and into my apartment. I locked my door then double checked that the locks were in place. Once that was done, I walked over to the fridge pulled out a bottle of chilled wine and began to drink straight from the bottle.

A knock on the door sounded ten minutes into my drinking and shaking.

"Who is it?" I asked, in what I hoped would sound like a calm voice.

"Nikolai."

Safe.

My mind whispered that word to me over and over again, until finally, I took the two steps to the door, unlocked it and let him in.

He looked like absolute hell.

From the dark circles under his eyes to the white shirt pulled out of his slacks.

Nikolai took one look at the wine bottle, swiped it off the counter, then started repeating what I'd done—drinking straight from the mouth.

"How is she?" I asked, joining him on the white leather couch, tucking my feet underneath me while he handed me back the bottle. I took a swig and waited.

He checked his watch—that was odd—then met my gaze with one of complete chilling indifference. "In exactly forty-two minutes, she'll be dead."

I gasped as he pried the bottle from my hand and took at least three long swallows.

"You… killed her?"

Nikolai laughed, actually laughed like I was making a joke. "What do you think?"

I gulped and shook my head "I really don't know what to think anymore."

"Did I pull the trigger? Stop the weak heart?" He cursed under his breath and ran his hands through his hair. It was getting long, I noticed absently, curling at the nape of his neck. I liked that; it made him look less controlled, more human.

He had a beautiful side profile, something that I imagined artists would kill to paint or sculpt. I reached out and touched his face.

His eyes closed as if my touch soothed him, and then he placed his hand over mine keeping it against the roughness of his five o'clock shadow. "You can touch me? You can bear to look at me? Even after all you've seen today."

"You helped them," I said in a weak voice. "Or are helping them…"

"Help—" He bit out the word. "—is such a weak, troublesome word, with such myriad meanings that I simply don't understand it anymore. Maybe I never did."

"Drunk already?" I joked.

He smiled against my hand. Then, as it dropped from his face, he clenched my fingers in his. "You're important to me, I hope you know that."

"Yeah," I croaked. "I think I do."

He caressed my arm and then frowned as he leaned down and examined the marks Jac's nails had made in my skin, along with the blood I still hadn't washed off.

"What is this?" His cold voice left me filled with dread.

I tried to jerk away. "Nothing."

"Maya," he growled. "Who the hell dared to lay a hand on you?" His voice was furious as his eyes flashed with rage. "Tell me. Now."

"Jac," I said in a wobbly voice. "It's like she just... snapped in the car, she kind of th-threatened me and then wouldn't let me go... I think maybe she's over worked or something because she's been acting weird all night... and at first she was so nice, I just—"

Nikolai interrupted me with a kiss, his mouth pressed so hard against mine that I fell back against the couch cushions, his warm body was both searing to the touch yet comforting in an odd way. When we broke apart for air, he cupped my chin forcing me to look him directly in the eyes. "I'll take care of Jac. Just do me a favor... don't allow yourself to be alone with her. Insanity runs in the family."

"You know her family?"

Nikolai hesitated than stated in such a quiet whisper I almost didn't hear him. "I am her family."

He looked away then moved to sit back so our bodies weren't touching anymore. "I'm her grandson."

A nervous laugh welled in my throat, but I suppressed it. "Didn't see that plot twist." I usually made light of a very scary situation with joking. I really needed to stop doing that.

"So she must be very protective of you."

He frowned, staring off into the distance. "She doesn't give a damn about me." His laugh was hollow. "She cares about… tradition."

"I'm not following."

"Every man and woman in our family has had the same occupation for as long as I can remember… my father broke tradition forcing my grandmother to take up the family…" He sighed deeply. "…business. I followed in my father's footsteps, not hers. She's been pressuring me to do otherwise."

I handed him the wine bottle. "You probably need more of this."

"Probably." He pushed it away. "But I'd rather drink from you."

"You want me to pour wine in my mouth so you can drink from me?" I teased.

He laughed, an actual laugh that echoed off the walls and ceiling only to wrap itself so tightly around me that I knew, I'd never be free of it, free of the feeling I had whenever he was near.

His laughter faded as his eyes darkened and met mine. "I want to drink you." He leaned forward, and his tongue slid against my neck. "Taste you…" His lips brushed a kiss across my jaw. "And not have any of the taste dulled by wine or anything so common as food or drink. I want your uniqueness to drown my senses and I want it right now."

Thrills rushed through me. "Demanding." It was the only answer I could give as he started pulling my white shirt over my head. Once my arms were free, he shrugged and then kept stripping me. I didn't protest, because I didn't want to. I just wanted him.

And the more I had of him, it was like the more I needed.

I popped my knuckles as a memory of white flashed before my eyes only to be replaced with dark brown eyes. "Let me taste you."

"Now you ask?" I groaned. "When you've been doing nothing but telling for the past few hours?"

"Pain I give... pleasure I seek," he answered. "Will you let me touch you, Maya? Will you allow it? Please say yes, I don't think I could survive with no."

"Yes." I moved for him just as he reached for me. "Yes." Our mouths met. *Yes, yes, yes.*

"Let me pleasure you," Nikolai whispered. "Let me see you, all of you, in the light, against the white."

I did as he asked, stripping free of the rest of my clothes.

Nikolai slid from the couch, moving to his knees, then grabbed my thighs, pried them apart and whispered, "And now, I worship at your feet."

"Blasphemy."

"Not at all." His eyes locked reverently on mine. "Blasphemy is replacing God... I'm simply honoring His most perfect creation in the only way I know how."

"With pleasure?"

"Always... pleasure I seek."

I froze.

So did he.

His mouth opened and then closed.

But instead of questioning him, or allowing myself to put two and two together, I closed my eyes and said. "What are you waiting for?"

"Oh Maya, it seems like I've been waiting years and years."

The last cognitive thought I had before his mouth was on me was the familiarity of his smooth movements.

And how being with him, felt like coming home.

As if I'd run away and gotten lost.

He'd given me a map.

And I'd found my way back.

CHAPTER THIRTY-SIX

You have to learn to walk before you can run. –Russian Proverb

Nikolai

SHE FELL ASLEEP IN MY ARMS... I tried not to fixate on the way her forehead furrowed while she dreamt, just like I tried not to feel guilty over the fact that her entire existence with me was a lie.

A giant test.

It all led back to keeping her safe.

I glanced around the white room.

So similar to the one she'd been placed in after she'd been kidnapped.

Similar to all the rooms Petrov used.

Right along with the sick bastard's white masks that he forced people to wear whenever they entered his parties.

His men never realized they were getting taken to me because they always assumed the masks meant that they were going to another orgy. Instead, the car would always take a detour to one of the many apartments.

My fixation wasn't with blood, like she'd guessed.

I absolutely hated white anything. Hated it with such a fiery passion that it took me years of conditioning myself not to puke every time I walked into a modern office with white fixtures, or modern apartments. I'd had to surround myself with it so I would stop reacting.

Petrov enjoyed watching the blood... he chose the white, not me. He loved to see how much he could make people suffer. And bleed.

And he always kept cameras trained on me when I did my work.

Except for one time.

One time, he made an exception.

He shouldn't have.

But I refused to work otherwise.

It was my gift to her. The only one I'd been able to give.

She moaned in her sleep, I knew the dreams that haunted her at night, and I was powerless to stop them.

With a sigh, I checked my phone.

Jac: Taken care of.

Nikolai: *Thank you.*

Jac: It's my job. Our job.

Nikolai: *Any word on the girl you claim escaped when you let her in the clinic?*

I knew Jac was lying, she'd had blood on her hands, the very same hands that had touched Maya. My grandmother was finally snapping. I added that to the list of things I could blame myself for.

Jac: I have no idea what you are talking about.

Nikolai: *Going to bed.*

Jac: Is she with you?

Nikolai: *Goodnight, Jac.*

She didn't respond. If I didn't do something, rein her in,

she was going to do something stupid, or end up getting herself hurt.

After being gone for so long I didn't think it wise to suddenly take another extended vacation to either kill my own family member or toss her to the wolves. I wouldn't be so callous, but I would take away her memories enough to settle her in a nice retirement home... she deserved peace. At least I could give it to her the right way.

The nightmares of my family's past had haunted her for far too long, the sins, she alone carried on her shoulders, it wasn't her responsibility, not anymore. It was mine.

One that would sure as hell end with me.

I lifted Maya into my arms and carried her into the bedroom, laying her across the down comforter, wanting so badly to tell her the truth but drowning in the fear of what that would mean for both of us.

Her father only agreed to our terms as long as I could prove the false memories had stayed intact.

I was supposed to report to him after a year.

What the hell was I going to say now? She remembers, but it's okay because I'm watching her?

"No loose ends," he'd stated over and over again.

The only answer was to find the last two houses in Seattle and burn them to the ground. Ending my research was a small price to pay to save her life... if the houses were gone, then she would no longer be a threat.

Because locked away in that mind of hers... was the key to her father's undoing... a girl seeing what she should have never seen.

"Bury it," he'd demanded. "I don't care how. Just bury it, or she dies."

"She's your daughter!" I yelled, already entranced with the girl I'd seen but a handful of times at her father's side. I protected her, it was part of my job, and now he was asking me to go back on my oath.

"She knows too much!" he spat. "Either you kill her, or you make her forget…"

"She's too young," I argued. "To alter her memories at this age… to replace them, I'd have to create real trauma, real memories to cover up the others, don't you see? Her brain is too strong, she isn't one of your foot soldiers. She could die!"

"I don't care if you have to wipe her entire damn memory, just make her forget. I pay you to make people forget."

She was blindfolded, tied to one of the metal chairs in the white room, bleeding profusely. If I didn't stop the bleeding, she would be too weak to go through the process.

"Damn it, Petrov, she's sixteen. Just bribe her with a new car." I paced the room, my knife clutched in my hand. I should have never said yes to him, should have never allowed myself to be bribed. Then again, had I not, Maya would have been dead. He didn't give a rat's ass about her. She was an abomination to him, born out of wedlock between his wife and an Italian Mafioso.

"No." Her father uttered a Russian curse. "She is a liability. Make it go away, or she dies, and her death will be on your hands."

I had no choice.

"Fine," I whispered. "But I work alone, leave me."

Petrov hesitated briefly.

I crossed my arms. "No cameras. The last thing you need is for this to come back to you."

She whimpered, her head falling forward. Shit, she was going to lose consciousness soon. What the hell had he done to her? The doctor in me screamed in outrage, the monster rubbed his hands together.

Petrov strode to the door and unplugged the camera next to it. With a final warning gaze, he stepped through the opening and shut the door behind him, blanketing us in darkness.

I reached for the white mask, hands trembling, then very slowly tied it around my head.

I apologized to her, in my head of course, and I swore that someday I would save her. Just not now. I prayed that she'd *understand, that one day she'd thank me.*

I expected Maya to pass out. She was only sixteen, beautiful, but so young. She lifted her chin as if to say, do your worst! And I had to respect her in that moment. Sweetheart, I would do my worst, and then, when she swore fealty… I'd do my best work, and save her life.

I stopped staring at her sleeping form, and backed up against the dresser, one of the white masks fell onto the floor.

I'd put simple triggers everywhere in the apartment and nothing… we'd made love a few times… and still nothing extraordinary other than Maya remembering her childhood friend.

Maybe, just maybe I was better than I'd originally thought.

I clung to that thought as I lifted the mask to my face and stared at her one last time, as the monster she had no clue she'd invited into her bed—into her heart.

CHAPTER THIRTY-SEVEN

A fool's tongue runs before his feet. –Russian Proverb

Maya

I WAS SO WARM. I CUDDLED back into strong arms and let out a happy sigh. Nikolai kissed my temple, I turned on my side.

"You are so beautiful," he whispered, his eyes glassy, like he hadn't slept all night.

"What's wrong?" I started to get up.

He opened his mouth to speak then shook his head. "We have to get back to work today... and I'm going to have a hell of a time keeping my hands off you."

I laughed, burrowing my face in his firm chest. "I gotta admit, I've always loved the whole forbidden office romance thing... Want me to pin up my hair with a pencil and wear some thigh-highs?"

He growled, covering my mouth with his, then pushed me back against the pillows. "We're going to be late."

"Look at you… so punctual," I teased, loving that he was finally letting his guard down with me, actually smiling, making me believe that even if he was in deep professionally with my father, he would do absolutely nothing to hurt me.

"Why does punctual sound so erotic coming from that wicked mouth of yours?" He nipped my lower lip then deepened the kiss, tossing the covers in a whoosh from my naked body while trying to strip himself of the wrinkly clothes he'd fallen asleep in.

Within minutes the barrier of clothes was gone, and he was lifting me up into his arms and carrying me into the shower. I let out a screech. "I thought we were going to have a lazy morning? What happened to having sex?"

"Whoever said sex always had to be in a bed?" came his answer just before he quite literally tossed me into the shower, then pinned me against the wall and shoved his tongue into my mouth.

It. Was. Everything.

He knew when to be aggressive, when to be soft, and I needed aggressive this morning after the episode with Jac.

With ease he lifted me into the air, pushing my back against the cold tile wall, then plunged into me.

"Whoa." I nearly slid down as the force of his thrusts had me seeing stars.

"This…" He captured my mouth again and again, matching his movements effortlessly, making me lose my mind, all sense of feeling. "I want this from you… every day… I want… you… I just…" He stopped talking, allowing his body to move in mine.

It was perfect.

He was perfect.

I was so close, my hands greedily trying to grab at anything I could to get more leverage when I finally found my release and accidently said out loud, "I love you."

It was impossible to see his face as I slid down the front of his wet body, I expected him to freak out.

"Good." He kissed my mouth softly, then exhaled as if he was relieved. "Because I've loved you for a very long time."

"What?"

"We should get ready." He pulled away from me, then slapped my butt playfully. "Don't want your boss to fire you."

"Nikolai, shouldn't we talk—"

"We will." He cut me off. "Just not now... but soon." His words said he was happy, his body language didn't match them; his movements were stiff, and then he let out another sigh as he showered the rest of the soap off his body.

What just happened?

****

THINGS GOT WEIRDER AS the day progressed. Nikolai, when he was in my office, was edgy, short, and then apologetic. I kept telling him it was fine, but something told me it was my fault, if I hadn't blurted out those three words.

"Idiot," I muttered to myself. I say I love you to the first guy I sleep with? Maybe my father had been right about keeping all guys away from me, at least Nikolai hadn't faced some sort of crazy accident because he'd shared my bed.

I could only imagine what my father would do if he knew Nikolai and I were involved, considering the contract specifically warned against it.

Speaking of the contract... was that void now? Was I still a prisoner? Did it matter? Would I stay if he ripped it up? I swallowed over a lump in my throat. Yes. I would stay. Because I did love him. I couldn't explain it, but it was like a part of me was tied to him. It was a scary thought, one that no matter how many times I tried to justify it, I couldn't. It was a feeling, deep in my soul, a feeling of rightness.

"Try harder!" Nikolai barked into the phone. He pinched the bridge of his nose as he glanced from me back to the window. "You're right. I'm sorry. Maybe it's not in Seattle." He gave a curt nod. "I know what your information says but we need…" An impatient sigh ended in a pithy curse. "Fine."

"Everything okay?" I asked, hoping he wouldn't bite my head off for asking. "Are… you okay?"

"No." He shoved his hands into his pockets and stared out the floor-to-ceiling windows, the Seattle cityscape was blanketed in rays of sunlight, bursting through the clouds. "I'm not."

"You can talk to me." I stood and slowly made my way over to him. "You know that, right?"

"That's just it…" He sighed, rubbing the back of his neck. "I can't… I really can't."

"But—"

"Maya." Nikolai turned. "I wish I could. Believe me."

I stared down at the ground, nervously popping my knuckles as he rocked back and forth on his heels.

The movement, so familiar… hypnotic.

Back and forth, back and forth.

I popped my knuckles again.

Nikolai grabbed my hands firmly. "What's going on?"

"Your shoes…" I felt my vision blurring. "Not your shoes. Sorry, just the way you're standing."

Realization crossed his features, though I have no clue why. I looked back down at his shoes. I couldn't help it.

Slowly, Nikolai raised his hand to my face. I thought he was going to feel my forehead, maybe I was getting sick?

Instead, he covered my eyes with his hand, making it so my only choice was to look down, at the movement of his shoes as they rocked back and forth across the floor.

And like a horror movie pressing play in my mind.

I saw blood on his shoes, drip, drip, drip.

With a gasp I pulled away.

"Maya, what did you see?"

"Blood." I gasped. "On your shoes."

CHAPTER THIRTY-EIGHT

Call me what you like, only give me some vodka. —*Russian Proverb*

Nikolai

I BIT OUT A CURSE AND removed my hand, her eyes were glassy with unshed tears. "Am I going crazy? Be honest."

If only it were that simple, make a simple diagnosis about mental instability, write her a script, and we move on with our lives.

No, her reality was so much more tragic that it hurt my entire being to think about it.

"Nikolai?" She pleaded, her voice small, afraid.

"No." I sighed, reaching for her hand, intertwining our fingers together. I could feel my heart beating as it thumped against my chest. I exhaled. I inhaled. I exhaled. And when I looked at her? It was as if all natural functions of my body needed more effort. I had to tell myself to breathe, force myself to think straight.

The information Phoenix had given me had been useless. While they'd succeeded in hacking the cameras that Petrov had… they were still having trouble tracking down the actual locations.

Each location researched was a false lead.

Phoenix believed that the actual location was trapped somewhere inside Maya's head… I agreed with him, because I was the one that closed the door and threw away the key, damn it.

"If I asked you a favor." I was going to lie to her… again. "But couldn't tell you why…"

She shrugged. "It would depend on the favor."

"Maya, I'm very good at what I do, why don't I allow you to into an altered state of consciousness, and we can talk through the blood, possibly discover why you're having those visions?"

She frowned. "I don't know…" Then she looked away. "My father was always really superstitious about hypnotherapy. He said it was the devils work."

Ironic, that the devil would warn against the devil. "It's completely safe," I reassured her. "And I do have an ulterior motive."

"Oh." She took a step away. "And what's that?"

I prepared myself for the lie, forcing my body to relax, allowing an easy smile to cross my face. "Well, Phoenix believes that your father is still keeping girls locked away in whorehouses, but every location we check into is a dead end. By the looks of it, there are still two houses in operation… They were able to hack the live camera feed, but the location is scrambled…"

"And you think I know where it is?" She asked in a doubtful voice. "Look, my father rarely allowed me near any of his businesses, and those were the legal ones… My mom

and I were trophies he paraded around at political dinners...
we never kept his secrets because we never knew any. He
never had a reason to tell them to us."

I pushed her more. "But, the mind..." I licked my lips,
hating myself all over again for trying to manipulate her... but
I needed her to say yes... if she said no, I would do it anyway,
and I wasn't sure if I wanted to go on living knowing
everything we had would be based on a lie. I wanted to tell
her, and I would, after I destroyed everything, after I gave her
a reason to stay.

After I proved that I would fight her father—and win.

"It's powerful, you may have seen something and not be
fully aware."

Maya held my gaze for a few seconds of silence. "Do you
love me?"

That wasn't what I expected. Not by a long shot. At least
in that I could give her an honest answer. "You know I do."

"Then I trust you."

She shouldn't.

Just like she shouldn't love me.

But I was in too deep, the dark waters washing over me,
washing over us... the only way out was to inhale–together.

"Thank you." I held out my hand again and led her out of
the office, on the way out telling my receptionist to hold my
messages while I took Maya up to her apartment.

I'd never been nervous about re-entering a person's
mind.... because it was on rare occasions that it happened. I
just needed to remember to stick to the box... that was how I
brainwashed. I didn't lock everything away together, but
separated it, giving each memory a different trigger.

The main memory was the sex... seeing her father have
sex with the prostitutes while men watched.

I needed to bypass that memory in order to get to the
previous one, which was, how did she happen upon the

whorehouse in the first place? She said she was looking for her father, meaning she knew who to ask and where to drive her brand new car.

"You look nervous." Maya said in a tight voice then laughed awkwardly. "Should I be worried?"

I smiled confidently. "It will be just like you've taken a short nap. I swear it."

She exhaled once I shoved the key into the lock and let us both into the apartment.

"So, where do I lie down?"

"You stand."

"What?"

"Kidding." Her stunned expression was priceless, and it put me at ease, "Why don't we go into the bedroom?"

Her heels clicked against the marble floor. I followed the sway of her hips as she marched ahead of me then kicked off her heels and lay across the bed, her hair a crowning glory across the pillows.

I was having second thoughts.

Third thoughts.

Maybe fourth thoughts? Was that possible?

"This okay?" She asked, on a swallow.

I closed the door behind me and lowered the lights then cleared my throat. "Perfect, Maya."

She shivered.

"You're cold." I noticed the goose bumps breaking out on her arms, quickly pulled the afghan from the nearby chair and covered her in it. "There's no need to be nervous... I'll be quick."

"Bet you say that to all the girls in bed." She winked. Her trusting smile nearly did me in.

Nearly.

"Very funny." I placed my hands on her right arm, on the first cut, the pressure would be familiar... though only in the back of her mind, in the forefront I was simply touching her arm, nothing more. "Now, close your eyes."

She did as I asked.

"I'm going to count to five, with each ascending number I need you to take a deep breath and exhale, can you do that?"

"Yes."

"Fantastic," I lowered my voice. "One." She inhaled then slowly exhaled. "Two." She repeated the process. "Keep breathing Maya, I want you to think about your favorite place in the world... I want you to go there, in your mind, right now." She sighed. "Do you have that place in your mind?"

"Yes."

"Three... inhale again, exhale slowly." She followed my instructions. "I want you to sit down in this place, then as you sit, focus on your breathing in and out, in and out... you exist to breathe, you exist to simply be."

Her body started relaxing, I pressed harder on her arm. "Four... inhale, now exhale. Your body is going to start feeling very heavy, this is normal, the pressure you feel in your arm is like sand getting placed inside your limbs, as I press your arm, imagine sand weighing you down, allowing your body to fully relax against the bed. You're so relaxed that even your breathing has slowed down, your chest rising and falling with slowness. You feel your heart rate match your breathing as your body gets heavier." I moved my hand to her chest and pressed down. "And heavier."

Her breathing slowed.

"Good Maya, you're doing so well. Remember, you're in a safe place, nobody can hurt you here. On the count of five I'm going to snap my fingers and you're going to go into a dreamless sleep, when I snap my fingers twice in a row, you'll wake up refreshed and energized." I held my right hand midair, unsure of whether I should proceed. But it was our only hope... discovering where the girls were taken, destroying them before Petrov discovered she was remembering. I had to be one step ahead of him.

"Five." I whispered then snapped my fingers.

Her body went completely limp.

"It's the day of your sixteenth birthday," I whispered. "You're so excited to meet your friends for the party in downtown Seattle. You want to drive, but your mother said you need to ask your father's permission first... but you can't find him, where is he?"

"I don't know." Maya said in a clear voice. "I've looked everywhere! Texted him, called, everything goes straight to voicemail."

"What do you do Maya? Can you walk me through it?"

All I needed to know was how she discovered his whereabouts. If I took her too far past that memory we'd meet the next box, where she saw her father at the whorehouse, and all the memories I'd locked away would shatter with that trigger, they were fragile already, too fragile.

"My mom doesn't care, and if I don't leave soon I'll be late... Father always refuses to let me into his office, it's always locked anyway, but I pick the lock... the men are gone and so is he. He's always been paranoid about technology and my mom gets him an old school planner every year for Christmas. Maybe it's in his office."

"Good, Maya, what happens after you pick the lock?"

"It's easy. Too easy." Maya moved a bit on the bed, her arms coming up off the mattress as if she was walking. "His office is very bare, no computer, just file cabinets and a desk. His desk has a lock on the middle drawer. I pick that lock too. When the drawer opens, I see his planner."

"Do you pick it up?"

"Yes." Maya started trembling. "I pick it up and quickly find the date... it says he has an appointment at three in the afternoon."

"Where Maya?" Unbelievable, her mental stability was astounding.

Maya didn't answer.

"Maya? Where is he?"

"He's..." Her eyes squeezed as if she was trying to repel the memory. "He's..." Shit maybe I had locked the memory away too deep. "Seattle." She shook her head back and forth. "No wait... there's numbers... and underneath it, it says new construction... I remember him talking about office buildings he was putting up in Everett, down by the docks."

"Well done Maya, is there an address with the numbers?"

"It's..." Her breathing was starting to accelerate. "So, dark."

"Not so fast Maya, remember you're safe, you don't need to visit that place... just tell me where it is."

"So dark!" She writhed on the bed. "I go in, I shouldn't go in, but I go in. What am I walking into? It looks abandoned, but I try the door anyway. It's dark around me, I try the first door, the second, the third building and see my father's Lexus, then the door opens. It smells funny."

"Maya, let's focus on your surroundings, do you notice anything different?"

"Fish." Her teeth chattered. "It smells like fish, and there are docks behind us, construction, but nothing's being built or maybe it's just too late at night. I walk in the door—"

"Maya why don't you take a step backward... don't go in the door."

"I have to!" She shouted. "I have to go in!"

"No." I sat back down on the bed and gripped her arm, pressing firmly against the scars, hoping mentally her body will remember the physical pain that manifested last time she was under, and pull back, instead she tries to jerk away from me. "Please! Please let me go in. Something's in there, someone's hurt."

My gut clenched.

"I need to help her! She's screaming!"

Maya was too far gone. I quickly released my hand and tried to talk over her. "I'm going to snap my fingers twice, when I snap my fingers you're going to wake up feeling rested and—"

Maya let out a blood curdling scream as her eyes flashed open.

"Shit!" I yelled, pinning her hands down. "Maya, focus, focus on my voice, I'm going to help you okay. I know it's scary."

"They're children!" She yelled. "Children! I babysat them once, I—" Her body trembled as her eyes rolled in the back of her head.

"Maya!" I yelled sternly in her ear. "Two snaps of my fingers, and you're safe, two snaps, ready?" I snapped my fingers twice to bring her out of the trance.

She immediately fell against me.

But didn't wake up.

Fear crept down my spine. Had I broken her? Was it too much? Had I failed in trying to save her? Save us?

"Damn it." I pressed a kiss to her forehead. "You're safe Maya, wake up."

She blinked open her eyes. "Thirsty."

"I'll get you water. Just stay here."

I rushed into the kitchen and filled a glass of water then hurried back. She was just sitting up, I handed her the glass

With shaking hands she sipped then handed the glass back to me. I went to put it on the dresser and accidently knocked over one of the white masks. Without thinking, I picked it up then locked eyes with Maya just as she let out a scream straight from the pit of hell.

One reserved for villains and monsters.

For people like me.

Who deserved it.

CHAPTER THIRTY-NINE

Love cannot be compelled — Russian Proverb

Maya

I COULDN'T STOP SCREAMING. THE SOUND coming from my mouth didn't sound normal, I was losing my mind, because suddenly I had visions of Nikolai hurting me, of him... taking off his mask.

"Pleasure," he whispered.

Nikolai held out his hands. "I can explain."

"Explain?" My teeth chattered as I pulled the blanket around my body. "Explain what, you bastard? That you tortured me when I was sixteen! The masks..." I pointed at the masks lining the dresser. "You kept trophies of it? Are you going to kill me?"

Terrified and nauseated, I tried to scramble off the bed, but my feet tangled up in the blanket causing me to fall to my knees on the floor. My entire chest hurt with the effort to breathe. I had told him I loved him! My captor! The person who'd... made me... forget.

Everything.

It was too much, the memories, as if someone had unlocked Pandora's Box, the pain in my skull so intense I was seeing double.

"Shh." Nikolai held up his hands in surrender and kneeled next to me on the floor. "It's normal to feel pain after the repressed memories come forward."

"Don't touch me!" I shrieked.

The scars on my forearms throbbed. How was that possible?

I scratched at them.

"No, no, Maya." Nikolai gripped my hands. "You're going to hurt yourself if you do that. Your brain is re-living the memories... and trying to manifest something in the present so that the pain makes sense. It won't, and... you'll end up killing yourself."

He pinned my hands behind my back.

I squirmed against him and screamed as hot tears ran down my face. Escape. I had to escape. I had to get out.

The apartment was white, it had always been white. Everywhere was white.

The masks.

The couch.

Bile rose up in my throat.

Before I could react any more Nikolai reached into the top of the dresser and pulled out a syringe. I flailed against him harder, but he was too strong.

"Don't! Please!" I sobbed uncontrollably. "Please! Nikolai if you love me at all you won't hurt me!"

His dark eyes closed very briefly as he looked away and stabbed me with a needle directly in my arm and pushed the plunger.

My vision blurred. And it was weird, in that moment, I wasn't afraid of what he would do to me. No, instead, my heart broke, because it meant he didn't love me.

****

I WAS TIED TO the chair. He had cut me six times on each arm. I counted. The pain was horrible. He said pain was one of the only ways to quickly brainwash someone because mentally you didn't think you could handle it, even though physically you could.

I asked him lots of questions.

He answered every single one.

"Why are you doing this?" I gasped as Nik made his final cut in my arm.

"You were in a tragic car accident" he said in a low voice. "Lucky to be alive, do you feel these cuts? They're deep, from the glass in the windshield."

"No." I shook my head. "No, you did this! I didn't mean to see it, okay? I'll tell my father, if I just explain to him that I didn't mean to."

"What you saw matters," Nik said tightly. "Your father cannot trust you not to say anything to anyone… your options are die, or this." He pressed his palm against my forearms, I was losing more blood.

"You beat me."

"No, that was him." Nik said sadly. "How do your arms feel?"

"Heavy."

"That's from the impact of hitting the steering wheel, the glass from the accident missed your main arteries, you're lucky to be alive."

"You already said that."

"Repeat after me." He ignored me.

I refused to repeat.

Then felt more pressure against my forearms. "Repeat it,

Maya."

"I'm lucky to be alive."

"Why?"

"Because the glass." I frowned. Why did I feel as though I was reliving something that didn't happen? "It missed my arteries."

"The building you ran into was empty, thank God," he said.

"Yeah." The building. What building?

"It was a motorcycle shop, remember? You drove by it in order to get to your party for your birthday."

"My birthday." I felt tears well in my eyes.

"Happy birthday, Maya."

I felt dehydrated, tired. Wait, where was I?

"Maya," Something wrapped around my arms, I think the bleeding had stopped. "Do you remember what happened?"

"Yeah…" I frowned against the blindfold, only able to see a sliver of movement underneath it, black shoes rocked back and forth, back and forth, they were covered in blood, was that mine? "I um, got in an accident."

"Lucky to be alive," we said in unison.

"So lucky," Nik whispered. "It's good your father found you when he did, he was so worried."

"My father?"

"Maya, how do you feel about ice cream?"

"Huh?" My mouth watered. I wanted something to drink and some food. Why wasn't anyone feeding me? Why did I have a blindfold on.

"I love it." I finally answered.

"Me, too." He sighed as if the thought saddened him. "I'm going to take off your blindfold now… And it's going to make you feel so much better."

"Do I get to leave?"

He hesitated. "Not yet, I'm going to give you a gift instead. Remember you're going to feel so much better once the blindfold is removed…"

"I'm going to feel so much better." I repeated then shook my fuzzy head. "Did you say gift?"

"Something so you don't remember the pain... so that when you dream, you dream of light."

I nodded, my body trembling but I wasn't sure if it was fear or excitement. "I would like that."

"Besides." His hands came around my head loosening the blindfold. "You've done so well, you deserve a gift. You've been brave, so very brave. And I want to reward you for that bravery."

"Really?"

The blindfold fell.

His mask was white, like something you'd see at a historic masquerade, the nose was elongated, at least four inches from his face, pointing downward, the mouth open so I could see his full lips and blinding white smile. It matched the mask.

Dark liquid brown eyes stared back through the two large holes next to the nose.

"Will you take off your mask?"

"I don't take off my mask."

"You can't?"

"I don't," he said in a simple nodding gesture, his smile easy. "For you I would love to, but I can't."

My body was heavy, so heavy.

"You're tired," he said. "At this point you've been awake for over thirty-two hours."

"What!" I tried to jump out of my chair but my body was too heavy, too tired, and full of so much pain.

"The car accident," Nik stated. "It was very traumatic for your body."

"Will I be okay?"

"Of course. I'm a trained surgeon. You're going to be just fine, but it's important that you stay awake for the next twelve hours just in case, do you think you can do that?"

"Yes." I nodded once, twice, maybe three times?

Every time I moved he mimicked my movements, it was weird, like I was staring into a mirror though that was ridiculous right? My brain told me it was ridiculous, but for some reason it put me at ease, made me think, he was just like me, trapped in some weird white room.

I looked down, but was met by soft fingertips. "I wouldn't... there is a lot of blood from your accident."

"Okay," I whispered, mesmerized by his dark eyes and the way his eyelashes seemed to stretch out past the confines of the white mask, he was beautiful, so beautiful, like a fallen angel.

"You are gorgeous, you know that?"

"No."

"But young." He sighed, sounding almost disappointed.

"I'm sixteen... I think."

"Your sixteenth birthday, remember? The accident? In your brand new car..."

"My father told me not to drive." I frowned. "But I did, because I wanted to make it to the party."

"Of course you wanted to make it to the party. You were going to be late, after all." His fingers caressed my face.

"That feels good."

"I'm glad."

"Will you keep touching me?"

His hand hovered near my cheek, as if he was hesitating. "I did promise a gift... and pleasure."

"Yes," I whispered. "Yes." This time I said it louder.

"Yes," he repeated. "Close your eyes."

"But—"

"I said I'd give you a gift."

"Okay..."

"But no sleeping."

"Alright..."

"Promise me, Maya, no sleeping... that is not your gift."

"I promise," I said in a shaky voice, closing my eyes. It would

be impossible to fall asleep sitting in a chair anyways.

"My gift is a story."

"A story?" I opened my eyes.

"Shh, don't you want to hear it?"

"Yes." I did. I wanted something to distract me from the throbbing in my arms or the way my body felt like someone had dumped sand inside it. "Sorry."

"Never apologize to me, Maya."

"So—" I shook my head. "Okay."

"Good." He sighed then ran his fingers down my face. "You are beautiful, young, talented. You will be able to do anything you want with your life, do you believe me?"

I shrugged. I'd always been into science but didn't get good enough grades, not that I was going to admit that.

"If you could do anything in the world, what would it be?"

"I think…" I chewed my lower lip, the pain so intense that I had to take a minute and remember to breathe. "I think I'd want to help people… maybe become a vet or a doctor?"

"Doctor," he said. "That fits you."

"You think?" Nobody had ever complimented me on my life choices, at least that I could remember, which wasn't much, everything was so blurry and out of focus.

"I know." He said softly, his fingers still caressing my face like I was precious, desirable. "Keep your eyes closed."

I squeezed them shut just as I felt his rough cheek against mine. I let out a little gasp as his mouth found my neck.

"Are your eyes still closed, Maya?"

"Yes." I exhaled as the sensation of his mouth against my skin felt like the most wonderful thing in the world. "Yes, my eyes are closed."

"When you leave this place… you'll feel determined… so very determined to work hard, to get good grades, to study, to prove to everyone just how smart you truly are. Do you believe me, Maya?"

"Yes." For some reason I did. I believed him. He was the only

lifeline I had after being in hell for what felt like days. He'd given me water, hadn't he? And he'd wrapped my arms after apologizing. He was... he was my everything right now, my life. "I believe you."

"People will try to stop you, but you'll continue on with your goals... even your father may try to dissuade you, and here's the gift I leave you with... He will never have any power over you. Do you understand?"

"Power?"

"Your father, Alexander Petrov will never own you, he will never be able to tell you what to do, there will be no fear when you look him in the eyes, only sadness that he is missing out on the wonderful daughter he could know if only he'd look past his own selfishness. The gift I leave you... is peace."

"Nik, I don't feel peace."

His mouth kissed down my neck again and then his warm lips moved across mine in a searing hot kiss. I wrapped my arms around his neck as he lifted me off the chair and into the air. My body ached everywhere but he felt so good, so warm, and I was suddenly chilled, my teeth chattering between kisses.

He placed me down on a couch and deepened the kiss then ran his hands down my hips. It felt so good having him in the places that hurt, knowing he would make it better.

I thought I heard him mutter a curse as he ran his hands up and down my stomach.

It was sore.

"Broken ribs... not by my hand, Maya, I would never hurt you in that way... In fact..." I could almost hear him thinking, I kept my eyes squeezed shut for fear that he would disappear or leave me if I opened them. "Every time you crack your knuckles it means you are remembering the bad, not the good. If you crack your knuckles I want you to pay special attention to your breathing then count to five and try to focus on your goals, focus on getting through school, focus on settling down, and focus on staying away from your father."

"My father?"

"Promise me, Maya."

"Okay." I swallowed the dryness in my throat. "I promise."

"Good."

"One more thing… and then no more talking."

"Yes?"

"Remember me…" he whispered, followed by another caress of his mouth. "Remember me in your dreams… not the pain, or the state in which you were brought to me, remember the pleasure, not the pain."

"Remember the pleasure…" I repeated like an oath. "Not the pain."

"Good."

"Now what?"

"Oh Maya, now I show you what I mean by pleasure."

My mind fast forwarded through moments where he cradled me, where he kissed my head, only to move down to my mouth. He only ever kissed me, barely touched me, but it was enough to fuel the fire of obsession for this man, the man who saved me.

The man who I thought had hurt me.

But had rescued me instead.

The hours went fast, my brain couldn't catch up.

When the door opened to the room, the blindfold was put back on my face, and I heard my father's voice.

"Is it done?"

"Of course," Nikolai said in a smooth voice. "You brought her to me half starved, sleep deprived, and nearly dead, it took me less than twelve hours to finish your task."

"She looks good," my father said. "Why is she no longer bleeding?"

"I didn't think it necessary," answered Nikolai. "Now, if you no longer need my services?"

"One last thing…" My father grunted. "If I find out that you double crossed me, I will kill her."

"Why should her life matter?"

"Because... I don't trust you, and I never turned off the camera, though the sound was too muffled, I saw you touch her, I saw your want. And I'm not stupid, she could easily be triggered by any of the things you did to her. If she relapses, if she remembers, I will kill her and I know, the last thing you want is her death on your conscience. Then again, what would it matter since not only would I kill her, but reveal your family's true identity to the media. Imagine what they would do if they found out who your ancestors were. You know, they still haven't found that serial killer last year, what was his name again?"

"Fine." Nikolai said in a cold voice. "But you have nothing to worry about, I did my best work..."

I was listening to them but it was almost like a dream.

I head more footsteps then Nik was next to me, whispering in my ear. "Butterscotch."

It was impossible to keep my eyes open.

The next thing I remembered, I was in a hospital room waking up from a coma, and my mother was crying by my bedside... my father said I suffered such psychological trauma from the brain damage that I was lucky I wasn't a vegetable. When I mentioned the man in the white mask, my father laughed and rang the nurse for anti-psychotic meds. They said to give me a while.

So I buried the memory and soon, it was nothing more than a weird dream induced by medicine, or so I thought.

With a gasp I woke up, to find Nikolai sitting on the edge of the bed, his head in his hands. "So now you know."

"How did you? I don't understand."

"Are you still afraid?"

"No," I said in a calm voice. "But I am confused."

"Hypnotherapy and brainwashing can work hand in hand but it's imperative that the brainwashing take place before the hypnotherapy. Otherwise, it won't last... you have to be open to suggestion and a strong mind is never open enough to suggestion or replacement of memories unless a severe trauma has taken place. The minute you left your dad's whorehouse, you were beat within an inch of your life, starved for a week straight, only given enough water to survive, and when you ceased to remember your own name, when you cried out for death, they brought you to me. I'm always in white." He shook his head bitterness twisting his lips into a non-smile. "Like an avenging angel... Your father has always been dramatic, the idea has always been so simple... take them from the depths of hell, give them heaven and offer them peace, and then, go through the stages of hypnotherapy. Did you know—" He laughed without humor. "—that ninety percent of people will agree with most statements if you repeat them more than three times? You have to be confident, convincing, but that's without brainwashing, imagine what could happen if you were weakened physically?"

"But..." I pressed my fingers to my head. "I remember the accident."

"I showed you pictures." He sighed. "Of your wrecked car, and I did..."He swallowed. "Inflict some pain, I made the cuts on your arm because regardless of your mental state, I needed to show you I was in control and usually the only way to do that is through some sort of pain, it can be minor, I'm sorry yours wasn't."

It was too much to process. Almost.

"How did you get me back?" I whispered. "Why am I with you now?"

"Because I lied and told your father that the Italians knew where the rest of his whorehouses were... he believed me because ever since he attacked one of their own a few months ago, some key pieces of information have been missing. I asked for you... and told him I would take care of the Italians in return."

"But you didn't."

"No... and there were... terms. He said I could have you

for a year but that if I touched you and triggered one of the real memories of seeing him in the whorehouse with the girls... he'd kill both of us, so..." He stood and spread his arms wide. "I re-created a nearly identical room to the one you were held in, even kept masks nearby." He walked over to the dresser then with a cry tossed it onto its side and slumped to the floor.

He was losing his mind.

Or maybe just allowing me to see he wasn't as in control as I'd always thought.

Slowly, I slid out of bed and joined him on the floor.

"You should go," he whispered.

"And where would I go? To my father's house? The same one who tortured me for a week? No thanks, I think I'll take my chance with the person who tried to save me."

My body trembled all over again at the thought. He might not be my flesh and blood but he was still a father, he was supposed to protect me, not break me and scatter the ashes while laughing.

Warm tears streamed down my face.

Nikolai pulled me against him, wrapping a muscled arm around my body as I continued to sob quietly against his chest.

"I didn't." Nikolai cursed under his breath. "I didn't save you. I made it worse, so much worse. Saving you, would have been trying to get you out of the building, saving you, would be handing you over the Italians and faking your death, saving you—" He turned to cup my face, his eyes filled with tears. "—would be letting you go, rather than keeping you for myself."

"What if I want to be kept?"

"You realize," he said, then swallowed slowly, his mouth inches from mine. "That you say you want to be kept by the very monster that made you believe you were in a car accident, by the same person who took advantage of a sixteen year old girl because he couldn't help himself."

"You kissed me, hardly a crime."

"I didn't just kiss you. I desired you. I wanted you, from the minute I saw you with your father that year, and it disgusted me that I was so much older yet was drawn to someone so young, so bright. You wore your emotions on the outside, while I'd been taught emotions were frivolous wicked things that would get me nowhere in life."

"And yet the beast somehow still managed to turn into a prince."

"I'm not your prince."

"You're right." I nodded. "I think the beast is hotter anyways."

He cracked a smile. "You should be sleeping, running, possibly screaming and pulling a gun on me."

"But I remember," I whispered kissing his mouth. "I remember you telling me to work hard in school... I remember you telling me how special I was... I remember everything..."

"I can make you forget again, it could be dangerous, and I'd have to disappear from your—"

I kissed his mouth hard, pulling him into my arms, our tongues tangled in a wild frenzy.

We broke apart.

"I had your picture in my room," I blurted.

His eyebrows drew together in shock. "You what?"

"In my room. You know how some people have pictures of bands or move stars? I had pictures of you... you'd always been my idol, maybe that's why I was so crazy to meet you, or maybe—"

"—maybe you just wanted to come home."

"You're my home," I whispered tugging at his shirt.

"God, I've waited years to hear you say that." His lips found mine again, and then he was tearing at my clothes, ripping them from my body as he laid me back against the cold slate floor. I didn't care, I needed him, wanted him, with such desperateness it was hard to breathe.

Clothes flew over his head and then his warm body was pressing against mine, our mouths fused as he thrust into me without warning.

My head fell back, brushing the slate as he made love to me.

The piece that had always been missing, finally, with a resounding click, locked into place.

CHAPTER FORTY

Ask a lot but take what is offered. –Russian Proverb

Nikolai

I BRUSHED HER DARK HAIR AWAY from her face and kissed her soft cheek, my lips sliding down to her mouth. I craved more of her with every breath I took.

"Nik?" She'd been calling me that since we made love on the floor, and this time, when she referred to me the way I'd originally instructed her to so long ago, I was okay with it, knowing she wasn't reverting back to some altered state of consciousness but completely aware that it was my nickname crossing her lips.

"Yes?"

"Tell me about the clinic."

I sighed, as the last bit of heaviness washed over me. It was my burden to carry not hers, and telling her only added stress to what she was already dealing with. "I study the girls, the ones given to me by your father, and when they can no longer work because of sickness, disease…" my voice trailed off.

"Nik?"

"Yeah?"

"You don't have to tell me the rest."

I relaxed, as if my body made a giant sigh against hers. "Maya?"

"Yeah."

"When you were under… I asked you about the addresses, do you remember?"

It was her turn to tense, and then turn around in my arms a frown marred her pretty face. "It was on the Pier, and I recognized Everett, but I don't remember the address, just thinking about it makes my head hurt."

"Sorry." I kissed her forehead.

"Why is it important?"

Burdens, so many burdens I was sharing, I hated myself for it, but maybe it was time to extend the weight and trust the other person wouldn't let it slip through their fingers. "You'll never be safe, as long as those houses exist. I want to destroy them… if they're gone, then I'm hoping you won't be as big of a threat to your father as he thinks… right now, if he saw you on the street, he'd recognize the fear, even if you tried to hide it. You'd flinch, you'd back away into another person walking in the other direction, you'd gasp, your eyes would widen, there are any number of physical responses you would have. And he would know, and he would either kill you, or capture you, then do it right in front of me to make an example. The only way to be free is to eliminate the threat, and right now, those two houses existing, making him a shit load of money…" I looked away.

Maya tilted her head thoughtfully. "You said the Italians owed you."

"I owe them."

"That's not what they said."

"I don't really think they see it that way, Maya. They're being kind."

"The Italians? The ones with the scary guns and weird even more terrifying tattoos and sneers, those people? You have seen that big guy right? The one with the permanent frown on his face?"

"Nixon?"

"No not the lip ring guy." She waved me off. "The other one."

"Tex?"

"No, the other one." She snapped her fingers. "With the…" She gulped. "Darkness, I know this sounds crazy but he has this… weird aura about him."

I nodded my head and whispered. "You're talking about Phoenix."

"Scary." She shuddered.

And in that moment it was like all the possibilities of how they really could help me were brought to light.

"His father and yours used to work together." I didn't want to give too much away, better she never find out about that. "He may be able to help more, but his wife's six months pregnant." I sighed. "I'll call him. I think that may be the only choice we have."

"Other than running away together," Maya whispered, brushing a kiss across my mouth. "That sounds good too."

"Someone like me… can't disappear without making CNN."

She sighed, pulling her mouth away. "I know."

"But…" I tilted her chin toward me. "We can stay here… for at least a few more moments, let the world go to hell… while I give you a glimpse of heaven."

"Arrogant bastard."

"I've never pretended to be otherwise." I full on grinned.

Her breath caught. "You're sexy when you smile."

"It's why I don't do it often, too hard to be taken seriously." I toyed with a piece of her hair.

"Wow look at you. Such a good mood, I wonder why."

"Sex," I said truthfully. "But first… love."

"First comes love?"

"Yes, Maya." I closed my eyes, breathing her in. "With you? First, always comes love."

CHAPTER FORTY-ONE

Another body has been discovered in Pikes Market, Jane Doe had no identification, and no missing reports have been filed. She was believed to be a prostitute and homeless. –The Seattle Tribune

Maya

WE TALKED ABOUT EVERYTHING THAT HAD to do with nothing important. And then, when we ran out of words to say and silence filled the air, we kissed, communicating with our mouths, hands, bodies, what we were feeling.

Sunlight crept through the window early that morning. I forced my eyes shut, not wanting to leave the bed or deal with the heavy stuff, the questions still rolling around in my brain, the memories, the flashbacks. Over the course of a few hours I felt like I'd regained my entire childhood only to wish it would have been kept under lock and key for eternity.

I shivered.

It wasn't pretty.

My memories had always been about the later years, when I pushed myself in school and sports.

The early years? Were filled with getting pushed out of the house at age five because my father's associates were coming to visit. *Why did it matter?* I'd ask my mom, what if I play quietly.

At such a young age I didn't understand, that those men, the ones that were in our house once a week, dealt child pornography to the masses, making millions off of a sick addiction that should equal the death penalty in my mind.

I stumbled past one of the men as my mom ushered me out the back door, he grabbed her arm, then looked down at me with a frown.

"Leave it," she snapped.

My mom was rarely rude, especially to my father's associates.

The man bent down to my eye level, his breath smelled sour and his face was white as a ghost. "So, you're the bastard."

Those were his words. I didn't know what the name meant, but the way he said it had made me think it was a bad name to be called. He also leered, made me feel like I should hide behind my mama's skirts or maybe just disappear altogether.

When I brought it up to Nikolai, he simply kissed me and told me he was sorry he couldn't keep the bad away—sorry that he had failed.

If anyone failed in this scenario it was my father… he was a complete lunatic. My only saving grace was that I wasn't actually related to him, only to my mother. Thank God.

My gut clenched. Was my mother even safe?

"You look very deep in thought." Nikolai said without opening his eyes.

"You can't even see me."

"I can feel you," he murmured, "and you feel stressed."

"I'm not stressed," I grumbled, frowning harder.

His eyes blinked open. "God, you're beautiful."

"I better be, I put on lip gloss and brushed my hair at least a hundred times throughout the night in fear you'd wake up and scream."

"Very funny."

"Don't believe me?"

He ran his left hand through my hair, and of course his fingers got caught in the tangles, I tried to pull away but he continued combing it with his fingers. "I think I like you messy... less polished. It fits you."

"Are you calling me a mess?"

"A hot mess. The adjective changes everything don't you think?" The corners of his mouth lifted into a heart stopping smile.

CHAPTER FORTY-TWO

An enemy will agree, but a friend will argue. —*Russian Proverb*

Nikolai

I HATED THAT I CALLED HIM in, almost as much as I hated the fact that I needed to ask for help.

Help had always been a weakness, as if I was down, bleeding out, and needed someone to put pressure on the wound in order to stay alive.

My blood heated at the thought, the mere, idea that I would need to call an Italian to aid me.

I glanced back at Maya as she slept in the bed.

I would do anything, anything for her. Legal. Illegal. There wasn't a line I would not cross, a job I would not do. A life I would not take.

The phone rang once.

"Yes?" The voice clipped on one end.

"I need you." Damn the words were out before I could

stop them, my hand clenching the phone as if it was the only object in my existence and the pressure aided by my fingertips only helped persuade the voice on the other end in saying yes, in making sure I kept the woman I loved safe.

"Okay."

A click. And the conversation ended. No persuading. No banter, nothing that would help me understand the situation further, just a simple okay.

I would have been a hell of a lot more at ease had he been argumentative.

I let out a sigh of frustration. I hadn't intended on relying on anyone else. I didn't trust people, but I did trust the Italians. And maybe that made me the worst betrayer of them all... the fact that I so easily trusted outside of the Russians, the family my father bet his very life on.

With a sigh I turned away from Maya as she slept and dialed Jac's number.

"Hello?" She picked up right away.

"Jac," I said relieved. "How are you?"

She was silent and then. "I haven't heard from you all day, will you be in tonight?"

I glanced nervously at Maya. "Of course, why not?"

"Well, a lot of things have been changing lately."

I rolled my eyes. "Jac, I will always do my research. You know this."

"Do I?"

A challenge. "Yes. You do."

"Fine." She sighed heavily. "I'll see you tonight at the regular time."

"Yes," I hissed. "And maybe, during that time, you can help me locate the missing girl?"

"Missing girl?"

"The one you led into the clinic the other night? The one who we can't find? That girl."

"What's one girl, Nik?"

"What is one girl, Jac?"

"What are you saying?"

"I'm not saying anything, merely asking... You led her in, did you see where she ran off to?"

The phone went deathly still as if Jac was holding her breath. "I don't like being attacked by my own family, my own grandson."

"Is that what this feels like? I'm asking a question. That's all."

Jac cursed. "You're accusing me. There's a difference, think I can't tell the tone you're using? The girl ran off, just like I told you. If you paid more attention to your own damn records, you'd know that. Now. Can I please get back to work? The real work we're supposed to be doing? As a family?" I didn't miss how she said that last part with venom, how she spat the word, disgusted with having to even discuss it with me in the first place.

"Yes." I nodded even though she couldn't see me. "Yes, get back to work."

The phone line went dead.

Maya made a small noise in her sleep. I'd exhausted her, so relieved that I could be with her that I hadn't given her a break at all, just taken my pleasure, offered her hers, and gone on with life.

The clock chimed three in the afternoon.

Our time would be up soon.

Our number called.

And as if her father could read my mind, a text sounded on my phone.

Petrov: *Tsk, Tsk, Tsk good doctor. Have your hand in the cookie jar, do you? Meet me tonight at Pier 49, 10:00. Being late, means her life... I'll find her, I always find them. I always succeed.*

With a curse I tossed my phone onto the bed and ran my

hands through my hair.

Maya awoke and squinted up at me. "Is everything okay?"

"Of course," I lied smoothly. "Just... anxious to lie next to you, to hold you in my arms. Can I do that?"

"Yes..." She yawned, stretched, then opened her arms. "Are you sure it's okay to take today off?"

"Yes," I snapped unintentionally. "Bosses orders, he's an ass after all."

She reached around and pinched my ass. "Yes, yes he is... better pull the wool over his eyes while we can."

I kissed her hot mouth. "Yes." I growled. "While we can."

I wished moments like that could last forever.

But my wish was in vain.

I couldn't be reborn, and ask to be part of a different family, ask to be something other than what I was.

I cringed, just thinking about what Jac was doing.

About what she'd been doing.

Maya moaned. "Make love to me again."

"Okay," I whispered against her lips. "Okay." I prayed she'd never find out the other half, why I agreed to Petrov in the first place, why I still allowed myself to be controlled.

It isn't money that makes the world go round.

It's knowledge.

And when it came to me?

He had all he needed to know.

Not just half of it.

All of it.

CHAPTER FORTY-THREE

So near and yet so far. –Russian Proverb

Maya

I ACHED IN ALL THE RIGHT PLACES. Did he have the same delicious afterglow I was experiencing? I reached across for his warm body, but my hands met the cool sheets. With a yawn I sat up, blinking against the light floating in from the hall.

He was gone.

I should have left with him, but I'd been so tired when he'd mentioned something about working at the clinic that he'd kissed me on the head and told me to go back to sleep, this time promising to allow me to do it the right way, the natural way, no finger snapping or trigger words. Was that hours ago? Minutes?

My feet touched the cold slate floor just as a throat cleared.

"I sure hope you have clothes on."

With a scream I jerked back against the headboard, pulling the sheets up around my naked body.

One of the Italians, the scary one, the one with the bird name, peered at me over a ceramic mug, his face a mask of cool indifference.

My eyes darted to the door, already planning my escape, if I needed to escape that is.

He sighed. "If I was going to kill you, you'd already be dead." He took a long sip out of his mug.

"How reassuring," I grumbled.

"That's me," he said in a low voice. "Reassuring."

My ass. "Why are you here? Standing in my room?"

"Guard duty." He looked away. "Nikolai called me in hours ago. I hopped on a private jet, and here I am."

My eyebrows shot up in surprise. "To protect me while I sleep?"

His lips pressed together in what looked like a hint of a smile. "Sort of." He ran a hand over his semi buzzed hair. "I'm Phoenix De Lange, you probably don't remember much about meeting me since it was such a... traumatic—" He seemed to choke over the word. "—week, but I'm the boss to the Nicolasi family and..." His eyes shifted from me to the floor like he was uncomfortable. "You know what, why don't you get dressed first, I'll make you coffee, and we can chat..."

"Chat?" I repeated. "Why do we need to chat? Aren't you just here to guard or whatever?"

He smirked. "Sure, I can do that, and while I'm at it, I'll be sure to fill you in on who your father is, I mean, unless you don't want to know?"

"What?" I clenched the sheet harder. "What are you talking about?"

"I'm good," Phoenix whispered a veiled threat. "At killing. At making it look like an accident. I'm the best at hiding when I need to... but my specialty, at least the specialty that's been passed on to me is that of secrets… it's how I make deals, how I trade. It isn't money that makes this world go around, Maya, it's information. If you own someone's past, you own their future."

I swallowed the nausea building up in my chest. "Are you telling me you know more about my past?"

"I'm telling you, I know everything… and so does Nikolai. Look, my wife wouldn't appreciate me talking to you while you have nothing but a damn sheet covering you, and I actually like staying alive. Wouldn't put it past Nikolai to get crazy and shoot me or inject me with whatever the hell new medical invention he has and make me talk like a chicken for the rest of my life, either. Get dressed, then we talk, sis."

"Sis?" I blurted out.

He nodded slowly. "Coffee's getting cold." And walked out.

CHAPTER FORTY-FOUR

Falling in love is like a mouse falling into a box, there is no way out.
—Russian Proverb

Nikolai

TWO BLACK ESCALADES WAITED BY THE Pier, how irritatingly cliché. I kept the engine running and slowly stepped out of the car, my pace unhurried as I slammed the door behind me and leisurely made my way toward the two SUVs. Gravel crunched beneath my shoes with each step.

When I was around four feet away, the door opened, and Petrov stepped out. His stomach protruded beneath a long leather coat, the inside was lined with fur. Amazing that he still needed warmth, one would assume the fat choking his organs would be more than enough to do the trick.

His *Sovietnik* approached from the other SUV, along with a handful of his muscle or *Byki*.

I smiled and nodded my head toward the five men, each

of them had their hands placed in front of their bodies as if to show me they had no weapons when we all knew they had enough ammo to take out the entire street. "Were they really necessary, Petrov?"

"You tell me." His cold eyes never left mine.

I didn't answer and refused to allow my brain to register that I was actually afraid, not for me, but for her, for what he would do to her if he knew the truth.

If I was dead I couldn't save her.

Then again, if I was dead, Phoenix would know what to do. That had been part of the conversation we'd had right before his plane landed. I wouldn't be able to welcome him to Seattle, but gave him strict instructions of who would pick him up from the airport and that he was supposed to guard Maya at all costs.

"How much does she know?" he asked in a calm voice that I knew took much control on his end.

"She knows about the girls, remembers me hurting her, but beyond that, I haven't told her anything. I thought it best not to dump everything on her all at once."

Phoenix sighed heavily on the other end. "So she doesn't know about... .me?"

I cursed. "Those are not my secrets to tell. They are yours and only yours."

"Damn it." The sound of something breaking cut into our conversation and then Phoenix began talking again. "I wanted this behind me, it is my past. Talking about it is nearly as bad as re-living it, you know this."

Yes, I did. Merely talking about a traumatic event was like experiencing it all over again, the human mind was incapable of logically telling the individual that it was just a memory being pulled. "Phoenix, I know. I wouldn't ask you to do this, if I wasn't desperate."

"Right." He hissed through his teeth, making the simple

agreement sound menacing. "Anything else you need from me? You know other than helping you save the world?"

At that I laughed. "Screw the world. I'd kill every last person on this planet to save her, you know that, because you would do the same thing, to protect the woman you love."

Phoenix was silent and then. "You love her?"

"I do."

"Well." He chuckled. "I guess that does change things.... people go to war over less..."

"There is no greater reason to stop someone's heart." I closed my eyes then opened them and glanced back at the bedroom door. "So that another may beat without interruption." I loved her. The thought was the only thing bringing my chilled body warmth. "Protect her above all costs, while you are here. I need you to protect her like she is blood."

I knew what I asked.

Italians cared for blood.

Anything outside of that was a gamble depending on their mood.

"You have my word," Phoenix said quickly, surprising me, "that I will protect her like she is my own blood, because she is."

I exhaled. "Thank you."

"I should be at your apartment within the next two hours. If I don't hear from you within twenty-four hours, I'm getting her to safety and calling in reinforcements."

"I'd like to keep this within The Family." I swallowed the indignation that I was referring to their Family and not my own.

"The Five Families are one," Phoenix said. "We are separate when we need to be, but lately more united than usual. Apparently, Russians force us to keep needing family reunions," he joked. "Go do what you need to do. Right now, Sergio's working on hacking the entire Petrov empire. He doesn't just mean to helps us discover the location of the two whorehouses. He means to drain all Petrov's resources and make it look like the Feds."

I let out a dark chuckle. "Wonderful, and I'm assuming the Feds will turn the other way when they realize our involvement?"

"But of course." Phoenix answered. "Try not to die, Nik. Love has a way of making things seem less dark... I would hate for you to stop breathing before you get the chance to experience sunlight for the first time."

My heart beat wildly in my chest—for the woman sleeping in the other room. I would live. I had to live. For her. I would find a way.

Petrov motioned for his men to step back as he reached into his pocket, pulled out a cigar and took his time lighting it, drawing a few puffs before addressing me again. "My daughter... she died."

For a minute I panicked then remembered Maya wasn't technically his, so he had to be referencing Andi.

"She died well." I nodded. "We attended the funeral."

"By we, am I to assume you took Maya with you?"

"She does work for me." I said in a bored voice. "So unless you want me to lock her in a tower for the next year, travel will be necessary."

"You touched her." Petrov motioned for one of his men, a cell phone was tossed into the air, he grabbed it then pulled up two pictures of us getting on the plane.

Thankfully, my hand was on her lower back.

Even better?

She looked pissed.

"Apologies." I fought to hide my grin. "By touching I thought you were referring to sex but were too polite to say so. Yes, I touched her, on the back, I've even touched her hand by accident while opening the door for her." I snapped my fingers. "Damn it, I've even seen her bare feet, so if you mean to kill me over an infraction like that, or rip up the contract simply because we had different definitions of the word touch, then by all means, pull out your guns and blast my ass off, but

275

know this." I took a step forward. "I always have a failsafe. Always. Do you really want to take the chance that upon my death, I rain hell on your empire by releasing every piece of information I've collected on you over the years? Worse yet, do you really want to take the chance that I haven't asked the Italians for help?"

"Even you wouldn't go that far." Petrov's face turned a deep red. "Working with the Italians…" His eyes narrowed and then he broke out into a smile as he patted my shoulder. "Enough of business… I simply wanted to make sure that you understood the terms of our agreement. If you've touched her in a way that causes her to remember… well… I may not be able to kill you, but I could kill her." I flinched. "And I do think that would be worse for you, would it not? Knowing it was your fault. Knowing that you failed twice?"

"She remembers nothing," I lied. "I even placed the very same masks in her bedroom… nothing has triggered her… yet."

"Yet?"

"I'm a doctor. Not God." My fists clenched. "And I can't read minds. I simply tell the weak ones what to do…." With a smirk I leaned forward and snapped my fingers twice. "Like this."

"Stop it!" Petrov stumbled backward. He'd always been afraid of someone taking over his mind, afraid that his mind was not his own, especially after seeing what I could do, what I did do to his soldiers for him. He had a very real fear of seeing me snap my fingers ever since I helped make his last *Sovietnik* jump off a twelve story building.

I smiled. "I believe we are done?"

Petrov adjusted his coat then slowly heaved himself into the black SUV, I imagined the leather made a stretching noise as his weight settled against it. He slammed the door behind him. I was just getting ready to turn around and leave when the window rolled down.

Shit.

One gun shot rang out and then he yelled. "A reminder."

The window slid up, and the car glided away with the menacing growl of its engine.

Never turn your back on a Russian.

I fell to the ground in a heap, grabbing my side, the bullet had gone in and out in one clean shot, but I needed to stitch myself up. I limped to the car then was hit in the back of the head with something hard.

Gravel crunched against shoes as my body fell to the ground. I looked up as five men descended.

I could kill. I could fight.

But not against five.

Not with a fresh gunshot wound.

I kicked away from them and stood, just as arms wrapped around me. Two of the men took turns hitting me in the stomach. I hissed out a curse as my wound tore open.

They laughed when my head fell back against the two men holding me. Nearly blacking out, I tried to flex, preparing myself for the hits, but they kept coming, and my vision was starting to fade.

A loud gunshot stopped the next man from hitting. At first I thought I'd been shot again, but with two of the men holding me, two hitting, and one watching, nobody had a gun.

They looked at one another in confusion, while I tried to think of a way to escape.

Someone whistled and then Tex Campisi stepped out of the shadows, giant grin on his face as he held a semiautomatic in one hand and a baseball bat in the other.

He shrugged and said. "What? I have a hard time choosing weapons." His grin grew. "Who's first?"

The men laughed, one stepped forward. "There are five of us. And two of you, one half dead."

"Damn it." Tex shook his head. "You know? For a Russian, you're super smart, I bet you even went to high school while dip shit over there couldn't make it past first grade. Here's a tip. You point the gun at the target."

One of the guys started charging him, just as another gunshot rang out, but Tex's gun was pointed at the ground.

The guy fell over clutching his chest. He couldn't have been shot by a semiautomatic, considering his body hadn't been cut completely in half.

"You know how long it's been since I've shot something that stupid?" Chase stepped out of the darkness.

"But you shot at Tex yesterday," Nixon countered, joining the line where Tex and Chase stood.

"So I think," Tex scratched his head and looked around. "That makes it, what? Three against four?"

"We will kill you." The man holding me spat on the ground. "Italian bastards!"

"Hey, that's offensive," Chase piped up. "Some of us *are* bastards."

The man holding my body pushed me to the ground. I coughed up more blood, great, and looked up in shock as Frank Alfero stepped in the middle of the guys then opened fire.

Two gunshots, three, four, five, and then six more.

"I think they're dead." Tex slapped Frank on the back.

"Yes," Frank nodded, his face serious. "But, I have not had live targets in a while and I'm to be leaving for New York soon. Trace has been saying my vision is not what it used to be." He turned to them and shrugged. "And I do not like doctors."

"Great." I muttered from a pool of my own blood. "Does that mean I get to be another target?"

"Hey, Nikolai, didn't see you there." Chase laughed.

I rolled my eyes. "I have no energy to respond with

anything but get me the hell out of here. Now."

Nixon moved ahead of the guys and leaned down. "Why didn't you fight back?"

I rolled my eyes, trying to get to my knees. "Probably because I was shot in the side first, then sucker punched from behind before I had the chance."

Nixon grunted as he helped me to my feet.

"Thank you." I leaned against him more than I'd like to.

"Sick ride." Chase opened the door. "I'll drive us."

"Us?" I repeated.

"Phoenix may have let it slip where he was going... and we like killing as a family... it's more meaningful that way," Tex said then called out shotgun while Frank kicked at a few of the bodies then pulled out his phone.

"Yes." Frank nodded. "Five bodies... right next to the ocean, quite convenient... Thugs, an easy accident. Thank you, Chief." He laughed. "I'll let him know."

My ears were playing tricks on me, weren't they? "Cleanup crew?"

"Hell, no." Nixon barked. "The cops."

"You called the cops." Even as I said it I couldn't believe it. "Why in the hell would you call the cops? On the Russians? The cops can't do shit to Petrov. It's his town."

"Hah." Frank climbed in the car next to me. "As of one hour ago, it is mine. We've bought six of his ports, turned over evidence to the FBI. We do still have some lovely connections there, just lovely." I had a suspicion the new head of the organized crime division in Chicago was a woman, a very attractive, woman. "And I've known Bart for years."

"Who the hell is Bart?" I gave Nixon an apologetic look then ripped part of his shirt and started bandaging myself up.

He shrugged out of it then started helping without as much as a blink.

"Police Chief." Frank answered. "Known that man

twenty years."

"They golf together," Chase said in a bored tone. "Every labor day weekend in Florida."

I bit out a curse as I touched my bruised face.

"Yeah, you look like shit." Nixon said unapologetically. "Good thing they didn't kill you, Phoenix would be pissed to have to protect another Russian."

"Technically…" I panted. "She's half Italian."

All talking in the car ceased.

"Shit." I was starting to black out. "Keep me awake."

"So, Maya's hot." Chase winked at me in the rearview mirror just as I lunged for him, pumping too much of my blood all over the leather seats.

Nixon smacked him in the back of his head. "He said to keep him awake not make him want to shoot you."

"I'm married. I was kidding, and look, his color's already better," Chase argued.

I groaned into my hands. "How did you buy out Petrov?"

"Sergio, snapped out of some of his… uh, funk, and got pissed, like real pissed," said Chase.

Right. I knew Andi's husband was an expert hacker who used to work for the FBI, but I also knew the guys were giving him time to grieve.

"The minute you left he started working on locating the last two houses, as you know, and ended up finding a lot of other information that we knew we could find extremely useful…" He paused and then added. "Not judging, but your grandmother is scary as hell."

"Shit!" I slammed my hand against the leather as my arm went completely numb. "I needed to be at the clinic tonight."

"In your condition." Nixon shook his head. "You aren't going anywhere, and unless you want stitches in the shape of a dick, I'd probably stay awake so you can make sure one of the guys can help stop the bleeding."

My vision clouded again. "Just text her for me tell her I've been shot… hell tell her I almost died, just make sure she doesn't…" I tried to find the right words, wasn't sure how much they knew. If Sergio really had dug up those files, then my name was in them, and so was hers, my family's, all of our secrets. I started sweating for an entirely different reason.

Nixon nodded to me then said in a lowered voice. "The evidence against your family… dynasty…" It seemed he was trying to choose his words carefully. "…was destroyed. Sergio mentioned something about her mental state. I'll be sure to let Frank send the text. He can handle things more delicately. Where's your phone?"

I held in another moan while I reached into my pocket, typed in my security code and handed my phone to Nixon. "He does know the definition of the word delicate? Because he just shot four men in cold blood for target practice."

"Good shots too. Right in the head and chest." Tex said approvingly while Chase chuckled.

Nixon's eyes didn't leave mine. "I'll send it."

"To Jac." I felt shame for my family in that moment, shame and relief, that for the first time in my life, I would no longer have to bear the secrets on my shoulders alone.

"We've got you." Nixon nodded then started furiously typing away on my phone while I gave in to the darkness.

CHAPTER FORTY-FIVE

When you meet a man you judge him by his clothes, when you leave,
you judge him by his heart. —Russian Proverb

Maya

HE SCARED ME. HIS ENTIRE PRESENCE felt... angry, tense. And he
also reminded me of someone, something, I wasn't entirely
sure what, maybe it was just the way he moved about the
room. He moved like a predator, like he was faking a calm on
the outside while a war was being fought on the inside.

"Sit." Phoenix was leaning back against the white leather
couch, his legs propped up on the table, everything about his
position appeared relaxed but his face was tight, his eyes
piercing right through me. He ran a hand through his semi-
buzzed hair and bit out a curse before muttering something in
Italian and standing. "You know what? I'll stand for this. I
think I need to stand."

I sat on the other end of the couch and folded my hands

in my lap.

"Wine." He said without looking at me. "I thought it might be better than coffee."

"Better for me or you?"

"Both." He turned on his heel, hiding a smirk from me as he cursed again and then finally sat down, leaning forward on his knees. "I'll say it once, not twice, so you need to listen and wait to ask questions until the end. It's the only way I'll get through this. Know that talking about my past isn't just something I don't like doing, it's something I don't do, not for anyone but my wife, and only because I love her and know it helps heal wounds that would otherwise fester if she didn't kiss the darkness away."

"You know, I think I'll drink first." I reached for the wine waiting on the table, gulped down four swallows then set it back.

"Better?" Phoenix asked.

"No."

He laughed, it sounded funny on him, like he wasn't used to it. He inclined his head toward me. "There's a lot of darkness in this world, a lot of bad... for a long time, my family was a part of it. Unlike the Russian mafia, the Italians have a pretty strict set of rules that run our organization. One of them being that in the beginning of our formation, we were to never involve ourselves with drugs or prostitution."

I snorted. "So what? You just involved yourself in money laundering? Extortion?"

He smiled. "Would it surprise you to know that most of our families own legitimate companies?"

"Yes."

"Well, then surprise." He shrugged. "Our family is not what it used to be, the five families have been forced to change with the times, but when I was younger... my family, the De Langes were the most hated because we were willing to do anything for a profit. And my father, noticing that we were losing the respect of the other bosses as well as money, decided to do something... different."

I had an idea what different meant, but wanted to hear him say it.

"Prostitution rings and drugs... both of which he involved himself so heavily in that he not only got hooked on his own product but started selling girls, their virginity, to the highest bidder. He..." Phoenix coughed, then hung his head. "He tried to sell my stepsister. And by the time I was ten, I'd seen more evil than people have seen in a life time. It was my comfort, all I knew. Darkness was my blanket, my sanctuary. It became my temple, because I knew if it didn't, he would kill me for it. There are things you don't need to know, but what you do need to know is that at one point, my father, did, in fact, sell his own daughter."

My stomach clenched, like I was going to puke. "Why would he do that?"

"Money. Always money." Phoenix said in a bitter voice. "I of course didn't know of her existence until I took over the Nicolasi Family just this last year. Secrets, as I said, are what I deal in. Luca Nicolasi was one of the most well-known bosses in the five families, and he left everything to me, but he did business in secrets, he has so many people by the balls, people you wouldn't even—" He stood abruptly. "He has what I call Black Folders on hundreds of individuals."

Phoenix walked over to black messenger bag and pulled out a sleek black folder, then dropped it right on the table next to my wine. It wasn't very thick, the folder, but it was daunting, almost like opening it would unlock things I wasn't sure should be known.

"Truth, always comes out." Phoenix towered over me. He was lithe, muscular, intimidating, and dark, so very dark. "One of the greatest lies you will ever believe is that you can sin in silence and get away with it. Because most of the time silence is the loudest, it demands to be known, to be heard." He sighed and leaned down opening the first page of the folder.

I leaned over, my heart slamming against my chest.

It was a picture of me.

And beneath it was a name.

Maya De Lange.

It was me, but there was a different name. I knew my father wasn't really my father, but... that would mean. I glanced up at Phoenix. "You're my brother?"

He winced, as if the word held nothing but pain for him.

"I don't understand," I whispered. "I don't..." My eyes felt blurry, my body heavy.

"Lay down." He instructed in a soft voice. "I won't let anything happen to you. Promise."

"I have a terrifying brother," I muttered as my mouth filled with cotton, a whooshing sound caused me to close my eyes.

"Thanks for the compliment," he chuckled.

The last thing I registered before my body gave in to the darkness.

****

I BLINKED MY EYES and winced as a man I'd only seen once had a flashlight pointed in my eyes. I pushed his arm away as tears filled my vision.

"Russians don't cry." He said it with a small smile and then tilted his head to the side. "Are you okay, Maya?"

"Yeah." I pressed my hands to my temples as Sergio slowly helped me to a sitting position in the couch. "Where's Phoenix?"

"Here." Phoenix said from somewhere behind me, soon

he appeared next to Sergio with coffee. "I added whiskey."

I pressed my lips together in a smile. "Smart man."

"My wife thinks so. That's all that matters." Phoenix's voice was still gruff, he and Sergio shared a look.

"She's fine." Sergio stood. "Just a little... stressed."

"No shit." Phoenix muttered. "I still can't believe you're here, why are you here?"

"I felt left out." Sergio shrugged. "And it's time."

Phoenix swallowed, looked away, then slapped Sergio on the arm just as the door to my apartment burst open revealing a bleeding Nikolai and Italians.

"Not on the couch!" Chase shouted. "It's white!"

"Who the hell cares?" Tex fired back. "Dead is dead! Save the couch or save the Russian?"

They all paused, like actually paused as if they were contemplating keeping the white couch pristine.

"What!" I shrieked, as Nikolai nearly collapsed against the floor.

"Sorry." Nixon grabbed Nikolai. "Old habits and all that."

"Damn it, let me sit!" Nikolai yelled, his face was bloody, his mouth swollen.

I lunged for him, but Sergio grabbed my arm. "Let me patch him up first, stop the bleeding and give him something for the pain."

"But—"

"Maya." Sergio shook his head once. "He knows. Believe me. And out of all these schmucks I'm the only one who actually has any medical knowledge that won't end up making Nikolai look like Frankenstein."

"Ha ha." Chase winked in my direction. "Tell me it wouldn't be hilarious if we had to start calling him that?"

Nikolai muttered a string of curses then tried to lean against the counter as blood dripped from a wound on his arm.

"I can walk." He grumbled half shoving half stumbling past the counter top and nearly falling into Sergio's arms in a brave effort to avoid the white couch.

Our eyes locked.

I knew why he would avoid it.

Because the blood on white made him sick—it was his thing, we all had them, and it hit me, in that moment, that maybe he was just as traumatized over our joint past as I was.

"Here." I quickly moved to his side and helped Sergio take him into the bedroom—my bedroom. It's where he belonged, with me, on my bed. Once he was positioned over the bed, I grabbed one of the red Afghans from the chair and tossed it over the white duvet in an effort to make sure he didn't see his own blood on the white—I didn't want to add emotional stress to his already physically stressed state.

"Sergio." Nikolai said his name like an angry curse. "Why the hell do I have six Italians in my home?"

"Seven." Sergio said in a bored tone just as Phoenix walked into the room with a large boxy briefcase, handed it to him and walked out. "Technically there are seven of us. Eight if you count Maya." He winked.

"Phoenix told you." Nikolai's shoulders slumped. "I'm sorry I was not here for you during that time."

"That's okay." I sat next to him on the bed and held his bloody hand. "You were too busy getting beat up."

"And by the looks of it." Sergio tore the rest of Nikolai's shirt with his hands. "Shot at."

"What!" I shrieked, grasping Nik's hand with more intensity than necessary.

"I'm fine," he assured me. "It went clean through."

"What the hell?" Sergio leaned down to examine the wound I guessed, then cursed again. "How did a simple bullet wound tear?"

"They beat the shit out of me and I tried to fight back. How else do you think it tore open?"

Sergio ignored him and placed the box on the floor, opened it, and pulled out a syringe.

My eyes widened, maybe too much because Sergio smirked in my direction. "Don't worry I'm not killing him, just giving him a nice dose of morphine that should make him dream of unicorns and shit."

"I don't need morphine," Nik grumbled as sweat started pouring down his temples.

I nodded to Sergio. "Give it to him."

"Maya I don't need—" He hissed as Sergio jabbed a needle into the inside of Nik's elbow. "I hate drugs."

"Always good when a doctor that invented his own special drugs actually hates them. That way you won't ever become an addict," Sergio said helpfully. "Now, you were only shot once, but I'm thinking..." His hands moved to Nik's chest and ran down. "Two broken ribs?"

Nik was silent and then, "One black eye, three broken ribs on my right side, possible internal bleeding, a pissed off kidney, and a giant gaping wound where I got shot. That's it. See?" He tried to get up, but fell back onto the bed and wheezed out. "I'm fine."

"Doctors are always the worst patients." Sergio grabbed another needle and jabbed it into Nik's neck, within seconds he was slumping back and then sleeping.

"What did you give him?" I asked in a panicked voice. I was surrounded by Italian mafia, and as much as I wanted to trust them, because Nik did, because my sister had, I was still apprehensive. There were seven of them, seven huge terrifying men in my apartment. What if they decided we weren't worth it? It's not like I wasn't aware of what Nikolai did now, or what my father had done to them, to Andi.

"Hey," Sergio drew my attention back to him. "Why

don't you help me wash off the blood so I can see where he needs to stitch?"

"He?"

"I highly doubt a surgeon as talented as Nikolai is going to want someone who dropped out of his fourth year of med school sewing him up. Besides, I'm hoping it doesn't look as bad once we get him cleaned up."

I nodded my head and went to the bathroom to grab a warm wet cloth, then made my way back into the bedroom and started softly wiping away the blood on Nikolai's side.

We worked in silence. I washed blood and Sergio did small sutures over a few cuts while simultaneously examining the bruising already forming across Nikolai's body.

After a few minutes of companionable silence. Sergio spoke. "She would have loved you."

My eyes filled with tears. "Do you think… it's possible to miss someone you never really knew?"

Sergio's hands froze. "Yes. I do. I think it's possible to miss someone simply from hearing memories from other people, knowing what that person was like, seeing someone talk about them as their faces light up with pleasure or excitement almost like the person is still breathing—living." He cleared his throat and started working again. "It's okay to feel loss, even though you weren't a part of her life." His eyes met mine. "I know if the situation were reversed, she'd feel the same way about you. She'd mourn you—because blood is blood, Maya. And we're all human… very breakable, most of us already broken, and she knew that better than anyone I'd ever met. She looked at the world like it deserves to be looked at."

"How?"

"With respect… with beauty."

A single tear ran down my face. I tried to wipe it away but Sergio grabbed my hand. "It's harder for those left behind then it is for those who leave. Just know… she laughed a lot, and drove me insane."

I licked my dry lips, a smile forming across them. "This world needs more laughter."

"It really does." He agreed as we both stared at Nikolai. "And he's going to need you…"

"He has me."

"Does he?" Sergio's eyes narrowed. "He's a killer."

"So are you."

"The very hands he uses to give life—he takes. You'll have to turn a blind eye… because it will always be in his blood."

"What will?"

Sergio shrugged. "Once you are in this life, you don't walk away, even when you want to. It follows you, tempts you, beckons you, promises you the world. He will always be mafia. So, I'd leave now if it's too much. I can make you disappear, and because of Andi, I'm going to give you that option." He stood. "You'd be in Canada by midnight, or Mexico if that's your preference, a house by the ocean, a new identity, passport, a new life, just say the word."

"But Nikolai—"

"He stays. This offer is for you. Not for him."

Panicked, I stared at Nikolai and stood, it was what he'd wanted for me, for us, to disappear, for me to be safe, but I didn't want safe if it meant I was away from him.

"My father, he will keep coming after Nik? After me?"

Sergio didn't answer.

"What would Andi do?"

Again no answer, he simply stared, his crystal blue eyes blazing holes through me.

I swallowed, straightening my shoulders and whispered, "If he stays. I stay."

"Thank God." Nikolai said in a hoarse voice. "And

Sergio, leave before I kick your ass."

"Hah," Sergio pulled out a needle and thread. "In your position you're more likely to fall on your ass and look stupid in front of the girl you love." He handed the needle to Sergio. "I'll let you do the honors."

"Thanks." He grumbled, "And Sergio?"

Sergio turned.

"Stab me with a needle again and I'm ripping out your throat while you're awake."

"Huh." Sergio nodded approvingly. "Succinylcholine, didn't know you were a fan."

"Out." Nikolai made a weird growling noise.

Sergio shut the door and yelled back. "You're welcome!"

CHAPTER FORTY-SIX

*We do not care what we have, but we cry when it is lost. –Russian
Proverb*

Nikolai

I COULD AT LEAST BE THANKFUL that Sergio hadn't used a full dose to knock me out, only enough to make the last ten minutes seem fuzzy. It had just felt better to close my eyes and relax back against the mattress as the drugs filtered through my system, the morphine, burned along my veins. I'd always had a terrible reaction to any opiates. They typically made me sick, which was a blessing, considering I had easy access to them at all times and thought myself a chemist when it came to making my JR serum.

I wasn't shocked he had offered her sanctuary.

What shocked me was that she declined his offer and stayed.

A smart woman would run far away, take the second

chance at a fresh start and never look behind her.

There was literally nothing but horror in her past, and I couldn't imagine the future would be roses and fairy tales either, not if she stayed with me. There would never be a time in her life that she wouldn't be reminded of her past, of our past, and I had to wonder if it would continually impact our present, filtering into our future.

With a sigh, I sat up as much as I could. "Maya, would you please grab a hand mirror from the bathroom?"

Frowning, she gave a simple nod went to the bathroom then returned with the mirror.

"Excellent. Can you please point it at my side, angle it down, a little farther." Her hands were shaking. I didn't blame her. I was a mess. "Thank you."

We didn't speak while I nimbly and quickly sewed up my wound in perfect sutures that would leave a slight white mark as if I'd been scratched.

Maya swayed on her feet.

"Maya?" I reached for her with my free hand, I just needed to cut the thread. "Are you going to pass out?"

She tugged her lower lip between her teeth and bit, causing my body, even numb with drugs, to tighten, to flush with lust.

"No." She shook her head. "That's just really… hot."

"What is?" I glanced down at my bare stomach. Surely she wasn't referring to me being shirtless? She'd seen me naked. I highly doubted my bruised body was doing it.

"That." She pointed to the hand still holding the needle. "You just stitched yourself up, perfectly, better than, well I don't even know, but it's just… sorry, is that inappropriate?"

"Very." I nodded seriously. "Let's be professional, Maya." My lips twitched in a barely contained smile.

"Right." She agreed crossing her arms. "Will that be all, Doctor?"

I let out a suppressed groan. "Hurry and cut this damn thread so I can kiss you."

"I didn't know Russians kissed Italians without protection." She ran her hands down her body, damn I would do just about anything for a taste, better than any drug.

"Very funny." I nodded toward the scissors. "Now, but before I accidently poke you."

"Hah." She wagged her finger in my face. "You mean like last night?"

I rolled my eyes and lay back against the mattress. "Go ahead, finish me off, kill me. I'll wait."

She gently crawled over me, careful not to put any weight on my body as she reached for the scissors and cut the thread. I grabbed her hand the minute it was free, bringing her fingertips to my lips, she tasted like home.

"How are you?" I wasn't that man, the one who asked emotional questions. I'd never cared, not until her.

Maya licked her lips, studying my mouth for a few seconds before answering. "I'm hanging in there."

"Well at least you haven't run away screaming yet."

"That would get me killed."

"Your father may be too busy to kill you right now... or at least too busy to threaten us, and when he does... I don't think we'll have problems finding people willing to fight for us. Apparently the Italians have been bored this last week, imagine that?"

Maya shuddered. "Bored means they haven't gotten to shoot something in a while? And seven days is a long time? Wow, talk about self-control. Should we give them a medal? Or at least gift them some wine?"

I burst out laughing, shocking myself at the fact I couldn't keep it in anymore. I'd gotten the shit beat out of me, one of my darkest secrets was about to get revealed to Maya, and I could laugh.

Because I loved her.

And when you have love—everything else seems to just fade into the background, the noise of your own heart beating, smothering out the screams of the past.

"Italians," I whispered tucking a piece of hair behind her ear with my good hand, "do love their wine."

She leaned down brushing her lips against mine. "And I love you."

My body hummed with pleasure and sang with completeness at her proximity. "You can say that... after everything? Even after the fear of tonight? After finding out your parentage?"

"You had nothing to do with my mom cheating and sleeping with Petrov's right hand man—absolutely nothing."

"No." I swallowed the lump of guilt. "But I knew. He was an outsider, trying to escape the pressure of his own crime family, and the sense of embarrassment he felt at being the poorest, most disrespected. I knew the information because of my father."

"Apparently everyone knew." Maya sighed. "In the grand scheme of things, does it really matter?"

"I don't know, does it?"

"Not really. No. If anything it just makes me thankful that I'm not blood related to a Russian gangster." I opened my mouth to speak but she pressed two fingers against it and whispered. "But I am in love with one."

I wasn't sure if it was the drugs or just having her close but my body felt warm the minute she said that. Still, she had to understand. "I won't ever be free of it."

Maya turned her head, giving me a view of her gorgeous long neck. I wanted to trail kisses from neck to navel, and then lower, drink her nectar until I was drunk on her. Her hand gently caressed the sickle tattoo. "I don't think either of us will ever be free of our pasts, but that doesn't mean we can't have a future, right?"

My body went rigid. There was one more thing, one more secret I'd kept close to me, a secret my family had kept even closer. It wasn't just something I could tell her, I'd have to show her the diary, explain to her the reasons, but worst of all. I'd have to make sure I talked with Jac first.

She was the loose cannon in all this, the very last part of my life that could unravel and destroy everything I held dear.

With a few simple words, strung together in one powerful sentence, my entire career would be over—my life, Maya's life, my reputation.

I shuddered.

"Are you cold?"

"No." I answered quickly, maybe too quickly if Maya's frown was any indication. "I'm just thinking."

"Well, stop." Maya sucked on my lower lip. I let out a moan and tried to pull her body closer but it hurt to move more than an inch. She smiled against my mouth. "It's kind of nice, having you semi-paralyzed while I take advantage of you."

I went still for an entirely different reason as my body went from hot to frigid. She had no idea what that statement meant to me.

Paralyzed, yet awake.

Woman's screams echoed in my head. I'd never been present for it, did that lessen my involvement? Make me any less of a killer?

"Maya, I need to talk to you about something." I grabbed her wrist pushing her back as much as I could without letting out a sharp cry of pain.

"Words can come tomorrow," she argued, her eyes drinking me in. "Right now, let me just love you. Whatever you have to say can wait, can't it?"

I was too exhausted to argue. "Yes. It can wait."

"Good." She kissed my forehead, "Now sleep, and dream of me."

"You're all I've dreamed of… since I saw you from across the room and my heart beat… mine." I drifted off with visions of Maya's smile.

CHAPTER FORTY-SEVEN

There is no evil without good. –Russian Proverb

Nikolai

A WEEK WENT BY, A WEEK where Jac refused to answer my texts, and the newspapers confirmed my worst fears.

The Pier Killer has been at it again, the crimes have been more abhorrent. Two female college students were found in the U district, their mouths taped shut, their eyes completely missing from their faces right along with every single female organ. Police are offering a monetary reward for any information. The total known victims of this serial killer now numbered twelve women.

I scowled and pushed the newspaper away. Most of the Italians had left, but Phoenix had stayed. I couldn't wait for him to leave. It was nauseating, hearing him talk to his wife on the phone all hours of the day. I told him we had things handled. Ever since Sergio helped take down Petrov's empires, I hadn't heard from him or from any of his *Byki's*.

I'd gone to the clinic four times in search of any information on Jac, but it was just as a I left it, the only change was that women were no longer getting brought to my door—which saddened me, not because it was part of my research but because I worried about them, worried about the women who at times, only made it through the night because they knew that when they came to my clinic I would make them forget.

It was my gift to them.

Because it was all I had to offer.

Heal them both physically and mentally, and if I can do neither… offer them another option.

I tapped my fingertips against the newspaper as anxiety built inside my chest. Maya was showering. She'd been inside the apartment all week, and I thought it would be nice for her to at least get outside and grab a coffee or something.

Phoenix walked back in the room and glanced down at the newspaper. "When are you going to tell her?"

Loaded question for seven in the morning. "I was going to tell her last week, then the following day, and the day after that, I don't even know how to start."

Phoenix pulled out a chair and sat. "Well you can always start with… you know those horror stories from the seventeen hundreds…."

"You aren't funny."

Phoenix shrugged. "Wasn't trying to be. It is the truth, isn't it? Sergio found some interesting shit on you, I'd have given my right arm to read that history… but some things are better left burned."

"Yes." Voice hoarse I shoved the newspaper off the table and covered my face with my hands. "I have to kill her."

"You have no other choice." Phoenix agreed. "It is what's best."

"But I love her."

"I never said you didn't… but she cannot go on like this, there's been too much psychological damage, she's… going to go insane, and—"

"I know." I was disgusted with the whole situation. "Just… give me some time."

He shook his head. "Not something you have in spades, man. Do it tonight, or I do it for you."

I jumped to my feet. "The hell you will!"

"Then get your head out of your ass and get it done." He seethed, stomping off into the living room.

I smacked my hand against the counter top just as Maya walked around the corner stumbling into the chair Phoenix had accidently kicked over. She looked pale.

"Are you feeling well?" I asked.

"Yes." She nodded her head vigorously. "You know, I really am… feeling…" She tugged at her shirt. "Hot and cooped up. You think I can just head down to the lobby and grab a coffee on my own? Maybe sit outside?" She swallowed like she was nervous as I stood. "By myself."

I narrowed my eyes. It's not that I didn't want her to have her freedom, I just didn't like the idea of her going downstairs without a bodyguard, and the original plan had been to get some fresh air together. Then again, there were security guards everywhere; I also had access to all lobby cameras. "Sure." Even as I said it, doubt crept in, making me anxious. I shrugged it off. "Just be safe, and bring your phone?"

"Great!" She smiled brightly and went to the door, opened it, then slammed it behind her while I was left wondering why something felt wrong.

Two minutes later I was still staring at the door when Phoenix waltzed back into the kitchen. "What crawled up your ass and died?"

"She didn't kiss me goodbye," I whispered.

"Is that not normal?"

"Maya's always been… emotional…" I sat and folded my arms then shook my head. "I'm reading into things."

Phoenix placed a glass of orange juice on the table and then set his Glock right next to it. "So, what will it be? You want her blood on your hands or do you need me to do your dirty work?"

"I'll owe you."

"You owe me about a bazillion favors, just add to the list, remember? I thrive off secrets."

"No." I pushed his gun away. "I'll do it, make it painless, she'll simply go to sleep and not wake up."

"Where's the fun in that?"

"Fun?" I had trouble controlling my voice as rage filled me. "There is absolutely nothing fun about killing your own flesh and blood—killing the person who basically raised you."

I stood to my full height, which matched his. I was just itching for a fight, I could feel my blood pressure rising as he smirked and inclined his head. "Good. Keep that rage in place, it's the only way you'll be able to do this without living with guilt for the rest of your life… sometimes it's best to fuel the rage with anger so that when you look back on this moment, it's not with regret."

"When the hell did you get so smart?"

"I read lots of books, doc." Phoenix slapped me on the back. "Now, it looks like we have a woman to hunt."

"I know where she typically waits for victims." I sighed. "I just…"

"We'll split them up and find her in no time." Phoenix grabbed his phone out of his pocket, but first we need to figure out a babysitter for Maya.

"Shit!" I shoved him away and limped toward the back room where I had left the iPad, I quickly logged in to the cameras and located the ones in the lobby.

Maya was sitting in a chair sipping coffee, I instantly

relaxed. Until I saw a familiar face in cowboy boots approach her table and sit.

"Phoenix!" I yelled. "Jac's here!"

CHAPTER FORTY-EIGHT

The tongue speaks but the head does not know. — Russian Proverb

Maya

I SIPPED MY DRINK—NOT EVEN sure what I'd ordered, numbness had overtaken me the minute I stumbled upon Nik and Phoenix's conversation. After everything we'd been through together—he was going to kill me.

Who else could he be talking about?

And why wasn't I running around screaming my head off? It's not like I could go to the police, I mean I could, but what exactly would I say? They'd have me file a restraining order, and who would actually believe me?

I shivered as I glanced down at my latte, it tasted like nothing.

Was it foolish of me to still be sitting in that building?

Stupid to think about going back upstairs and trying to convince him that I wasn't so psychologically damaged that I was going to snap.

How could he possibly believe that? After everything that had been dropped into my lap over the last few weeks most people would be committed! I'd done well all things considered.

"I love you," he'd whispered.

Tears stung, causing my vision to blur as I tried to keep myself from choking out a sob, it hurt my throat, but it was nothing compared to the slicing pain I felt through my chest as my heart crumbled into a million pieces.

Most girls crying over broken hearts didn't have to worry about being killed, but maybe it would be less painful.

Because how, after knowing everything I knew, could I possibly live without him in my life? A few tears escaped as I covered my face with my hands. Of course that was it.

I was certifiably insane.

Because I was mourning my killer.

Maybe I did deserve to die.

Maybe I'd just lie down on the bed like I've lost every ounce of sense and hand him the knife to stab me with.

I was being dramatic as fear and sadness kept me rooted to that seat like I had no other option but to sip coffee and think about all the times he'd whispered his love out of one side of his mouth while the other continued to warn me against him, warn me of how dangerous he was.

Sergio had said Nik would always be mafia, always thirst for blood.

And now he wanted mine.

There was nothing romantic about it, nothing.

It made me angry, frustrated, terrified, and if I was being honest, I was sorry for myself, sorry that the same man who breathed new life into me, was going to be the one to take it.

Run! My mind screamed.

Stay. My heart whispered.

"Maya!" A female voice interrupted my inner battle. "Over here!" Jac waved a hand up at me and approached the table. "Oh dear, he told you, didn't he?"

"Told me?" Everything about Jac set me on edge, like she was a drunk tightrope walker just waiting to take the plunge.

"About me." She sighed sadly. "About our family."

"Um, no, but, you know I really should get back." This was danger. This woman sitting in front of me with the friendly smile and bright pink lipstick, this was wrong, everything about the way her cold eyes stared right through me caused panic.

I would run back into my killer's arms—away from her, any day of the week.

I made a motion to stand, just as something pricked the inside of my wrist. With a curse I jerked back my hand. "What the hell did you just do?"

"Shhh." Jac smiled warmly. "It's finally going to be okay. You'll be safe now. I promise. You'll finally be safe."

"I am safe!" With him, I was safe. Safer than with her. My vision blurred as my heavy body leaned against the table, I tried to hold myself up with my hand but it missed the table completely. Jac very smoothly moved beneath one arm and started walking me out of the building.

People would see us right? They'd see my struggle.

I fought to keep my eyes open and moaned out, "Help," as we passed two large figures.

They did nothing.

"Help!" I tried louder this time while Jac talked over me about the pitfalls of drinking in the morning, first scolding me about being publicly intoxicated and then saying good thing you have family like me to help you out!

"No." I shook my heavy head as my chin drooped to my chest.

"Ah, it's working so much faster than I thought. I only

stole as much as I could carry without him noticing, though he'll for sure notice now." She was breathing heavy and then we were in the alleyway between the two office buildings, the trunk of her car was already open. I had no strength left, a cold prickling sensation ran down my legs and then they gave out just as she pushed me against the back. Why was nobody coming after me? This wasn't normal! It was daylight!

Maybe that was the danger, my mind whirled as my mouth filled with cotton, the danger in profiling. You always assume the homeless man on the street has a knife, never once looking at the seventy year old woman with heels and a gun.

"Shhh, now." Jac pressed a finger against my lips. "Make sure you take long even breaths, don't want you to hyperventilate or anything."

I moaned.

"That's it, sweetie." She patted my check, hard, really hard, I could tell because of the force but the sting wasn't there, why was my cheek numb? Like I'd gone to the dentist and lost all feeling in my mouth, my tongue was heavy too. Her silver blue eyes narrowed. "That's it, dear."

The trunk slammed shut blanketing me in darkness, freaking the hell out of me, I willed my feet to lift to kick the taillight, like I'd seen in the movies but no matter how many times I tried, no part of my body moved.

I could still breathe, but would that go too? If my muscles were paralyzed did that mean my organs were going to be too?

Tears stung, the only reason I knew I was crying was because I couldn't see anymore, only blurry black.

Minutes went by that felt like hours, and then the car stopped. I tried to scream but only small moans and whimpers escaped. Sunlight burned my eyes as the trunk was opened again. Jac put her hands on her hips and stared at me. "Now, to get you out, that's always the trick! Be right back!"

She walked away, I couldn't see where, only blue sky telling me we weren't completely outside of the City yet if the seagulls and noise were any indication.

Jac pushed a gurney that was level with the trunk right up to the car and then pulled my body toward it. I fought her, or at least I tried to but she was stronger than she looked, easily heaving me onto the gurney and strapping me down.

Terror shot through me in that moment.

She was batshit crazy.

And she was going to kill me. I had no doubt, that this wasn't some sort of funny prank or idea she'd had because I'd somehow touched her grandson and it pissed her off.

Humming, Jac pushed the gurney toward the back of a large red house, why were we passing the house? I heard the sound of a waterfall and clenched my eyes shut hoping and praying that didn't mean she lived on water and was about to push me into it—drowning terrified me, not breathing or moving was right up there. I continued to struggle against the restraints but again my body didn't move.

"Succinylcholine." Jac leaned down and patted my cheek then laughed out loud. "Only about one hundred milligrams or so do the trick well, though you never want to administer too much lest you kill the patient before the cleansing begins."

Cleansing?

"You should be able to talk though." She tilted her head. "I think I may have given you a bit too much, which just means we'll have to wait until you can participate."

Participate?

"It's always better to confess your sins aloud before you die." She opened a large door and pushed the gurney into the dimly lit room.

Lights flickered on around me, bright lights, like the ones you'd see in an operating room.

Everything was white.

I felt sick to my stomach, but held the coffee down. If I puked, I'd just suffocate, right?

I squeezed my eyes shut again, and thought of Nik, of the way he kissed me, touched me. Was this really how my life was going to end? At the hands of some crazy lady? I'd do anything—anything to be back in that apartment, even if it meant I was on the other end of the trigger, awaiting my fate. Better to die in love, than in fear.

Jac continued to hum while I heard the clatter of metal against metal. Finally, after a few minutes, she started talking again. "I warned him. I truly did. I warned all of the men in my family. Don't get too close, but they did, all of them, too close."

What the hell?

"We must keep the memory of our ancestors alive and cleanse the world of evil... of promiscuity. It is the only way for us to make it, to redeem the earth. It is up to us. Pity." She sighed. "Because I truly liked you. I liked all of them."

All of them?

"Oh I didn't kill them all, I simply... scared them into running off, it was easy. Though the bad ones, the ones with disease, I always end them, it is our legacy, after all." She peered over me, her pupils mere pinpoints. "Do you know who I am, dear?"

Satan. She was Satan.

"It was August, 1888, the date of the first kill. Funny, how so many historians and scholars assume that only a man could do such work." She scowled. "Mary Ann Nichols, that bitch had it coming." Light flickered off a silver knife that Jac waved in the air. "But he was weak, so weak, he cheated on my great-great-great-grandmother. Cheated on her several times actually, though it took years to find all the women, and oh she had to be careful, so very careful. That first kill was her first taste of revenge, of blood, and when she returned home

Andrew asked what she'd done, why was she covered in so much blood."

Jac pulled up a rolling stool and laid the knife on the table. "And you know what she told him? She told him that she was going to cleanse the city of its darkness, one by one, and she would start with every woman he'd ever been with. Of course, his immediate response was to beg forgiveness, but do you know what that bastard did that next night? He went to warn another woman, leading good old Grandmother to her next victim. She didn't attack that night, merely watched and waited, she was patient like that, so very patient. It's been an issue in our family, infidelity. It matters not, now…"

What was she talking about?

"Oh…" She patted my head. "You look confused…didn't you ever pay attention in school, dear? Listen very carefully…my grandmother wasn't just any killer, she was a serial killer." Jac chuckled, a sinister sound that shot terror into my heart. "All the women in our family have carried on the tradition… Do you know who I am?"

No. And I didn't want to. I just wanted to escape, go back in time to where I was lying in Nikolai's bed.

I closed my eyes.

"Open your eyes," she commanded.

I tried to shake my head.

Sudden pressure against my neck had me opening my eyes. "Oh good, you're starting to feel again, but the sad part is, you still won't be able to move, you'll simply feel everything but be unable to run away. Wonderful, isn't it?"

"No." I finally got the word out.

She smiled warmly. "Honey at least your death will be honorable, a penance of the sins of our family. If I do not kill, then our family is not successful, the one woman who tried to go against the tradition ended up getting killed in a freak train accident along with everyone in her family but her two children, me and my sister, rest her soul. We are history in the making. Think hard… prostitutes being killed… London."

I let out a gasp.

"I'm Jack the Ripper…" she whispered in my right ear. "And I will listen to your confession—before I cut you apart."

CHAPTER FORTY-NINE

The end is the crown of any work. — Russian Proverb

Nikolai

WE MADE IT DOWN TO THE lobby just in time to see Jac's car speed away. I couldn't exactly run down the street, I'd end up doing more damage to my body, and I suspected I'd need my strength for the upcoming battle.

Phoenix grabbed his cell and started barking orders into it while I reached for my own phone and stared down at it. If Jac really had snapped, there were only two places she would take Maya, two places where she could do her work.

The clinic.

Or her house.

The one I had bought and paid for.

Along with her operating room, where all the murders of the sick girls had taken place and now, I imagined, many more. I'd turned a blind eye because of the guilt, because of the love I still had for the woman who had helped raise me.

But she had just stolen my reason for living.

So I was going to rip her lungs out through her throat while she watched.

"Phoenix." I snapped my fingers. "I'm texting you the directions to the clinic. If Maya's there, make sure you call an ambulance after you bring down Jac, I don't know what drugs she gave her. Typically, she gives the type that paralyzes your body, but if given too much Maya could die."

"Where are you going?" Phoenix's eyes were crazed.

"Her house. There's only two safe locations where she has the right instruments to..." *Torture. Kill. Maim. Destroy.* "Do what she does."

"Be safe." Phoenix slapped me on the shoulder then went running out the door while I went in the opposite direction, half stumbling toward the parking garage so I could grab my car.

Rage filled my line of vision, bloody rage, a rage I could barely control as I finally stumbled into my car, started it, and sped toward Jac's house.

I would end her.

And I would do it slowly.

The clock on my dash blinked back at me, and I prayed, I prayed that Maya would be strong, that she would fight back, but most of all I prayed I'd have time to save her life, even if it meant sending her away so the reminder of whose blood pulsed through my body didn't haunt her every breath.

CHAPTER FIFTY

One does not look for good, from good. —Russian Proverb

Maya

STAY ALIVE, STAY ALIVE, STAY ALIVE. I was singing the mantra in my head, actually singing it, hoping that if I just kept singing then it would be true and Jac wouldn't use the knife she was currently holding over my head.

I closed my eyes and prayed just as the knife sliced across my hand. I screamed as loud as I could—which, thanks to the drugs, still wasn't very loud.

"Just checking to see if the medication has worn off." Jac gave me a freakish smile. "You know, I didn't choose this life. It chose me." She wiped my blood across her hand then lifted it to her mouth. "If it wasn't for me, Nik wouldn't have the career he does, nor the success. It is up to him to continue the family name, or birth a female who is stronger, who can do it for him."

"You're sick!" I yelled. "You're going to get caught."

Jac burst out laughing. "We haven't been caught for over a century. Grandmother was married to a surgeon, she aided in all of his research. She was more brilliant than he any day of the week. We've always been a family of medicine, and those who practice medicine may as well be gods as we hold lives in the palms of our hands." My blood dripped off her fingertips, she rubbed them together, examining it. "I grew tired of killing prostitutes... tired of killing the sick. Where's the fun in killing those who are already knocking on death's door?" Her gaze met mine. "But killing the pure? That's a challenge. It takes finesse, finding the right people, snuffing their lives out at the very last moment." She leaned over her breath fanned over my face. "You will scream. It will hurt, and then?" She shrugged. "You will be no more. I'm sorry it has to be this way, but I can't afford to let him develop a conscience. I can't afford to lose my grandson just because he thinks himself in love with you."

"He'll kill you," I said, my voice filled with tremors.

"Hah!" Jac waved the knife over my body. "He adores me. I raised him to be what he is today... I've saved him, and you've done nothing but confuse him." Her eyes narrowed. "And for that, you will die."

Light flickered off the knife as she raised it above her head. "One cut, slightly to the left of the navel, and then, I'll open you up, and remove every last female organ you have... I do this first, in honor of my family, in honor of my grandmother, and then. I kill you."

The knife dove toward my skin and then hovered as she leaned over and sliced across my stomach. Unbearable pain washed over me. I wanted to thrash, instead I screamed until my voice was hoarse as the burning, tearing sensation got worse.

"Drop the knife." Nik's authoritative voice sounded from

the door. "Now."

Jac turned, bloody knife in hand. "Oh, good! You're just in time. I needed an assistant, if you'll just grab an apron so you don't get blood on your clothes I'll—"

Nik lunged for Jac shoving her against the gurney and pulling the knife from her hands then turning it on her.

Her expression was one of shock, disbelief. "You don't mean to harm me, do you?"

"Not at all." He said in an empty voice, confirming my worst fear, that he wanted me dead, that maybe he was just as bad as he'd said. He leaned in then ran the knife very slowly along her neck and said in a low voice. "I mean to kill you."

Her eyes widened and then one slit to her neck, it was quick too quick for Jac to do anything but gurgle out a bloody. "Nik…" Before falling to the floor as she choked to death.

I couldn't see, but I could hear, and those sounds would probably haunt my dreams for an eternity.

Nik stepped over her and turned his eyes to me.

"No!" I yelled. "Don't hurt me please don't hurt me!"

His face fell. "Maya, I love you, I would never hurt you."

Panicked, my eyes filled with tears. "You said this morning…." I couldn't get the words out. "You would kill me, you said!"

Nik cursed, cupping my face with both hands. "I said I was going to kill her—Jac—not you. I wouldn't harm a hair on your head. I love you."

Tears made it nearly impossible to make out his face. "But, you said her past and—"

"I imagine she told you enough about her past for you to know how crazy she was… how crazy my bloodline is." He swallowed. "But that's my burden, not yours. My father…" He licked his lips and slowly started undoing the straps around my body. "He was… sickened by what our family did, he joined the mafia in hopes that it would protect us when Jac

RIP

went insane, when she went after us. We also needed protection from the feds, from the police if they ever discovered the truth. A trade was made, but my father, he knew too much, he was killed leaving me to pick up the pieces to make a deal with the devil in order to protect the woman who'd helped raise me. I never believed it, believed she would go crazy."

My body was free from its restraints but I still couldn't move anything. Nik lifted me into his arms and carried me out of the building, I was able to see more, see the large barn next to the house and Nik's waiting Audi.

The minute I was safely laid across the back seat, he reached for my stomach, his hands came back bloody. "It's not deep, superficial, probably hurt like hell."

My teeth started to chatter. "Y-yes."

"Shhhh." He kissed my forehead. "You're going into shock, just listen to my voice. I want to take you away from here, somewhere safe, it's best I treat you... understand?"

I couldn't nod but I managed a weak whimper.

He kissed my mouth. "Just stay awake, talk with me."

CHAPTER FIFTY-ONE

Falling in love is like falling into a swimming pool. — Russian Proverb

Nikolai

I MADE HER TALK ABOUT FRIVOLOUS things like her favorite restaurants in Seattle, all the places she wished to visit— anything to keep her talking and coherent. I'd already sent a text to Phoenix that we were on our way back to the apartment. I kept emergency supplies, enough to be able to stitch her up without having to worry about her having scars or being in pain.

It took me a good fifteen minutes to finally get her into the apartment and over to the couch.

"No!" She gasped. "It's white. Not the couch."

Guilt slammed me in the chest, stealing my breath away. "Maya, it's fine... I need to lay you down now."

"You hate red on white."

"I also hate butterflies."

"What?" She gasped.

"It was a joke." I smiled. "Now lie down."

"But—"

"Don't argue with your doctor."

"Horrible bedside manner." She shivered.

"Now, Maya." I set her down carefully while Phoenix shared a look with me and left the room. "You know that's not true."

Her teeth wouldn't stop chattering.

"Maya." I grabbed a syringe of morphine. "I'm just going to give you a little bit to numb the pain while I stitch, it will also relax you."

Without waiting for her answer, I injected her.

She went silent, her eyes boring holes into me as I slowly stitched up her stomach. Six stitches. Nothing huge, nothing life altering, but enough to pray that Jac rotted in hell for putting Maya through what she had.

"I can take it away," I whispered, hating that the words were coming out of my mouth. "But I have to take it all away."

"What are you talking about?" Maya blinked, tried to sit up then winced and lay back down as I knelt next to her on the couch.

"The memories." I was an ass. "Just say the word, and I'll make you think you've been in another car accident, I don't know if it will work but I can try, I can take away the bad."

"Oh, Nik." Maya placed a hand over mine. "You can't do that."

"I can try."

She smiled. "Life is hell."

"Yes."

"It sucks."

"These aren't exactly points in your favor."

"My point..." Her lower lip trembled. "...is you can't

take away the bad, without taking away the good. The good is you. If I need to keep the bad memories in order to keep you. Then I choose the bad."

"But—"

She pressed a finger to my lips. "Kiss me."

"My grandmother almost killed you. I'm not just part of the Russian mafia but I'm guilty of turning a blind eye while my own flesh and blood went on a killing rampage, and what's worse? I encouraged it, because I wanted no part of it. And you want me to kiss you? Still?"

"Not just still," Maya whispered. "Always."

"But—"

"Damn you're argumentative. See? Horrible bedside manner."

I rolled my eyes. "Maya, be serious. Our life... it will never be easy."

"Who wants easy?" She shrugged. "Give me hard." With a grin she slid her hand down to the button of my slacks.

"Very funny."

Her hand inched further. "And true."

I groaned. "What the hell am I going to do with you?"

"Love me." She sighed. "Keep me safe."

"With my life," I vowed. "I'll do both."

Maya drifted off to sleep, not a drug-induced one, not one that was pushed upon her, but one of absolute exhaustion. Her body needed to heal, her mind even more so.

"How is she?" Sergio was the first to ask when I emerged from her room two hours later for something to eat. She was still sleeping, but I had forgotten to eat and knew that if I didn't take care of myself there was no way I could take care of her.

The rest of the guys had gone to the hotel across the street, Sergio had stayed behind to make sure that the security at my apartment hadn't been infiltrated from the outside. I assured him that I had the best of the best.

Which earned a smirk and a, "Clearly not, if it wasn't me who did it for you." I let the arrogant ass take a look, too exhausted to do anything except grunt and give him all of my passwords, reminding myself to change them later since the bastard would probably memorize them as I said them.

"Good." I finally nodded, rummaging through the fridge for something to eat that wasn't a fruit or vegetable.

I felt a pat on my back as Sergio handed me a hot Panini.

"Did this just appear out of thin air?" I asked taking the sandwich.

"Phoenix dropped off food." He shrugged. "I kept yours wrapped in foil in the oven just in case you were going to be a while."

"The same Phoenix who kills for fun and wears a permanent smile while pointing a gun at your head? That Phoenix?" I asked dryly.

"The very one." Sergio managed a small smile. "Would you believe me if I told you he used to only eat the color green, freaked the shit out of him to eat anything with color, like he didn't deserve color in his life. Therefore, he didn't deserve it in his food."

I pulled out a bar stool and sat. "I've heard worse."

"Oh yeah?" Sergio sat next to me and continued typing on his laptop, the screen was black, his fingers were typing in code so fast that it was hard to keep up. "Let's hear it."

"I hate vodka."

Sergio's fingers froze in a hover position over the keyboard as he lifted his chin in my direction. "No shit?"

"I prefer wine."

"Hell, Tex is right. You really are going Italian aren't you?"

I rolled my eyes. "Don't insult me."

"You should be so lucky, Russia," Sergio said and then

hung his head and whispered. "It slipped, calling you Russia. It was my nickname for Andi." His voice cracked. "You know, for a psycho doctor you really do have a good point. Some days the memories hurt so bad that it's hard to breathe."

"Only real memories can do that," I murmured. "The fake ones don't hurt... the smoke screen rarely causes a physical reaction that you feel from your chin down to your feet. The more powerful the memory, the stronger the connection."

"Good to know it's normal that I want to puke all the time when I think of what I'm missing, when I wake up and she's not taking up the space next to me, when my hands ache with the memory of hers."

I couldn't speak. I'd never understood love, not really. Not until Maya, that moment when I thought I was going to lose her, I couldn't think of anything except what if, what if I don't get there in time, what if she dies, what if I lose the only reason I have for breathing?

"I have to hope," I finally answered with a sigh. "That it will get better and that a girl like Andi would be pissed as hell that you're sitting here whining like a girl."

Sergio burst out laughing. "Shit, she'd kill me if I ever shed a tear over her. I promised her I wouldn't, and I've broken that promise more than I'd care to admit." He typed a few more things into the computer then slowly shut the top, turned to face me and stood. "I'd like to say it's been a pleasure but..."

I held out my hand. "But?"

"It's been interesting... your fire walls are solid, big brother isn't watching and I've deleted your family's virtual thumbprint from the Internet. You can thank me later." He heaved his bag over his shoulder. "I'm off to New York, text me if you need me."

"New York?" I parroted. "Not Chicago?"

"Secrets." Sergio nodded. "It seems a bit of our family has

gotten… out of hand. Guess who was voted to go enforce the law?"

"Try not to leave too many bodies in your wake."

"True or false, you told someone to walk into a fire and watched them burn alive? Calling the kettle, doc?"

I didn't answer, instead shifted uncomfortably on one foot then the other.

"That's what I thought." He smirked then called back. "Stay out of prison… and Nik?"

"Yeah?"

Sergio took in the large apartment, his eyes flickering from one object to another. "She would have been proud to see you settle down… Domesticated."

"Hah." I nodded. "Andi would have laughed her ass off then asked who I hypnotized to be in a relationship with me, at worst she would have asked if I paid someone."

"Sounds like her." Sergio whispered, then gave me a middle finger salute—not that I expected anything different—and shut the door quietly behind him. I went over and locked it then finished eating my sandwich.

CHAPTER FIFTY-TWO

You will only understand your misfortune when you fall in love —
Russian Proverb

Maya

THE ROOM WAS DARK, MAKING IT impossible to know what time
it was or how long I'd been sleeping. Memories assaulted me
like automatic gunfire: of my attack, of Jac, of Nikolai rescuing
me. I shivered just as the door to the bedroom opened.

Light flooded through, casting a shadow of Nikolai's lean
sexy body. I let out a huff of air as he made his way toward
me, his stance cautious, as if I was an animal that was about to
attack.

He reached out his hand, caressing my cheek with his
fingertips. "Are you okay?"

"Not yet," I said truthfully. "But later... yeah."

"I love you," he whispered. "Forgive me?"

"Forgive you?"

With a deep sigh, he sat on the bed next to me. "Forgive me for not telling you the complete truth about my family? About Jac?"

Just hearing her name shot tremors of fear through my body. "You mean about her being...." I couldn't finish the sentence.

"Jack the Ripper." Nikolai licked his lips glancing at the wall, away from me, his body no longer touching mine. "She told you how it started? With jealousy?"

"Apparently it's a powerful emotion." My voice cracked. "Were all the women like this? In your family?"

"No," Nikolai said quickly. "Jac was unable to have children after my father, leaving the job to him... he refused to carry on the tradition. By then Jac was still working, and he realized he wanted more for our family, but he was cut out of her will... he needed money... and so he started working for Petrov." Nikolai leaned back on his hands, raising his chin toward the ceiling and inhaling deeply through his nose. "It's a long complicated story. Believe me when I say now you know everything."

He turned his gaze to mine.

Eyes so dark, so haunted, like they were begging me to understand him, begging me to accept him even though he came with so much baggage that it was hard to see everything he was carrying on his shoulders.

"Yes." I whispered.

He frowned, "Yes what?"

"I still love you."

"I didn't ask."

"Your eyes did," I whispered reaching for his hand. "It's not your fault she was crazy, and it would be stupid to hold your past against you, ruining both our futures."

"I'd let you go." Even as he said it he was pulling me into his lap, kissing my neck, his lips grazing by my pulse. "It would destroy me, but if it's what you wanted, to be away from memories of me, your father, Jac, I'd let you go."

"My place is here." I turned my head so I could meet his mouth. We kissed, and then I placed my hand on his chest. "And here."

His hug was so tight it was hard to breathe. "I'll protect you with my life."

"Good." I laughed through my tears. "Because apparently I'm a wanted woman."

A low growl issued from his throat. "I want you every second." His mouth covered mine and then pulled back. "Of every day."

"That's a lot of seconds."

"Eighty-six thousand four hundred." He kissed my neck. "But who's counting?"

"Who knows those things?"

"I'm a doctor."

"Is that going to be your answer to everything I don't understand?"

"Yes." He licked where his lips had just pressed. His touch was driving me crazy. I tried to pull off my shirt but he pinned my hands down.

"Oh, sorry, I thought all that math talk was foreplay," I teased, wondering how I was able to even do that after the traumatic day I'd had.

"You'll know when it's foreplay." He snaked his arm around me and lifted my body back against the pillows. "Now, shall I force some chicken noodle soup down your throat?"

"Why is it always chicken noodle? What if I wanted clam chowder?"

"Then I'd get you clam chowder."

"Really?"

He slid a cell phone out of his dark jeans and held it up in the air. "Really."

"In that case... I want clam chowder, sourdough bread, and a brand new Mercedes."

His smile was gorgeous—dazzling as he leaned forward and kissed my chin. "A Mercedes huh?"

"A new one."

"Figures."

"Part of the new contract?"

"You wish."

"You are still paying me half a million..." I teased. "Even though I'm technically your girlfriend now?"

"Let's start small, with the clam chowder. Later we'll talk cars and... payment."

"A guy who doesn't want to talk cars in bed? My, my, where have you been all my life?"

His eyes met mine. "I'm here now. That's what matters."

"My contract specifically says I'm not to have any sort of dating relationships." It was fun getting him upset, ignoring the darkness of the day and focusing on us, on our reality, our future.

"One tiny indiscretion after a near death experience doesn't count." His mouth found mine again. "I'll explain to that pretentious boss of yours."

"Please do, and while you're at it tell him to buy me something red."

Nikolai growled low in his throat. "I'd kill to see you in red."

"Too bad, the boss says only black."

"The boss had his reasons."

"The boss is an ass."

"He has reasons for that too."

"Hmm." I licked his lower lip and tasted. I was acting like an insane person. I would never get tired of his taste of the dominant way he returned each kiss like he was trying to remind me I was his.

My life stopped making sense a long time ago.

But his kisses always eased the cobwebs and helped me focus on what was important.

"Maya…" He groaned. "If you keep kissing me like that—I won't be able to control myself."

"So lose control."

"Easier said than done." He pulled back slightly. "You need to eat and then we'll discuss… all bedroom activities."

"Ah, so the boss means to put his cranky pants back on."

"When did the boss take his pants off? Just curious."

I peered down. "Must have been my overactive imagination."

"You're cute."

"Am I?"

"And dangerous…" He sighed, "So very, very dangerous."

"Maybe that's why Jac wanted me dead."

"No." Nikolai said it so quickly it was as if he knew I was already going to say that. "She was clinically insane, out of her mind. She finally snapped the minute I let you in my life, the minute she was no longer number one, but she was slipping even before that. Only, I ignored it, and for that I'll never forgive myself."

"And my father, if he ever finds me? Discovers I'm alive and breathing?"

"He'll die… besides he'll be too focused on staying out of prison. Sergio truly did a number on your family." Nicolai shrugged. "You'll be happy to know your mother wasn't implicated."

"I stopped having a mother a long time ago." Fresh pain washed over me, but I pushed the thoughts away. What good would they do anyway?

"You still want to stay? With me?"

"I'm still holding your hand aren't I?"

"Yeah." He squeezed and then lowered his head to brush a kiss across my knuckles. "You are."

CHAPTER FIFTY-THREE

Life is not a bed of roses. — Russian Proverb

Nikolai

I MADE A QUICK CALL TO have soup and bread delivered and made sure to start the bath for Maya so that she could soak and relax.

A half hour later, I knocked on the bedroom door then pushed it open with my foot while I carried the food tray in.

"Finally." Maya stood completely naked in front of me.

The tray crashed to the floor.

I didn't have time to stop it.

"Wow... even bruised and bleeding I look that good?"

"Maya." I croaked out her name. "You have stitches... you need..." I couldn't speak. "Rest."

"Rest with me?" She held out her hand.

"You're out of your mind if you think I'll be able to keep my hands off of you."

"Then don't." She took a step toward me.

I took a step back.

"The great Nikolai Blazik, scared? Of a mere woman?"

"You've never been a mere woman... you're my fantasy, my love, my perfection, living and breathing. A woman I don't deserve but want anyway..."

Her lips parted as she let out a little gasp. "Nik... I need you."

"But—"

"Your grandmother nearly killed me while I was trapped in my own paralyzed body, my father nearly killed you, we've had crazy Italians with large guns and no respect for censorship in our house for two days." I loved how she said our house already. "And I'm still freaked out. I want you, inside me, right now."

I was walking and then with a lunge I pulled her into my arms and gently laid her across the bed. "I love you." My mouth found hers in a frenzy while she ripped at my clothes.

"I love you too," she breathed, our teeth knocked together as she struggled pulling my shirt off.

I gently pushed her back and peeled my clothes off as fast as possible then pulled her into my arms, our bodies fit, our skin sizzled on contact.

"Now."

"You're not ready for me—"

"Nik." She patted my cheek softly with her hand then harder. "I've been ready for hours... I need you, desperately. Don't make me beg."

I smirked. "But you do it so well."

"You're an ass." She started moving her body against mine. "And I'll make you pay for it later."

I lifted her hips into the air and settled her on top, thrusting into her as she came down on my lap. "Hmm make me pay for it now."

I moved her hard on top of me, careful not to touch any of the bruising on her body, bruising I blamed myself for.

Maya's hands found my head, and then her lips were on mine, and we were moving in perfect sync.

The world around us faded.

And I realized I needed her just as much, maybe more, because in that moment I'd needed to know that if everything else went to hell—we'd still have us. We'd still have that very real connection.

With a small cry she bounced up, sliding down, her hair kissing my face with each movement, I kissed her neck and then held her in place even though she tried to move.

"Feel," I said through clenched teeth. "Feel."

She let out a sob as her body clenched around me.

"We were made for each other, Maya." I held her for a few more seconds, until I thought I was going to explode, then thrust one last time.

Her strangled cry mingled with mine as we clung to one another, the soup was all over the floor, the bath was probably cold.

And the world was still an evil place.

But with her—I didn't see spilled soup, cold water, murderers and blood... for the first time in my entire life, when I looked at the world.

I saw hope.

A dangerous thing hope...

A beautiful, wonderful, dangerous idea.

One I would hold on to, as long as I had her in my arms for they came hand in hand, I just never knew it.

AUTHOR NOTE CONTINUED...

WHOA! YOU GUYS MADE IT! Curious about other books in the Eagle Elite series? ...want to know Phoenix's story? Maybe Nixon's or Tex's? Awesome! you won't regret it. The Italian mafia... well, I'm obsessed. That's all there is to it!

The *Eagle Elite Series* reading order is as follows:

Elite

Elect

Entice

Elicit

Ember

Elude

Empire (out May 2016)

Enforce is a companion novel to *Elite;* it's from the guys' POV should be read after you read the first two books or at any point within the series. *Enchant* is part of the series prequel. *Enamor* takes place after *Elicit* and is a short Nixon and Trace novella.

Want more Nikolai and Maya? Make sure to let me know! I love to hear from readers, and if you want more Russian mafia, your wish is my command! As always follow me on Facebook www.facebook.com/rachelvandyken or join Rachel's New Rocking Readers — my fan group on Facebook! I'm also on Twitter and Instagram @RachVD.

If you want mindless updates on all my new releases, simply text MAFIA to 66866!

Hugs,
RVD

ABOUT THE AUTHOR

RACHEL VAN DYKEN is the *New York Times*, *Wall Street Journal*, and *USA Today* bestselling author of regency and contemporary romances. When she's not writing you can find her drinking coffee at Starbucks and plotting her next book while watching "The Bachelor".

She keeps her home in Idaho with her husband, adorable son, and two snoring boxers. She loves to hear from readers.

You can connect with her on Facebook at facebook.com/rachelvandyken or join her fan group *Rachel's New Rockin Readers*. Her website is www.rachelvandykenauthor.com.

ALSO BY RACHEL VAN DYKEN

The Bet Series
The Bet (Forever Romance)
The Wager (Forever Romance)
The Dare

Eagle Elite
Elite (Forever Romance)
Elect (Forever Romance)
Entice
Elicit
Enforce
Ember
Elude

Seaside Series
Tear
Pull
Shatter
Forever
Fall
Strung
Eternal

Wallflower Trilogy
Waltzing with the Wallflower
Beguiling Bridget
Taming Wilde

London Fairy Tales
Upon a Midnight Dream
Whispered Music

The Wolf's Pursuit
When Ash Falls

Renwick House
The Ugly Duckling Debutante
The Seduction of Sebastian St. James
The Redemption of Lord Rawlings
An Unlikely Alliance
The Devil Duke Takes a Bride

Ruin Series
Ruin
Toxic
Fearless
Shame

The Consequence Series
The Consequence of Loving Colton
The Consequence of Revenge

The Dark Ones Series
The Dark Ones
Coming Soon:
Untouchable Darkness
Dark Surrender
Darkest Temptation

Other Titles
The Parting Gift
Compromising Kessen
Savage Winter
Divine Uprising
Every Girl Does It

www.rachelvandykenauthor.com

Made in the USA
Charleston, SC
14 January 2017